I0733959

Paths Not Taken

Anne Louise Bannon

HH
Healcroft House, Publishers
Altadena, California

Contents

Acknowledgements

Where to begin? I don't think I'd be assembling this book except for the incredible generosity of so, so many people.

Losing not only your home but also your neighborhood to the ravages of a wildfire is truly awful. There are worse things and my husband's and my situation could be more miserable than it is. But we're scraping the bottom here.

The reason things are not the absolute worst is that we are blessed with several communities that have not only reached out, they have gone above and beyond to help us get back on our feet and me to a point where I can work again. Kristen Shubert, Elissa Rosenberg, Ralph Koek, Traci Locke and Robert Grossman, Robert and Jill Crudup, and Mark and Robbie Dawson of the Los Angeles Cellarmasters, reached out and took good care of us. Naomi Hirahara who volunteered at the evacuation center that first day and made sure that Michael and I had something to eat, then brought more food a week later. Cassy and David Muronaka not only took us shopping in the early days, they set up the GoFundMe (now stopped). The dozens and dozens of donors who contributed. The Garden Christian Fellowship, whose gift was so generous, and my cousin John Mason, who initiated it. Jasper Dickson and Amy Luftig, of Angeleno Wine Company, who spread the love around. Holly Wolcott, Petty Santos, Maribeth Olivieria, of the City of Los Angeles. Our beloved Repair Cafe community, especially Michael Starch and Lan Dang, who not only set up our new tech, but built my desk. Susan Strother Carrier and Kelly Russell. Our pet sitter Robin Hollis, who was at the evacuation shelter with us, but did not lose her home, and who is now babysitting our traumatized dog. Ellen Byron for her generous gifts and spreading the word around. The Sisters in Crime, for their much-needed grant, and Nancy Cole Silverman for telling me about the grant. Meredith Taylor, who gave us her husband's bed and a table to eat at. Susan Kitchens who brings us citrus. Stuart Byles, who is drawing up the plans for our new place. And Michael Pauls and Alicia Ley, our inside connection to the county permitting and zoning process. Tracey Phillips, G.P. Gottlieb, and the rest of the Blackbird Writers, who made it possible for me to go to Left Coast Crime.

And, finally, my editor Carol Louise Wilde and her husband, Gerry Wuenschell. In the early days of the crisis, when Michael and I utterly overwhelmed with our loss, they not only did the leg work to find us an extended stay room, they loaned us the cash to pay for it. Then gave us more furniture.

I am sure that I have left out several folks – for which I profoundly apologize. Things have been such a blur. But we are coming back. We are Altadena Strong, thanks to the wonderful people surrounding us.

To the people of Altadena, California

May 13, 1988

“**I**’m done!” I hollered into my truck’s cell phone. “It’s over. I’m done.”

Sid, my darling husband, chuckled. “We knew that, sweetheart.”

“Yes. But it’s official now. I finished Casey’s exam and got my paper back from Barber. I am done for the semester.”

“Great. Stella called just before you did.”

Stella is Sid’s aunt. She raised him, so she’s more like his mother than an aunt.

“Oh?” I asked.

“She’ll pick Nick up from school, along with Darby and Josh. She got tickets for the game tonight.”

My gut clenched in spite of my earlier glee. “Will she take them overnight?”

“I, um, may have made that a condition of her taking them.”

Nick is Sid’s and my son. Darby and Josh are his best friends, although Darby is also my nephew and Josh’s mom is one of my closer friends. All three boys were in the last few weeks of their freshman year of high school and were devout baseball fans. They had in Stella not only a fellow fan, but one willing to indulge them endlessly.

Given Stella's leanings toward Communism on the political side, it had completely surprised Sid and me that she loved baseball as much as the boys did. The problem is that when you indulge three adolescent boys to the extent that Stella does, the result is frequently wired teens with tummy aches.

"Is it safe to say that Mae and Lety are on board with that condition?" I asked.

Mae is my sister and Darby's mother. Lety is Josh's mother.

Sid laughed. "Hell, yes. How long before you get here?"

I glanced at the clock on my dashboard. "Probably another half hour or so. The last traffic report didn't mention any problems between here and there."

Such is driving in the Los Angeles region. I had the news station on my truck's radio mostly for the regular reports of what accidents were where, not to mention all the other congestion that regularly clogged the freeway, in the hopes that I could avoid those spots. [And people wonder how we got so dependent on Google Maps. – SEH]

"Okay," said Sid. "I'll see you then. I love you, sweetheart."

"Love you, too, darling."

I grinned, giving my shoulders a quick roll as I hung up the phone, then concentrated on weaving my way through the lines of cars on the freeway.

"...The House Committee on Intelligence announced a plan today to increase penalties for people convicted of selling American technology to the Soviet Union," the announcer on the radio said. "Congressman Dale O'Connor, speaking on behalf of the committee, said that sales of computers to the Soviets have escalated in recent years and need to be stopped."

"It is absolutely critical to our interests to stem this tide," O'Connor's voice said. "Stiffer penalties will make it less attractive to sell our technology to our enemies."

I rolled my eyes. If I weren't so worried about missing news of the latest accident, I would have turned the radio off. What Dale was spouting was pure nonsense. Nobody in the intelligence community gave a rat's patootie about the Soviets getting their hands on a few IBM PCs or Apple Macintoshes. Nuclear secrets? Satellite technology? We were concerned about the Soviets getting a hold of those, but more because they'd sell them to Iran, China, or India. Thanks to the chaos going on in the Soviet Union, there wouldn't be much they'd be able to do with it, and Dale knew it.

Sid and I know Dale O'Connor, although we're hard-pressed to call him a friend. One of the reasons he's on the House Intelligence Committee is that he's a member of the U.S. Intelligence community, overseeing covert operations going on in both the CIA and the FBI. It also makes Dale one of our bosses.

Within the structures of the FBI and the CIA are several smaller agencies, so top secret that only their members and a few key liaisons know they exist. Sid and I belong to one such agency called Operation Quickline. We're mostly couriers, but Sid and I and our team often get pulled into investigations that are too hot to handle by local law enforcement.

As annoyed as I felt by the news, it didn't do much to dim my cheerful mood. When I got home, I hurried through the house to the office I share with Sid. He was waiting for me and kissed me soundly.

I grabbed for his belt buckle. I was a little surprised when he caught my hands and held them.

"As much as I want to celebrate the end of your semester with you right now," he said as he winced, because he really did want to celebrate. "You've got to call Dr. Clemmins."

"What?"

"He said he needs to speak to you today before five and it's after four-thirty now."

I groaned. With Nick out of the house, Sid and I wouldn't need to worry about where we messed around. And I was certainly more interested in messing around than calling Dr. Clemmins back. However, Dr. Clemmins was one of the members of my graduate committee and given the trouble I was having with the head of that committee, I couldn't afford to blow him off.

I picked up the phone and dialed. Dr. Clemmins, fortunately, picked up right away.

"Lisa," he said, awkwardly. "I, uh, have some bad news. Dr. Barber is recommending that you be put on academic probation."

"I see." I pressed my lips together. "And what is he basing this on?"

"Your last paper."

"Oh, for crying out loud!" My temper flared. "I did what you told me to do, to the letter. You saw it. It was exactly what he asked me to do."

"I know. You're— You're absolutely right."

"Dr. Clemmins, I'm sorry. This is not about me being a dilettante. This is about me being a woman."

"Well..."

"Is he recommending Miriam Parsons for probation?" I had a strong suspicion that Dr. Barber had.

"Uh... I'm afraid so."

"What about Dave Robbins?"

"Uh... No."

"Then this settles it. I have to call the Dean's office."

"Eh, Lisa, he is a preeminent scholar in the field. You told me he was why you came to this school."

"That was before I found out that he's also a sexist jackass. How many dissertations by women has he passed in the last ten years? Like none?"

"I appreciate the research you did in that respect."

"I just wish I'd done it before I got there. Well, thank you, Dr. Clemmins. You've been very helpful."

"You're not going to leave us?" He sounded very anxious.

"I don't know yet. I'll talk to you later."

"Sure."

I put the phone down as Sid shook his head.

"Probation?" he asked, sliding his arms around my shoulders.

"Barber's recommending that I be put on academic probation." I blinked back tears. "It's the first step to kicking me out." I shook my head quickly to clear it. "I've got to call Miriam, then we've got to call the Dean's office."

Miriam had already heard about being recommended for probation and was fit to be tied.

"But, Lisa, what can we do? I mean, do we really want a reputation for causing trouble? You know how hard it is to get a job."

"How are we going to get the jobs we want if we can't get our doctorates? And you know that son of a sea horse is not going to pass our dissertations. He's counting on us not wanting to cause trouble in the hopes we'll pass, then he's going to screw us in the end. Miriam, that's why he gets away with this nonsense. He's got to be stopped."

"Not by me." She sighed deeply. "I'm sorry. I need a job when I'm done."

"I get it. But you're not going to be able to get your degree."

"I'm transferring to another school. I'm already accepted. It will put me behind, but I should be able to land on my feet. If I don't make trouble."

"That's great. Really." I grinned in spite of my anger. "Their enrollment numbers are going way down. Clemmins is worried that I'll take off, too. Best of luck to you. I've got to call the Dean's office."

"I'm glad, Lisa. You're right about reporting Barber, but you're about the only person who can do it."

So, I called the Dean's office. Miriam was right. I was about the only person who could raise hell about Dr. Elias Barber's sexist behavior, because I am, in fact, a dilettante. I was not working on my PhD in English Literature, with an emphasis on Shakespeare, because I needed a new job.

Sid and I need to have some sort of occupation to cover what our actual jobs are, and that's been freelance writing. But we really don't need even that. To be blunt, we are independently wealthy. The writing thing has come in handy when we need to ask people questions without looking suspicious, but we don't have to do it for a living.

Even so, I was going back to my original career plan of being a college professor, which had been interrupted when cutbacks at the community college where I'd been teaching put me out of work. Then I met Sid, who recruited me into his spy business. Then he got me into freelance writing, as well. Then we got married.

As far as my life aspirations and plans were concerned, being married with a kid was pretty far down on my list. But Sid and I had to fall in love with each other, and I ended up adopting his son, and there I was. Married with a son in high school. Not a bad situation, by any means, since I deeply love both Sid and Nick. It was just not at all what I'd planned for my life. The doctorate was.

I hung up the phone after my conversation with the Dean's office, feeling completely let down.

"Hey, Lover," said Sid softly. "It will be alright."

"Thanks, but that's not what's bugging me." I winced as I slid into his embrace. "It's that I don't have to do this. Why am I putting myself through this torture? Half of it's boring as spit. Then Barber being such an ass."

"Well, maybe that's what you need to be thinking about over the next few months. You've got 'til the end of August before school starts again. It's possible you're in the wrong program. Or maybe you just didn't want to be a college professor as badly as you thought you did."

"Possibly."

I reached over and kissed him, my hands again sliding toward his belt buckle.

"And as much as I wish we had time." Sid grabbed my hands again. "We have to get out of here for dinner with your parents. It's just after five and we've got to be in Burbank by six or so."

I groaned, but he was right. Fortunately, I was wearing a denim shirt dress, which meant I didn't have to change for dinner. Sid had on his usual dark two-piece suit with a snowy-white shirt and a colorful tie that I'd made from a Liberty cotton. Sid is not a big man, only about three inches taller than me, and I'm average. He has dark, wavy hair, gorgeous bright blue eyes, and a cleft chin. I couldn't help smiling at him.

"Alright," I said. "Let me get my purse."

We got to the restaurant in Burbank closer to six-thirty. It didn't matter. My parents had flown down from their resort in South Lake Tahoe earlier that afternoon and had rented a car. They were ensconced in the restaurant's bar, a chain steakhouse with a kitschy Western flair, sharing a plate of appetizers with another couple.

There's only one way to put it. When Sid and I saw the other couple, our blood ran cold.

I'm not going to say that we regard Dale O'Connor as Evil Incarnate. He's hardly that and believes in keeping the U.S. safe from enemies and so forth. But Sid and I do not like him for a lot of reasons, and one of those reasons is that Dale is one sexist pain in the backside.

Sid had known Dale, though not well, for years before I met the man. We later got to know Dale when we'd been promoted to our current position two years before. Not only did he oversee a lot of covert activity, he was also a key liaison between Quickline and the rest of the intelligence community. Dale is also the congressional representative for the district that includes my parents' home in South Lake Tahoe. [Funny how we accepted that initially as a coincidence when it turned out to be anything but. - SEH]

Sid and I had wondered in the past whether my parents knew Dale. Sadly, that night, we were confronted with the fact that they obviously did.

"If it weren't for your parents," he grumbled.

"Even with them," I said. "I am not up to dealing with Dale tonight. Let's leave— Shavings!"

Mama had seen us and waved us over. I glanced at Sid, who shrugged.

"Will it blow our covers if I smash his face into the table?" I asked as we threaded our way around the tables.

My parents didn't know about Sid's and my spy business. Sid just chuckled, but once we'd hugged and kissed Mama and Daddy, and shaken hands with Dale and his wife, Adrienne, Sid made a point of seating me next to Daddy and as far away from Dale as possible.

"Looks like there's a good, long wait for a table," said Dale jovially. His reddish gray hair, what was left of it, sat in a ring around his bald spot, and he held himself ramrod erect like the former military man he was. "What do you two want for a drink? Sid? Scotch and water, right?"

"Bourbon and water," Sid said quietly.

Adrienne blinked at us sleepily from where she sat next to Mama. She looks a lot like a former model still keeping herself up, with full brown hair and perfectly made-up face. She doesn't generally seem tuned in to what's going on around her, but the last time Sid and I had talked to her, we'd gotten the impression that she was a lot more alert than she acted.

"Lisa?" Dale asked, waving for a waiter.

"A glass of white wine, thank you," I said.

Mama had a glass of what was most likely white zinfandel in front of her that she wasn't drinking. She's short and pert and usually bubbling over, although she wasn't that night. Daddy, who is as tall as Mama is short and as laconic as she is talkative, smiled, but had a wariness to his usual reserve. Not that Dale or anyone else would have noticed the wariness. Daddy plays poker insanely well and taught me to play. We're about the only people who can read each other's tells.

Sadly, the dishes holding the onion rings and shrimp cocktail looked very picked over. When the waiter showed to pick up our drink orders, Dale requested a second appetizer platter, and ordered scotch and water for Sid and a white zinfandel for me. Which explained why Mama had the white zinfandel, which she really doesn't like.

"Excuse me," I said to the waiter. "Actually, I'll have a white wine, my mother will also, and my husband will have bourbon and water."

"Uh, chardonnay okay?" asked the tired-looking young woman.

I glanced at Mama, who nodded. "Perfect. Thanks."

I smiled at the waitress kindly.

"I'd like a glass of the bourbon, too, please," Daddy said.

He pushed away the short tumbler with something amber in it as the waiter scurried away.

"Well, Lisa," Dale said. "Why haven't you told your folks that we're all friends?"

I glanced over at my parents and shrugged. "It just never came up."

"Oh, for Heaven's sakes, Dale," Mama said, her usual Southern drawl getting just a touch icy. "We never mentioned to Sid and Lisa that we knew you and Adrienne."

"So, what brings you to Los Angeles, Dale?" Sid asked.

"I'm coming home to Tahoe for a few days," Dale said. "I've got a couple of meetings with constituents. Flew in this afternoon and met Adrienne here."

She smiled and blinked. "I left early to get some shopping in."

Dale chortled loudly. "And how much of my money did you go through today?"

Sid gave me a quick once-over to be sure I was still in my seat. I really hate Dale's big joke about how much his wife spends.

Mama jumped in. "Dale told us a month or so ago that he and Adrienne are part of that travel club you two belong to."

The travel club existed. It's just that a good two-thirds of the members are also members of various intelligence organizations around Europe and the U.S. It's a way of making sure the people who supervise the four different routes that make up Quickline know enough about what's really going on so that they can get packages and information where it's needed.

"Anyway," Dale said. "When I found out I was flying in, I checked in with your parents, Lisa, and found out they were coming down tonight, and I suggested we meet. Looks like your father and I might be going into business together."

Daddy shrugged. "Well, you have an interesting idea about the resort restaurant."

"Sid, you used to be in the restaurant business, right?" Dale asked.

"I write about it, but it's been quite a few years since I last waited any tables," Sid replied.

We paused as the waiter brought our drinks and the extra appetizers.

"Still, you should join us," Dale insisted. "It'll be great. I mean, I can't be actively involved, so you won't have to worry about that. And I'll bet you'll be able to get this plan up and running in no time."

"I'll have to talk it over with Bill first." Sid glanced my way. "And with Lisa."

"Dale," Adrienne blinked and stood. "I'm done eating."

Dale glanced at his watch. "Yeah, and we've got a flight up north to catch. You think about that plan, Bill. Lisa, Sid, good to see you."

There was almost an audible sigh of relief once the pair were gone, and a moment later, the hostess told us our table was ready. Sid grabbed the appetizer plate and his drink as he got up.

"You don't have to do that, sir," said the hostess.

"It's no trouble," Sid replied, pasting a nicely sensual smile on his face.

The hostess smiled back. "Oh, and your friend has already put his card through for your dinners. In fact, we could have seated you a few minutes ago, but he asked us to wait until he left."

The four of us looked at each other but followed the sweet young thing to a table in the main dining room.

"So, Dale is coughing up," I said as we got ourselves settled and looking at the menus. "Should I go for the surf and turf or the double prime rib?"

"Now, honey, you don't want to take advantage," said Mama.

"Oh, yes, we do," Sid replied. "And it's not like Dale hasn't seen Lisa eat before."

"You don't seem to like the congressman," Daddy said.

"As one of our other friends in the club put it, some of the members are an acquired taste," Sid said. "And we're not acquiring one for Dale."

"Adrienne is not so bad," I said.

The dinner waiter, a young dark-haired kid with classic actor features, came up to get our order. I got lobster and prime rib. Sid opted for roasted chicken. Daddy went with the double prime rib. Mama had grilled salmon.

"Anyway," I said after the waiter had gone. "You've met some of the others from the travel club. They were at the wedding."

Sid and I had gotten married two years and some months before.

"I'm trying to remember now," Mama said.

"There's Hattie Mitchell, who used to be one of our editors," I said. "Lillian Ward. She's the one who got Uncle Leonard in the choke hold."

"I'd like to shake her hand," Daddy said with a grin.

Leonard and Steven Caulfield are my mother's twin older brothers and they're... Well, they make Dale look pleasant.

"And Marian and Andrew, the British couple," I finished.

"They were quite charming," Mama said.

Daddy grunted. He didn't take to Andrew flirting with Mama. Mama hadn't noticed the flirting and couldn't understand why Daddy had taken such a strong dislike to Andrew.

The waiter came by with our salads and offered us ground pepper. Sid and Mama went for it. Daddy and I didn't.

"So, what's this big deal that Dale is trying to pull off?" Sid asked.

"He wants to invest in improvements to the restaurant," Daddy said.

I gaped. "You're not going to let him buy in, are you?"

"Oh, hell no."

"William," Mama hissed at him. She does not like foul language.

"But he sure seems to want you involved, Sid." Daddy looked at us curiously.

Sid just shrugged, and we chatted a little about the project, then moved on to other subjects. But something was up, and I had a really, really bad feeling about it.

June 16-20, 1988

I can't say I was in the best of moods that Thursday afternoon. I had been looking forward to our trip to Bordeaux that year for the annual Travel Club meeting. Dale O'Connor notwithstanding, Sid and I like the other members, and it is kind of fun to talk about the spy biz with other folks who know what you're talking about and who aren't going to kill you.

But that morning, before we left for the airport, I got a call from Dr. Clemmins, then another call from my parents.

Apparently, Dale's big plan for the restaurant at my parents' resort was to upgrade the service and make it fancier. Daddy had hired a new chef back in February, a youngish woman champing at the bit to upgrade the dinner menu. Which doesn't sound all that complicated until you consider the upgrades to the china, tablecloths, and flatware, pulling together a wine list, and a bunch of other things that I had no clue about.

Sid and I had checked in with Lillian Ward, the head of Quickline, right after that dinner with my folks in May. Lillian told us she didn't know exactly what was up, but that Dale had some sort of plan and he expected us to be part of it. Which meant that we didn't have much of a choice but to work on it.

Then Sid got interested in the project. We'd gone back and forth to Tahoe several times and, after we'd talked, Sid told Daddy that we'd be there through July and most of August. Sid even got Nick hired as a busboy, much to Nick's dismay.

That morning, however, Daddy called with some bad news. Neff and Mary Nelson were this elderly couple that had worked as caretakers and managers at the resort. However, Neff had died the previous spring. Mary had stayed on, supposedly supervising the housekeeping staff. Only Mama had taken that over, because Mary was not even close to being able to do it.

The problem was that my Grandma Caulfield (Mama's mother) had decided it was time to finally clear her house out in Southern Florida and sell it and wanted Mama to go help her do it.

"Why now all of a sudden?" I asked Daddy. "She's only been letting it go for the past two years since she moved in with you."

"Stephen called this morning," Daddy grumbled. "He and Leonard and your aunts are going to be here next week. They want to take your grandma back with them. Only she said she isn't going without your mama to help, and your mama said she'd better or that house will never get packed up."

"This time of year?" I groaned in shock. "Mama hates being in South Florida in the summer."

Daddy chuckled. "She hates being in South Florida, period. Anyway, Mary's son finally convinced her to move to a senior's home near him. But that means I don't have anybody to fill in for Lourdes on her days off, and you are going to be up here starting next month."

Lourdes Manusco was the housekeeping manager.

"Me?"

"Honey, you did it back when you were in college that one summer, and worked the store, too." Daddy had also owned a souvenir and sporting goods store that he'd recently sold to the man who'd been managing it for him.

"But what about Mira?"

Mira Arguello was the assistant manager for housekeeping.

Daddy hesitated. "She, eh, takes off on her own and that upsets Lourdes."

I sighed deeply. Suddenly, it felt like smashing Dale's face into something wasn't enough.

"I haven't managed housekeeping for a lot of years, Daddy."

"Hasn't changed that much."

I sighed again. "Alright. I may as well. I'm pretty hopeless on the restaurant side."

Sid had already tried training me during a couple weekends that past month. It was a disaster.

[You are one of the most competent people I have ever met. That you couldn't handle taking orders and getting them served correctly shocked me to my core. - SEH]

Later, I told Sid about the two phone calls while we waited for the plane to Paris. He sympathized, but was glad that I had something to work on while we were at my parents' resort.

Nick wandered over from the window where he'd been watching the planes. He's got Sid's dark, wavy hair, cleft chin, and near-sighted blue eyes, although Nick prefers wearing glasses. Fifteen years old, he had all the ranginess of a growing young man. Not to mention a few dark hairs on his chin, with the occasional whitehead.

"Hey, Mom," he said, flopping into the seat next to me. "You okay? You don't look too happy."

I shrugged. "It's nothing serious. I'll just be doing more work at the resort this summer than I thought." I smiled. "I may as well. In the meantime, I just want to forget all that and focus on enjoying myself in Bordeaux."

"And Paris," said Nick with a grin. "That's going to be a blast."

Hours later, on the plane as it began its descent into Orly airport outside of Paris, Sid woke up. He sleeps on planes and rarely wakes up until right before we land. I was looking out the window when he woke and didn't realize that he had a little early.

"You're looking a little pensive," he said. "What's going on?"

I jumped, then winced. "Nothing I should be worrying about."

"Dr. Clemmins' call, perchance?" He smiled softly, then got his contact lenses and the wetting solution out of his jacket pocket. Sid hates how he looks in glasses.

"Yeah." I sighed. "I just can't help wondering about what you said that last day of school, that maybe I don't want to be a college professor that badly, and never did. I feel like I've shot myself in the foot by filing that protest over Dr. Barber."

Sid shrugged. "It's possible. But it's like you said, the reason Barber keeps getting away with that nonsense is that no one will hold him accountable. And in a way, Clemmins is just as responsible for the problem because he's using fear of rocking the boat to keep you and other women like you in line."

"But the rest of the committee?"

"Them, too. You're just lucky you take good notes and do the research."

"I suppose." I shook my head as Sid blinked to make sure he'd inserted the lenses over his corneas correctly. "Between school and working the resort this summer, I almost feel like I'm moving backwards. How much longer before I'm a moody teenager writing bad poetry again?"

Sid chuckled. "That would be the two of us, lover. We're both going back to our teen years, in a way. I'm pretty sure I'll be waiting a few tables before we're done."

"But you weren't moody and writing bad poetry."

"Okay. I skipped the bad poetry. But don't try to tell Stella that I wasn't moody as hell." He glanced across the aisle at our son, Nick, who had the headphones to a Sony Discman on and was just waking up.

"I take it you were comparing notes with her."

"Uh, not quite." Sid grinned and shuddered. "Let's just say that Nick has found a friendly ear in her, and when I complained about what a pain in the ass he's been lately, she laughed."

Nick, who turned fifteen that past February, had been pretty grumpy ever since he'd found out he'd be working at the resort for the summer instead of going to science camp and the week-long teen retreat our church puts on at a camp on Catalina Island.

I rolled my eyes. "I'm not surprised. You probably were a pain in the you-know-what when you were a teen. And Mama seems to think all the adolescent angst sloshing around is a hoot."

Both Nick and my sister's son, Darby, are the same age, which meant there was plenty of angst.

"Revenge being the key word, I would imagine." Sid glanced over at our son.

I gazed fondly at the kid, too. His hands had sprouted out some, and he was already as tall as his father, possibly taller.

Some minutes later, we were on the ground.

Neither Sid nor I are overly fond of Paris. We usually had a good time when we were there. But as European cities go, it's not our favorite, which I understand makes us certifiably nuts. On the other hand, it was the first time Nick had been able to visit the city. Since we had to be in Bordeaux by Sunday, Sid and I had decided to take an extra day or two to show Nick Paris. It was Friday by the time we landed, and even though it was early in the morning when we did, half the day was gone by the time we reached our hotel.

It didn't matter. We spent the afternoon on a boat tour on the Seine, then did a full-day tour of the city on Saturday. Nick, bless him, forgot the angst and had a genuinely good time. Sid and I were thrilled that he was turning into quite the tourist.

Sunday, we took the train to Bordeaux and got ourselves settled into the hotel where the other Travel Club members were staying. That evening, Nick joined us as we met with the other twenty-five people that were part of our group.

Not everyone there had come as members and liaisons of our network. Some had come as the spouses of some of the spies. The other six people were simply ordinary people who acted as cover for the rest of us, even though they did not know they did.

For the next five days, the spies would group and re-group to learn about various operations in Europe, South America, and the Middle East. Quickline's couriers didn't generally serve operatives from the Middle East, but we had several connections with the Mossad, which is the Israeli intelligence agency. Those of us who were floaters, or line supervisors, would touch base with each other about upcoming investigations and what special skills their team had to offer.

We also got to eat amazingly well. Admittedly, that's easy to do in France. But two of the driving forces behind the Travel Club are Lord Andrew and Lady Marian, the Earl and Countess of Graymere. They are two of the most unpretentious people I've ever met. They are also gourmands in a big way. They're not above eating street food or hitting a local dive. But if they do either of those things, you can be sure that street cart or bistro has the absolutely best crepes, sandwiches, whatever, that you have ever eaten in your life. Even Sid eats with reckless abandon when Marian and Andrew are hosting, and he's normally pretty fussy about eating healthy, skipping red meat, sugars, salt, fats, artificial additives.

We started that Sunday night with a full thirteen-course dinner in the traditional style, complete with matching wines. There wasn't much discussion about the real reason most of us were there. Instead, Marian asked me about my Ph.D. program.

"As I understand it, you're studying Shakespeare, aren't you?" she said as we started dinner.

We were scattered among three round tables in a private room. Sid was at another table with Andrew. Nick, who had proven the year before that he could behave with the proper decorum, was at the third table. Pedro Delgado is Lita Delgado's husband and a member of Quickline even though Lita and Barb Wasserman are the floaters on their team, which is the Yellow Line. Pedro had landed next to Marian, and I was on his other side.

"I'm told having a rough first year is not unusual." I made a face. "My first semester was surprisingly boring. But then I took a class with one of my graduate committee members, who was out to get me and the other woman in the class. Turns out he's a sexist pig who doesn't believe that women should be studying the Bard."

"Oh, my god," said Pedro, his dark eyes flashing with glee. "He's lucky he doesn't know Lita."

Marian's eyes flitted over to the table where Nick was sitting across from Dale O'Connor, who sat near our good friend, Henry James. Danielle Connelly, a cover member, sat between them. Lita was at the table with Sid and Andrew. She seldom sits anywhere within reach of Dale.

"That would be an amusing confrontation," Marian said, then ate a delicate little crab puff. "Mm. Lovely. However, I do not understand why the professor would object to you studying Shakespeare."

I smiled. "I don't, either." Shrugging, I glanced Dale's way, as well. "But then it's amazing how few guys have the first idea of just how sexist they are."

Pedro snorted with laughter. Some years before, Dale had grossly offended Lita, and she'd smashed his face into a table. When Dale had gone after Lita, Barb Wasserman, her partner and friend, had kicked him where it hurts. At least, that's what Sid and I had been told.

I had to admit that the thought of either Lita or Barb landing a swift kick into Dr. Barber's private parts was rather gratifying. Lita had gone blonde that meeting - her hair is actually black. While she is fairly short with some curves, the last thing you want to do is underestimate her or Barb. Pedro and Moishe, Barb's husband, are the hub team on their line, which is the Yellow one, but they frequently show up at Travel Club meetings as cover.

The next day, I had my first mini-meeting, this time with Dale O'Connor and Lillian Ward, who is the head of Quickline, Barb, Elena Montoya (one of the floater team for the Blue Line), and Steve Parsons (one of the floaters for the Green Line). We went for a walk around the town square, then settled in a small, outdoor cafe close to the cathedral, getting a table on an outside corner of the eating area. It didn't matter that we only heard French being spoken around us. We still kept our voices low.

That's when I finally found out what Dale's big plan was. He started out by complaining about the ongoing sale of American technology to the Soviets, then announced that Sid and I were going to catch at least one of the KGB agents doing the buying.

"We've got a fairly straight-forward sting that we're setting up," he said. "We're staging it in South Lake Tahoe. I've got it all arranged. Besides Sid and Lisa, we have an extra operative staying at Wycherly's Family Resort. Plus, there's a kid who's going to turn state's evidence for us and is already working there for the summer."

If I could have caused Dale to spontaneously combust at that moment, I would have. Without question.

"That's my dad's place," I said, my teeth gritted.

"That's why it's perfect." Dale grinned. "You and Sid will be there, and no one will automatically connect you to your father."

"What do you mean they won't?" I was about five seconds short of leaping out of my chair and strangling Dale, never mind that I was also still trying to keep my voice from rising.

"Nobody is going to care about Lisa Hackbirn hanging around on the resort." Dale sat back, utterly confident that he'd made his point and then some.

Somehow, he didn't notice everyone else at the table rolling their eyes.

"Which might be the case if my name were Hackbirn," I growled. "But it's still Wycherly. I never changed it and I'm not going to."

Dale shrugged. "You sure about that?"

"Not for you, not for anybody," I said. "Besides, my parents would ask why and what am I supposed to tell them? Never mind. Don't answer that." I looked around the square and then at Lillian, who was giving Dale the evil eye. "Is there anything else you need to cover?"

Lillian smiled apologetically at me. "I think that will be all for now."

"Good. I think I'll take a walk." I got up and left.

Dale scrambled up behind me. "I don't get it. Why are you so mad about the set-up?"

I turned on him. "You are using my parents' business as a safe house and inviting potential enemies there for a sting operation. Good lord, Dale. You own an entire chain of motels. Why couldn't you have set this up at one of them?"

"I want you and Sid there. We need the backup."

"But it's my parents' business. You're exposing them to all kinds of danger and risking blowing our covers at the same time. How could you have possibly thought that was a good idea?"

"It'll be fine." Dale was about to pat my shoulder, but pulled his hand back just in time.

"It's not fine, Dale." I blinked back tears. "One of these days, you're going to assume that you know it all, and you won't, and somebody is going to get hurt that didn't need to be."

Dale glared at me. "Collateral damage happens."

"Not when you're talking about exposing my family to it." I pressed my lips together. "We're not chess pieces. We're not assets. We're not even soldiers. We're human beings, and my parents and grandmother are innocent, at that. It's bad enough that you blithely make decisions for Sid and me. But you have no right to include the people we love or care about in that."

Dale swallowed, then rolled his eyes. "I make the best decisions I can in the interest of keeping our country safe. I know things you don't, and part of that is what one of our operatives is working on. It's a guidance system for our nuclear subs. It's critical to keeping our guys alive and the other side from launching nukes at us."

"Fine. That's critical. I get it." I shook my head. "But you still should have talked to us about it before making your grand plan. There might have been a better alternative, and you would have gotten better cooperation. What if Daddy didn't want to work on that restaurant project? Did that occur to you?"

"I know how to make things happen, Lisa." Dale looked away and then at me. "I've been doing it since Korea. You might want to try trusting me sometimes."

"You might want to try trusting me, too."

I stalked off.

Later, before dinner, Lita caught up with me.

"I heard that you're not happy about the big sting this summer," she said softly, as we made our way into the hotel lobby for the cocktail hour.

"Can you blame me?" I asked.

"Hell, no." She giggled. "I'm surprised that Dale isn't singing soprano right now."

"It was a near thing, as Marian would say."

Lita grew serious and put her hand on my arm. "It's worse than you thought." She glanced around. "We've gotten some noise that some Cubans are involved. How, we don't know. But they're looking to shore up their relationship with the Soviets."

"But with everything going nuts over there..."

"That's exactly why." Lita frowned. "The ex-pat community is thrilled with Glasnost, but Fidel isn't, and that isn't just a rumor."

Being from Miami, Barb and Lita had good access to intel out of Cuba.

"Yeah, I'd heard that," I said, sighing. "But thanks for confirming it."

"Hey. We all Need to Know more than they think we do. We'll keep you posted."

"I'll let you know what's going on, too."

Sid noticed immediately that I was not happy but didn't ask about it until we were getting ready for bed. I told him everything as we got undressed and he rolled his eyes.

"What a jackass," he growled. [Not the actual term I used. - SEH] "The problem is, you're both right."

"I know." I shuddered as I pulled the covers on the bed back. "Obviously, he knows things we don't and probably can't know for various reasons. But he really should check in with us and the others, because one of his schemes is going to blow up in all our faces. Or worse. Let's face it. With Dale's kind of knowledge, if he makes a mistake, it could cause World War Three."

Sid chuckled and pulled me onto the bed. "I think he's well aware of that. Which, I admit, does not help with his God complex." He paused, then slid the covers over us. "The strange thing is, I think Marian is getting a little fed up with it."

"What do you mean?" I asked, running my fingers through the hair on his chest.

He purred for a moment, then kissed my fingers. "Well, it's not as though Dale has ever been that much of a team player. But Marian thinks he's gotten worse about it lately. Setting things up on his own without consulting any of the others."

"You mean like his game for my dad's place."

"Exactly." Sid softly kissed my forehead. "Anyway, Marian asked me to keep an eye on him. Not that there's not much we can do about it."

"And it doesn't do us much good to worry about stuff we can't control." I sighed, then snuggled in next to him. "Is Nick asleep?"

Nick was in a room that connected to ours.

"He was when I checked him a few minutes ago." Sid's eyes gleamed lecherously. "And he's wearing his headphones."

I laughed, then yelped in joy as Sid's hands wandered. We are pretty noisy when we mess around.

Over the next few days, we heard about tensions escalating all over Eastern Europe. I don't want to sound callous - it was not good news. However, it wasn't anything we hadn't heard before, and really, our major concern was which agency or group was handling what and where they were. And who among our group would handle what investigation and when. Steve and Roy, for example, would be in Chicago for an extended period of time, starting in September working undercover as visiting curators at the art museum there trying to find out who was behind a counterfeiting scheme, probably financed by the Chinese.

We got a few more details on the technology sale scheme, but not many. I was still upset about the way things had been set up at my parents' resort. There wasn't anything I could do about it. It wasn't the first time Sid and I had had to work as ourselves on something that had landed in my hometown. We'd make it work out because that was our job. But I did not have to be happy about it.

"Order up!" Felix Arias called, sliding a plate onto the stainless-steel shelf between the waiters and himself and the other line cook.

Sid looked at the small group of filled plates, checked the ticket with them, then looked around.

It was Monday afternoon, near the end of the lunch rush. It tended to be the slowest period in the restaurant because if guests were exploring the sights, going to the beach at the lake, or doing other things away from the resort, they generally went during the day. Sid had tucked into his khaki slacks a light blue polo shirt with the resort logo on the chest. Actually, all the staff wore the same polo shirts in varying colors. I had on a green one tucked into khaki shorts and running shoes.

Daddy had bought the resort when I was around two years old, and I don't remember living anywhere else but in South Lake Tahoe. Over the years, he had expanded the number of rooms in the main lodge, fixed up the cabins, added a play and crafts room to the lodge, plus an indoor swimming pool, and completely re-did the playground.

One of the first things he'd done was add the restaurant space in the main lodge. However, he'd always leased that part of the business to various other people so that he could offer meals without having to run a restaurant himself.

Only that winter, the man who'd most recently been leasing the space decided that he'd had enough, which is when Daddy had hired Bracha Solomon. Bracha was an Israeli woman who had gotten her start as a cook in the Israeli army, then moved to the U.S. where she'd worked at several different restaurants all over the country. She also wanted to start her own place, but didn't have the capital to do it. Daddy had no interest in running a restaurant, so it was a good fit.

"Nick," Sid called. "Have you seen Marina?"

"She's trying to take an order from that kid who won't make up her mind." Nick slid a tub of dirty dishes onto the wash station and waved at Jorge, one of the two dishwashers working that shift. Nick had on a dark purple resort polo shirt and the same khaki slacks his father wore.

Sid cursed. "All right. I need you to deliver her order."

Nick's eyes rolled.

"Son," I growled. "It's not a good idea to roll your eyes at your boss."

Nick heaved a sigh. Sid had the dishes on the tray, having chosen to ignore Nick's behavior.

"It's going to table eleven," he told his son.

Nick's eyes suddenly lit up. "Sure!"

He hoisted the tray, grabbed the dish stand, and headed out to the dining room.

"Another one?" I asked.

Sid shrugged. Being the utterly charming kid he is (not unlike his father), Nick had scraped up a girlfriend a week from the various guests at the resort. I was glad to see it, too. I'd done the same thing when I'd been in high school.

Nick's flirtations had mitigated not going to science camp, where, as Sid had pointed out, the boys outnumbered the girls twice over. I was pretty sure the little romances were no more than flirtations.

Sid grew up sleeping around. He'd been raised to believe in free love and lost his virginity when he was thirteen. So far, Nick did not seem to be emulating his father, which relieved Sid and me. We were both worried about him picking up AIDS, and did not want our teen-age son getting into the kind of trouble kids get into when they get sexually active too young. [How I escaped that, I do not know, but am profoundly grateful I did. – SEH]

I stood in the doorway between the restaurant kitchen and the employees' break room. The break room had been placed there so that the employees could order lunch for free during their breaks. It was only one of many reasons why so many of my daddy's staff had been at the resort for a lot of years.

Sid had sunk some of his own money into the new restaurant. We'd told the staff, however, that he was there as a consultant. There had been enough grumbling among the wait staff about all the changes happening during the busy summer season. Sid needed and wanted to get their cooperation as quickly as possible. Being a co-owner that had only waited tables some years ago would not have gotten him much respect. A consultant was bad enough.

However, Sid really did know what he was doing. Yes, there had been a lapse in time since he'd waited. [Almost nine years, and that was that case that I worked in San Diego at Marge Benson's restaurant. - SEH] But as a freelance writer, he wrote a lot about the restaurant business, mostly for trade magazines. Which meant he also read the magazines. Between that and his own experience, he knew what needed to be done.

Bracha had already gotten the kitchen staff up to speed. Sid had worked with her first and the two were very much on the same page about how to run things. Sid's focus was on the front of the house (or dining room).

He'd been working with the management team so that they could train and supervise the rest of the wait staff, especially the dinner crew since they suddenly needed to know how to flambé, toss salads table-side, serve alcoholic beverages, and just generally be more formal. In fact, Sid had started with the dinner crew. However, it was time to focus on the daytime staff. He'd gotten the respect of the dinner staff by working several shifts with them first to get a feel for what they were doing. He was doing the same with the daytime crew.

Marina Jones, tall with skin the color of light coffee and black hair she wore in braids, stormed into the kitchen. Her polo shirt was white that day, and she'd chosen to wear shorts.

"I repeated the order back. I waited!" She pounded the keys on the newly installed computerized order machine. "And her parents have, like, no clue what that little brat is doing."

"Or don't want to know," Sid sighed, as the printer whirred and spit a ticket out for the line cooks.

That was one interesting thing about working at the resort. Sid was exposed to the entire range of parenting practices and was not impressed.

"They'd better not send it back," Marina grumbled, going through her other tickets. "What happened to table eleven's order?"

"Nick's delivering it."

Marina scurried off to check the front.

My walkie-talkie squawked, although Sid couldn't hear it. It wasn't for me, anyway.

"Anyway," I said. "Guess who I saw checking in a little bit ago?"

"No idea." Sid looked over the kitchen, then smiled at me.

"Dr. Miles Lipplinger."

Sid frowned, then remembered. "Didn't they ship him off to Europe?"

"That doesn't mean he didn't come back."

"Housekeeping One, are you there?" said a voice in my ear, where I had the earpiece for the walkie-talkie. It sounded like Irene on the front desk.

I removed the mike. "I'm here. What's up?"

"I have a guest in Room 305, Dr. Lipplinger. Says he wants to know where there's a desk for his computer."

"I'm on my way." I held up the mike for Sid. "And it sounds like Lipplinger hasn't changed either."

Sid shook his head and laughed. I hurried out of the restaurant and upstairs to the third floor, feeling rather nettled. I had no idea what Sid thought was so funny about Lipplinger, but I suspect it had to do with the reality that I was going to be dealing with the royal jerk and Sid wasn't.

Back in the fall of 1982, I'd been out of work for a year and had gone on a blind date just for the meal. I had to ditch the date, and Sid rescued me. Being into sleeping around at the time, Sid put the moves on me but backed off when I made it clear I did not sleep around. Instead, he was impressed, and a few days later, offered me a job as his secretary. There were two catches, of course. The first was that I had to move into his house, but that wasn't a big deal because I had my own bedroom, from which Sid was barred. The second was that Sid was actually recruiting me into his spy business.

A couple of months after I'd been hired and started my training, Sid and I were given the job of protecting Dr. Miles Lipplinger, which ended up meaning that we kept him at Sid's house. The man was a demanding, whiny, sexist, rude jackass. [As usual, my darling, you're being too kind. That doesn't come close to how god-awful he was. - SEH] Which is the long way of saying that I was not at all happy about him turning up at the resort and had to believe that he was there as part of Dale O'Connor's grand plan to catch the person selling U.S. technology to the Russians.

I took the back stairs to the third floor of the main lodge, then blinked as I went from the bright, utilitarian stairwell into the muted light of the third-floor corridor. There's a heavy emphasis on log cabin style across the whole resort, so there are lots of exposed posts and beams of dark wood in between the lathe and plaster walls covered in calming tan paint. The third floor tends to be the quietest, with twelve rooms evenly split between single beds and doubles.

The door to 305 was open as I walked up, and I could see Lipplinger, a stooped man with white hair and glasses, pacing and grumbling.

"Good afternoon," I said, smiling in spite of how I felt.

He looked up and glared at me. "They told me they were going to send a manager."

"That's me," I said slowly. "How can I help you?"

He didn't seem to recognize me at all, which was odd, since he spent several weeks at Sid's house. He had kept mostly to himself, and he probably hadn't paid too much attention to me since I was only Sid's secretary at the time.

"I need a desk," he snarled. "How am I supposed to work without a desk?"

The room was a single, with one king-sized bed, covered in a dark brown satiny bedspread. The bathroom was near the room's door, and a large window looked out over the front of the lodge. Along the wall across from the bed was a low chest of drawers, in the middle of which was a good-sized TV. Under the window, a small table sat with two chairs and a table lamp nearby.

I pointed at the table. "Won't that table work?"

"The outlet is too far away," Lipplinger shook his head as if it were perfectly obvious. "And it's too small and rickety. I don't want the computer falling off."

I looked at the unit he mentioned. It was considerably smaller than most computers I'd seen, but somewhat bigger than a nine by twelve manila envelope and at least a couple inches tall, if not taller. Which meant that Lipplinger had a point.

"Well, I'm sorry, Professor, but this resort is mostly a vacation destination." I shrugged. "We don't get much call for outlets to plug-in computers. We have a small office center downstairs. You can use the printer there for ten cents a sheet, which can be charged to your room. We can also get you an extension cord as a courtesy."

"I need space!" He glared at the TV set. "You've got to get this thing moved off this dresser."

"I can remove it entirely, if you prefer."

"No! I want to watch it at night." He pointed to a corner by the bedside table. "Just put it over there during the day, then move it back while I'm at dinner."

As annoying as his demand was, I had to be grateful that he wasn't going to move the TV himself. All the room and cabin televisions were hooked up to Cable TV. It was a limited package offered by the cable company, but it meant that we could have HBO, the Disney Channel, and a few similar channels in the rooms. It also meant that the televisions were hooked up with a special cable in the back. It wasn't that hard to undo, but it was better when someone who knew what they were doing disconnected everything.

I stepped into the hall and got on my walkie-talkie and called the facilities head, Ty Larson. Ty paged one of the college kids who were there to work for the summer.

Some minutes later, Dusty Simpson came out of the stairwell, his brown hair tousled, his green eyes blinking behind his perpetually dirty glasses, and wearing a yellow logo polo shirt over jeans. He didn't look like he had much on the ball, but he was a wiz at fixing things. I figured he and Lipplinger would get along just fine, what with Dusty being smart but quiet and, well, a young man rather than a young woman.

"I'll let our guest tell you what he needs," I told Dusty.

He nodded and shrugged. "Sure."

"Professor," I called into the room. "This is Mr. Simpson. He'll help you with your television set."

"It's about time," Lipplinger growled as Dusty went into the room.

The door to room 304 opened at that moment, and a man in his middle forties, with dark hair, dark eyes and a deeply lined face, stepped out.

"Good afternoon," I said, smiling, as I tried to remember his name. It's a small detail, but Daddy always says it makes a world of difference. "Mr. Lane, right?"

"Yeah." He smiled briefly. "Um, I hate to ask, but could I get an extra blanket tonight, please?"

"Of course." I nodded. "I'll get it myself right now."

Mr. Lane looked briefly at Lipplinger's room where we could hear Lipplinger telling Dusty how to unscrew the cable, never mind that Dusty probably had a better idea of how to do it than Lipplinger did.

"Thank you," Mr. Lane said quietly.

I went off to find the blanket from the upstairs linen closet and returned with it promptly. Mr. Lane was standing just inside his door. Lipplinger was loudly going over exactly how he wanted Dusty to deal with the TV and when. Mr. Lane thanked me again and went into his room.

He was a pleasant fellow who had been taking a room every couple of weeks. Given that the resort caters to families primarily, most of the people in single rooms are young couples, usually with one or two small children. But there were those folks, like Mr. Lane, who liked the atmosphere and came to relax. Ms. Sanchez was another and was currently in 306.

My walkie-talkie squawked again, this time with a request from the ground floor. My friend Judy Osbourne was there. Judy had the contract for maintaining our TVs and VCRs, along with providing the stock for our small library of videotapes. We'd known each other in high school and hadn't been close or anything. But since I'd been back at the resort, we'd gotten friendlier and had gone to lunch together a couple times.

She was a tall, blond woman with glasses and an athletic build. That day, however, she seemed nervous.

"I've got the invoice for this month's service," she muttered, showing me the paper.

"Thanks." I looked at her as I took it. "You okay?"

She winced. "I was just re-stocking your library a little while ago when I saw something." She shook her head. "It's okay."

"Alright." I watched her leave, wondering what was up.

That was the worst of Dale's big plan. Sid and I knew that Dusty Simpson was the kid we were there to keep an eye on. Dale didn't entirely trust him to sell the plans to the submarine missile guidance system to the KGB agent at a time when Dale or the other agent he had here could bust the KBG agent. However, we had not been told who the other agent was. Or who the suspected KGB agent was. Or anything else, for that matter.

Which meant that I spent a lot of time suspecting just about everyone and everything that I came across.

I took Judy's invoice to the business office where Irene Wu was glaring at the reservations print-out and a rack of paper slips with other reservations printed on them. That meant only one thing: Lyle Weaver, our chief front desk clerk, had messed up once more.

"Oh, dear," I said as I slid the invoice into the accounts payable inbox. "Did he overbook us again?"

"For the fifth time this summer." Irene shook her head, her short black hair swishing gently. "I keep telling him not to make reservations, but he does, anyway. I think we can squeeze it. But this can't go on."

"I know." I plopped down at a nearby desk. "Daddy's trying to figure something out. The problem is the guests love him. And he's been here since..." I frowned. "I think he may have been here when Daddy bought the place."

Irene, who was in her forties and had a couple rolls on her shortish frame, glared again at the reservations print-out.

"That's exactly my point," Irene grumbled. "He's got to be in his seventies by now." She winced. "I know Lyle is thinking your father will let him work until he dies at the desk, like he did with Neff."

"Yeah, but Neff kept his marbles together," I said with a sigh.

"And Lyle hasn't." Irene waved her hands in frustration. "I hate to say it, but it's true. We haven't been able to book cabin ten all summer, thanks to him. I almost turned away the Wrightmans, for crying out loud, and we can't afford to lose customers like them."

"I know." I rubbed my forehead.

"Let's just hope that the Elizondos are going to be more forgiving that the Wrightmans." Irene shuddered. "The good news is that we'll be clearing cabin ten this weekend after all, so the Elizondos should be happy, even if the Wrightmans are in twelve."

"They should be," I said.

The Elizondo clan had been spending a week at the resort every year since I was a teenager. I'd even had a brief flirtation with the youngest son, who I'd heard had gotten married and now had two kids. We had twelve cabins on the resort, most of which could sleep up to eight people. Cabins ten through twelve were the really big ones, though. They each slept up to twenty people, and cabin ten was considered the overflow because along with a large open area, the four rooms each had two queen-sized beds and locks on the doors, as if the cabin was a mini-hotel.

The Elizondos, whose family had expanded several times over, usually booked cabin twelve. But the Wrightmans had not been able to check into ten because Lyle had double-booked a couple rooms, and we'd put the extra families in ten. The Wrightmans had not been happy, but accepted cabin twelve for their two weeks with us.

"Do we have any more double bookings?" I asked Irene.

She shook her head. "I don't think so. Unless Lyle checks in somebody without a reservation."

"Let's pray he doesn't." I got up and checked my watch. "I'll be on the radio for a while yet, if you need me."

"Thanks," Irene said.

Besides being the reservations manager, Irene was angling to take over as manager of the resort. That position had been Neff's since I'd been in college. Daddy had taken up the day-to-day management since Neff's death. Rumor had it that since I was there, he was hoping to get me to be manager. I knew it would make him happy if I did, but I was pretty sure he knew that I wasn't likely to.

I wandered over to the activities center, which was basically a crafts room and mini-library. My niece Janey was there, as usual, helping Ms. Wanamaker, who was the summer activities director. Ms. Wanamaker taught at the local elementary school and since we only needed activities directed during the busy summer season, she was happy to work when school was not in session.

Janey, just shy of her twelfth birthday, had decided to help out at the resort that summer. She looked up at me with a grin, her hazel eyes sparkling and her long brown hair in a ponytail. She wore a pink polo shirt over her shorts.

"Hey, Aunt Lisa! Are you off work yet?"

"Not really." I couldn't help but smile back at her.

"Uncle Sid told me this morning that when he and Nick are done for the day that they'd meet me here," Janey said. "We have to figure out dinner."

I tried not to make a face. I hate cooking. I hate keeping house. I am possibly the least domesticated person I know. Mama usually takes care of the house I grew up in at the back of the resort. But she was in Florida. Fortunately, Daddy and Sid were paying to have a couple of the college kids who were there working for the summer to clean both the family house, where Nick, Janey, and my father were sleeping, and the staff lodge. The staff lodge was a large house on the edge of the resort, near the horse barn. Most of the college kids who worked the busy summer season stayed there. Mary and Neff's apartment had been there, as well, and that was where Sid and I were staying.

I'd been cooking while Sid was working the dinner shift. Sid had announced the night before that he would take over getting dinner cooked to the general appreciation of the rest of the family. I'm not a bad cook, but I'm not a good one, either.

Sid walked into the small room filled with craft supplies, tables, chairs, and shelves of books and videos. Ms. Wannamaker's eyes lit up as she saw him. I couldn't entirely blame her for her crush on my husband. Sid is one gorgeous, sexy man.

"So, how did it go?" Sid asked me after giving Janey a warm hug.

I tried not to roll my eyes as my walkie-talkie squawked. I picked up the mike, waving Sid off. Sure enough, it was Lipplinger again.

"Room 305 and you-know-who," I told Sid softly, turning for the door. "He wants to know why the restaurant is closed."

Which it was so that the dinner crew could set up, there not being any business to speak of around three in the afternoons.

Sid smiled at me. "Did he talk to you?"

"He didn't even recognize me." I rolled my eyes.

"Tell you what." Sid glanced upstairs. "The restaurant is my bailiwick, and if he won't talk to you, then I probably should."

"Okay. What do you want to do about dinner?"

Sid sighed. "I'm beat. If your dad's okay with it, why don't you get takeout from that Mexican restaurant we like?"

"Sure." I looked over at my niece. "Janey, you want to come with me to get dinner for everyone tonight? I mean, if Grandpa doesn't mind getting it to go."

"He won't," Janey said.

Which he didn't. Mondays at the resort are more like Fridays in normal life because the weekends are so busy and we're all off on Tuesdays and Wednesdays. Daddy, having taken over active management, was pretty tired on Mondays.

Janey double-checked with me, Sid, Daddy, and Nick to see what they wanted and called in the order. The second I could get away, we took off with me driving Sid's BMW, which we'd driven up in, figuring we'd probably need at least one set of wheels at our disposal.

It was a pleasant but quiet meal that evening. Sid and I headed back to what we still referred to as Neff and Mary's place even before it was fully dark, at nine-thirty. Neff and Mary's place had been cleared by their son and his wife after Mary had been moved to the care facility. Mama had added a few pieces of furniture, such as a bed and sofa, but not much else.

Sid went first to the bathroom and got his contacts out, then came into the tiny bedroom and sank onto the bed without getting undressed first.

"I can't believe it, but days are even more exhausting than dinner service," he grumbled.

"Well, you're working two meals and longer hours," I said.

"True."

"Did you talk to Lipplinger?"

Sid called Lipplinger something truly foul. "I have no idea how, but he's even more of a jackass than he was."

[I did not say jackass. - SEH]

"I know, but did he say anything about why he's here?" I stretched and sat down to get my running shoes off.

"He's got the plans to the guidance system, and he's going to use them to set up the sting with Simpson." Sid took his shoes off. "Beyond that, all we need to do is stay out of his way."

"I'm happy to do that," I said. I went over and pulled Sid's shirt over his head.

Sid's grin got enticingly lecherous. "So am I."

And that would have been it, except that three days later, Lipplinger was dead.

T hursday mornings were the all-management meeting. The breakroom was barely big enough for the entire team, but there was coffee in the breakroom and usually snacks. That Thursday, Sid had put out a large bowl of fruit salad. Most of us grabbed the donuts that Lourdes had brought in.

"I've got The Sound of Music for the movie tomorrow night," Ms. Wannamaker told us.

"And I'll be smoking beef brisket for the picnic," added Bracha Solomon. "With Bill's help, of course."

Bracha and Daddy often worked together on the food for the Friday night picnic and outdoor movie because Daddy is amazing when it comes to smoking meat.

Sid looked over his list. "We have three seatings almost completely reserved, mostly two-tops."

Which meant that a lot of parents would be dropping their kids at the picnic, then going to dinner by themselves. That was okay. Several of the college kids would be there to keep an eye on the little ones.

"Sounds good," said Daddy. "What do we have for Saturday?"

That was the really, really busy day. All of the cabins and most of the lodge rooms rented from Saturday to Saturday, so except for those families staying more than one week (and we had two staying for two weeks, another staying through mid-August, and one family there for the whole summer), there would be a lot of people checking out, then just as many checking in.

"Three-oh-five and three-oh-six are staying through," Irene told us. "Three-oh-four checked out this morning. Two-eleven is staying. Everything else, except cabins three, eight and twelve are vacating."

Lourdes, a medium-sized woman in her late 50s with dark hair and eyes, nodded.

"We'll have the full crew ready to go at seven," she told us. "Let's just hope that folks get out early."

Both hers and my walkie-talkies squawked at the same time.

"Lisa? Lourdes?" said Mira's voice in my ear. "Can you get Bill and get up here to room three-oh-five?"

"What's going on?" I asked.

"You'll see when you get here."

I looked over at Daddy.

"Bill, we've got a problem upstairs," Lourdes said, heading out of the room.

Daddy and I were on her heels. Outside room 305, Mira held Donna Mars, a college kid, whose face was utterly ashen.

"What the hell?" Daddy growled.

Feeling my stomach doing three kinds of flip-flops, I pushed ahead into the room. I probably shouldn't have. You see, I have this little phobia of dead bodies, which is really odd given my business. But I had a bad feeling that I would need to see what was in the room. Well, apart from the body.

And it was a body, Lipplinger's, to be exact. He lay on his back, eyes open and staring. The television was unplugged and had fallen on its side, as if Lipplinger had started to move it when he collapsed. The rest of the room looked pristine. That was as far as I got before my stomach started heaving. Somehow, I kept it all down and got out of the room. Daddy cursed under his breath.

"Mira, shut the door." Daddy sighed deeply and shook his head. "We'll have to call the paramedics and the police. It's sad, but these things happen. Lisa, can you get the emergency information from Irene? And I know it will be hard, but let's try not to upset the other guests in the meantime. It's not their fault."

I sort of already had Lipplinger's emergency information, but I went downstairs and asked Irene for it, anyway. She led me to the reservation office and got the number from the computer. Sid showed a moment later as Irene went back to the meeting.

"They said there's a stiff?" Sid asked, his face creased with worry. He knows me and bodies mostly because it was working for him and the spy biz that started the phobia.

"Lipplinger," I said softly, blinking my eyes. "Daddy's acting like it was a heart attack, and that almost makes sense."

"He wasn't a young man." Sid sighed, then put his hand on my arm. "How are you doing?"

"Shaky, but okay." I swallowed. "I didn't barf, and I saw him."

"That's good." Sid shook his head. "I can't help but feel for Hattie. All the same, this is not good timing."

"We'll see." I swallowed again. "Speaking of, I've got to call Hattie."

Hattie Mitchell was Lipplinger's younger sister. In fact, our adventure with Lipplinger was how Sid and I initially met her. She lived in Washington, DC, although she traveled a fair amount.

I had to wait for one of Hattie's staff to get her, but it wasn't that long before she picked up.

"Hello Lisa, what's going on?" she asked. "It's an emergency?"

"I'm afraid so, Hattie. Sid and I are here in South Lake Tahoe."

"Yes. Miles is supposed to be there, too."

"He was. Umm, Hattie, I'm so sorry. He died either last night or this morning."

"Oh." There was a long pause on the other end of the line. "Um. Do you know what happened?"

"I'm afraid not. We just found him in his room. The paramedics and the police aren't even here yet."

"Hm." There was another long pause. "Well... Hmm. Um. I suppose I'd better head out there. Have you talked to Dale yet?"

"You're the first person I called. I'm not even sure where Dale is."

"I think he's in DC. He should be. Congress is still in session for another couple weeks. Are you sure it's Miles?"

"Yeah. Pretty sure. I mean, he doesn't have a look-alike, does he?"

Hattie let out a bitter chuckle. "One of him is more than enough." She hemmed for another minute or so. "I'll call Dale."

"Are you going to be okay?" I asked.

"Of course. I'll let you know when I get there."

"Okay. Have them radio me if I'm not at the front desk when you arrive." I paused. "I'm so sorry, Hattie."

"Thanks, Lisa."

By that time, the paramedics and the police had arrived, and I let them in through the back and upstairs in the freight elevator. The nice thing about cops and fire people in South Lake Tahoe is that they're really sensitive to the tourist trade. It's not an everyday kind of thing, but people die in hotels often enough that the local authorities know how to be discreet about it. And people dying in hotel rooms is one of those things that freaks the guests out, even if the hotel has nothing to do with it. And it usually doesn't.

The paramedics seemed pretty sure that Lipplinger had died of natural causes, and the cops agreed. At least, that's what Daddy told me. In any case, Lipplinger was hauled out of there pretty darned quickly and quietly, and for that, I was grateful.

My next job after that was getting the room thoroughly cleaned. Mira, fortunately, volunteered to do that, and I helped. However, while she scrubbed and vacuumed, I went through Lipplinger's clothes, suitcases, and brief-case. Ostensibly, I was packing, but it also gave me a chance to search the dresser, closet, and bedside tables, looking for his personal items. Together, we remade the bed and replaced the towels.

I sent Mira to page Dusty so that we could replace the TV. I figured the one that had fallen wasn't going to work anymore. While she was gone, I moved most of the furniture and searched behind and under it but didn't find anything.

Once Dusty had brought the new TV, I went downstairs to find a place for Lipplinger's stuff to wait until Hattie could claim it. Then I went to get lunch since it was after one already and I was starving. In between orders, Sid volunteered to look at Lipplinger's computer to see if there was anything on it that we should be hiding. I was happy to let him.

Almost the entire staff was acting off because of the death. It's as though we all felt guilty because we had all disliked him so much and now he was dead.

Nick, however, didn't seem to have any feelings about it.

"I don't know," he said to me that afternoon as we walked back to my parents' house after he'd gotten off work. "I mean, he was a total jerk, and it's not nice that he's dead, but it doesn't really affect me."

I couldn't help chuckling. One of the things that both made me crazy about teenagers and that I loved about them was their amazing self-absorption. Nick stopped walking.

"It's not making your life harder, is it?" he asked, frowning.

Okay, maybe he wasn't totally self-absorbed. I smiled and ran my fingers through the lock of dark, wavy hair that constantly fell over his forehead.

"It is, and it isn't," I said.

"I'm sorry about that." Nick sighed, then grinned. "Grandpa said that he's going to teach me to drive next week."

"What? You're not fifteen and a half yet and you don't have a learner's permit."

"So? Grandpa's not worried about it."

I glared at him. "And what does your dad think about this?"

"Dad said okay."

I started to feel really steamed. It wasn't like Sid to make snap decisions about raising Nick without checking with me first, but it did sometimes happen. Just like I sometimes made snap decisions about raising Nick, I reminded myself. That didn't make up for much.

That's when three of the four dogs staying at my parents' place started howling and barking. Spot and Richmond belonged to my parents. Motley and Bowser belonged to Sid, Nick, and me. I'd gotten Motley in the fall of 1983. Sid's aunt, Stella, had given Bowser to us after she'd found him abandoned behind her music school when we were still in Europe. Bowser was probably whining along with the other dogs, but given that he was a 12-week-old puppy and living in a dog crate in the living room when Nick wasn't around to keep an eye on him, he wasn't making much noise.

Hearing the dogs barking gave me an idea, though.

"Nick, we'll put the driving on hold until I've had a chance to talk to both your father and grandfather, okay?"

"Mom!"

I held onto my temper with both hands. "It won't take long. Trust me. Now, you go feed the dogs and make sure Bowser has plenty of time outside and give him extra praise when he does his business out there."

"I know, Mom."

He ran ahead while I contemplated tanning his fanny. I don't believe in hitting kids, but there are days when it's tempting. I tried to banish adolescent angst from my mind as I got through the gate in the fence separating the back of my parents' house from the rest of the resort.

Motley, my liver-colored springer spaniel, came bounding up to me. Spot, an almost-two-year-old Dalmatian mix, and nine-year-old Richmond, a tan mutt, were both dancing around Nick. I found Motley's leash on the hook next to the back door into the house's kitchen, then clipped it onto Motley's collar. He whined a little. It was dinnertime, and I was taking him for a walk?

"Come on, boy," I said, leading him out of the yard into the resort. "We've got some work to do."

The guests were pretty well used to seeing dogs all over the place, mostly because we allowed people to bring their dogs as long as they were kept on a leash while outside and not left by themselves in the rooms or cabins, or in the guests' cars. Spot also got a lot of attention by running with the horses on rides. Richmond had done the same, but at his age, he was turning into quite the couch potato.

Motley, however, had been restricted to my parents' yard unless I or Sid had him on a leash. Oddly enough, it wasn't that Motley was badly behaved. In fact, it was the opposite. Motley was not only very well behaved, he was very well trained at finding illegal substances, specifically cocaine.

Sid and I had acquired Motley when he was a little over a year old, while working a case in Tahoe that had involved several packages of white powder. Motley had proven very adept at finding said packages of white powder. And right after he got to the resort this summer, he proved he was still very adept at finding said packages, not to mention packages of marijuana.

You might wonder who brings drugs to a family vacation spot? You'd be surprised. People do all sorts of stupid things, and there's really not much we can do about what they hide in their luggage. If somebody is obviously stoned or drunk in one of the public areas, we have to intervene, but beyond that, we have to let it go.

So, when Motley ran loose that first day there, then went into conniptions at the door of cabin eight, the guest at the time got extremely peeved. I later went in and found the cocaine behind the front door and had reason to believe that particular guest hadn't hidden it. Sid and I also decided that it would be safer for Motley if he didn't wander around loose to find things he probably shouldn't. After all, people hiding drugs are not usually very nice about it when you find them.

I headed first to my father's private office in the main lodge and found Sid there, pulling a three-and-a-half-inch floppy disk from Lipplinger's computer. I left the door open so that I could see outside to the main office just in case my father decided to come in.

He sighed. "I have no idea what's on this."

"Can I borrow one?" I asked.

"Sure." Sid handed the plastic disk to me. "Giving Motley a chance at turning something up?"

"Why not?" I said. "Um. Nick said you'd told Daddy it was okay for Daddy to teach him how to drive."

Sid chuckled and shook his head. "Nick was overstating it. Daddy mentioned it to me this morning right before the meeting. I told him I had to discuss it with you first and was going to as soon as lunch rush was over. But then things blew up."

"I guess they did." I sighed. "How do you feel about it? I mean, the driving thing."

Sid snorted. "I'm perfectly happy letting your dad teach him. I don't need another reason for Nick to be pissed at me."

"But he's not old enough for a learner's permit."

"He's got less than a month." Sid shrugged.

I folded my arms across my chest. "Are you trying to indulge him to make up for making him work this summer?"

"Possibly." Sid sighed. "Probably." He looked at me and winced. "But again, he is at the age for it."

I snorted and looked away.

"Lisapet, is there a reason you are looking so disgusted right now?" An almost sly smile crept across Sid's face. "Such as maybe your father's attitude about you driving when you were Nick's age?"

"I was a very good driver," I snarled.

"I'm sure you were." Sid smiled softly. "And you still are, by the way."

I couldn't help chuckling. Neither my mother nor my sister thinks that about the way I drive now. More than a few car chases have had their effect on how I handle traffic.

"That being said," Sid continued. "Let's just say I'm getting a good idea of how your father felt back then."

I rolled my eyes. "In my case, my gender may have played a big role, too."

"True. But your father told me something last spring, and Stella did, too." He winced a little. "One of the problems that you and I will have with Nick is that we've had so little time with him. Other parents have known their kids since infancy. We've only known Nick since he turned eleven."

Which was when Nick's first mother finally let Sid know that he had a son. Rachel had passed away three years before, which was when we took custody.

"It's going to make it a little harder for us to let go," Sid said.

"Which is exactly what we're supposed to be doing," I grumbled. "You've got a point. But driving?"

"Yeah, I know. Which is kind of why I'm happy to let your father deal with it."

I couldn't help making a face. "Fair enough. I can't say I want to be teaching Nick to drive, either."

"So, we tell Daddy yes." Sid smiled softly at me. "How about if I make you happy?"

"You already do," I said, smiling back.

"That's not what I meant, and you know it." Sid reached over and touched my cheek.

"What's going on?" I asked. "You don't seem that horny."

"Not any more than usual." He sighed and shrugged. "It's Lipplinger, I guess. I know you got thrown off by it, and I'm feeling a little strange, too. I'm just thinking that maybe celebrating our love for each other might make us feel better."

"You mean making love as a way of being life giving in the face of death."

Sid's eyes shone with warmth. "Yeah. Exactly."

I smiled back at him. "After dinner?"

"Now." He gently pulled me into his lap.

Motley flopped onto his belly with a soft snort while I returned Sid's kiss.

"This is not a good time or place," I whispered.

"Just a little quick one." He nuzzled my ear, then kissed me again, his hands wandering.

"Oh, for crying out loud!" snarled a cranky, older voice.

Lyle Weaver stood in the doorway to the office, glaring at both of us through his faded blue eyes. What there was left of his hair was light gray and standing up all over his head.

"I told you." I slid off Sid's lap. "Can I help you, Lyle?"

"I need the reservations book," he grumbled.

"The printout with today's reservations is on the front desk," I nodded at the front.

"I've got a request for next month that I need to reserve."

"Then you need to check the computer. Do you want me to show you how again?"

Lyle's eyes shot to the phone on the desk, where a line had lit up.

"Damn it. That Irene has taken over again."

"It's her job. She's the reservations manager."

"Don't you talk down to me," Lyle snapped. "You're not too big for your daddy to take you over his knee. And he will when I tell him what you said just now."

He stomped off to the front desk. Sid rolled his eyes.

"We do not need him at the front desk," he said.

"He's very pleasant to the guests. And, technically, he's not our problem." I grabbed the disk that had landed on the desk right about the time I'd landed on Sid's lap. "This is. We'll see about giving life to each other when we get back to our bedroom tonight."

Sid sighed a little, then smiled. "I'll be looking forward to it."

I went upstairs, Motley on my heels. As we walked down the hall, Motley began sniffing at all the doors. I opened the one to Room 305 with my passkey, and Motley bolted inside. He ran straight to the closet door and barked at the upper shelf.

"Quiet," I ordered.

Motley stilled, but stayed looking at the shelf, his stump of a tail wagging furiously. I ran my hand across the top of the shelf, then pulled the room's chair over to the closet, and stood on it to get a good look. There was nothing up there but the plastic laundry bag we always left and an iron, its cord still neatly wrapped. I looked under the shelf and didn't see anything. But Motley was sure there was something up there and Motley had never been wrong before.

I ran my hand along the underside of the shelf and found a bit of tape. I slid under the shelf and saw that a piece of silver duct tape had been stuck to the bottom. The shelf was intact, so there was no reason for the tape. I pulled it free and sighed deeply. A small plastic-wrapped bundle remained stuck to the tape. I debated yanking the plastic free from the tape, but didn't want to risk getting white powder all over the room's floor. Assuming there was a white powder inside the package. I hoped it was a micro-dot, but Motley didn't usually alert on those unless I'd given him a similar one to sniff and told him to find it.

I presented the dog with the floppy disk.

"Okay, Motley, find," I commanded cheerfully.

Motley went happily sniffing all over the room. He paused at the end of the dresser, where Lipplinger's computer had been set up, and sniffed that extra thoroughly. Looking up at me, he sat and whined disconsolately.

"You're still a good boy," I said, scratching him between the ears. "You're my good boy. I love my Fool's Motley."

Motley and I left the room. I relocked the door, then headed over to my parents' house. Sid was in the kitchen, making dinner with Janey's help. I shook my head at him and fed Motley.

Hattie showed up at the resort that evening around seven, right after dinner. I did not know how she'd found the right combination of flights to get to Tahoe, but I wasn't going to question it. My biggest problem was where to put her.

"We're filled to the rafters," I told her very quietly, the front counter between us. "The only room open is the one your brother had."

Hattie is a tall woman with gray hair and an incredibly calm demeanor.

She smiled. "That's exactly what I want."

"You're not feeling creepy about it?"

Hattie shrugged. "I'm sure if Miles could find a way to haunt me, he would. But as it happens, I do not believe in ghosts. Furthermore..." She lowered her voice and looked me in the eye. "I need to spend some significant time in that room in a way that will not be remarked upon."

I sighed. "Okay. Just so you know, I already went through it twice and Sid opened up every file he could find on the computer and the disks he had."

"I'll need to look at those, too." Hattie glanced around, but the lobby was empty for a change. "We need to get those plans he had before the target gets a hold of them or we'll be in deep trouble."

July 22, 1988

I couldn't help but remark on how beautifully blue the sky was. It was a perfect day. Nick got behind the wheel of a dark sedan, waved at me, and drove away along the seaside cliffs. The road curved, but the car didn't turn. Instead, it went straight off the side of the cliff and sailed into the air...

I woke up, gasping.

"You okay?" Sid asked.

He gently rubbed my back as I sat, trying to get my breath back.

"Nightmare," I said.

"The usual?"

There's a specific nightmare that I'm prone to having when I feel stressed. This time, however, I shook my head.

"No." I swallowed, then told Sid about the dream.

"Oh." He pulled me into his arms and squeezed me. "You are really not ready for this, are you?"

"You're not either."

"And yet we gave him permission to learn tonight."

I shuddered and shook my head. "We might as well have. Let's face it, Sid. Neither of us is going to be ready to see Nick driving, but it is inevitable unless we want to cripple him emotionally."

"There is that." He yawned and blinked. "What time is it?"

I looked at the glowing numbers on the clock radio next to Sid's side of the bed.

"Two-thirty."

Sid cursed. "Think you can sleep?"

"Sure." I laid back down.

He kissed me softly, then slid down next to me. Sid and I do like snuggling, and we will sometimes fall asleep that way. However, we rarely sleep tangled up with each other. We keep waking each other up when we do.

Sid was out cold and talking in his sleep within seconds, and I smiled as I looked at him lying next to me. He had been especially tender and warm as we'd made love earlier that night.

The alarm, however, was anything but tender and warm when it went off at four-thirty. Sid slapped it off and got out of bed while I rolled back over and tried to go back to sleep. Sid is a morning person and is almost always awake by five. Since he'd taken on the morning and day shifts at the restaurant, he was getting up at four-thirty so that he could get his daily run in, get showered and dressed, then over to the restaurant by six for set up before the restaurant opened at seven.

The housekeeping staff wouldn't even be at the resort until eight-thirty. They only started at seven on Satur-days because there were so many check-outs, which meant more time cleaning each room. I yawned. I'd still have to get up at six-thirty so that I could get my run in, then get dressed, eat breakfast, and be functional.

I didn't stagger downstairs to the housekeeping office until eight forty-five, but I'd stopped in the breakroom to get an extra-large cup of coffee. Lourdes was handing out room assignments to the crew. As she assigned Donna Mars several of the cabins, Mira rolled her eyes. Lourdes saw it and glared back. I sighed. The morning was already off to a flying start.

The housekeeping office sat next to the resort laundry in the basement of the main lodge. As the crew left to go upstairs, Mira glared again at Lourdes, who stalked off.

"Lisa," Mira groaned. "You know Donna can't handle the cabins."

Donna did have a lot of trouble working around any toys that got strewn over the floors, which was a much more significant problem in the cabins than in the lodge rooms because there was so much more floor in the cabins.

"How did that happen?" I asked Mira.

"Donna said she didn't want to work the third floor, and then Yesmenia and Irina said that they didn't want to give up the second floor, so Lourdes just caved right in." Mira folded her arms across her chest.

I sighed. "I'll go give Donna a hand later."

"That's just it." Mira threw her hands in the air. "You shouldn't have to. I mean, I totally get that Donna doesn't want to be on the third floor after yesterday. But we could have coaxed Yesmenia and Irina along. Lourdes won't do that. She just lets everyone walk all over her. It's almost like she doesn't want the job."

I bit my lip. As it happened, Lourdes hadn't wanted to be head housekeeper.

"Well, consider her position," I told Mira. "She had the most seniority, and she didn't want to lose that."

"But she totally sucks at it!"

I nodded. Lourdes didn't totally suck at the job, but she wasn't as good at it as she should have been. Mira, on the other hand, was an excellent manager, and with Daddy needing a new manager for the housekeeping department, you could tell she was salivating.

It was just one more headache that my father was dealing with that summer, right along with finding a new overall manager. I couldn't help making a face as I headed upstairs. After the previous few days, being manager of anything at the resort was the last thing I wanted. Which also made me feel guilty. [I don't see why. Your father knew you far too well to have those kinds of expectations, however happy it would have made him. - SEH]

After grabbing a snack and another cup of coffee from the kitchen, I made my way to cabin four, where Donna stood over the vacuum cleaner with tears in her eyes. She had reddish blond hair that she kept perpetually in a ponytail. Her frame was slight, but she could lift a king-size mattress long enough to get a sheet on in no time.

"What's the matter?" I asked, trying to sound as soothing as I could.

"I broke it!" Donna sniffed. "I vacuumed over some Legos again. You're going to fire me."

"I'm not going to fire you." I sighed. "But, yes, we did warn you about that."

"I'm no good at this."

I winced. "That's not true. Admittedly, you've got a problem working around toys, but your bed-making is gorgeous and you're very good at getting through a room quickly. In fact, that may be why you're having so much trouble with the toys on the floor."

She took a deep breath as I got on the radio to page Dusty, who appeared within seconds, it seemed like. Dusty smiled shyly at Donna, then went to work. I focused on showing Donna how to check for Barbie shoes, Legos, and other small items on the floor before vacuuming. It's a lot harder to do than you might think, especially if you're prone to moving quickly, which Donna was.

"All done," Dusty announced, and the vacuum roared to life and started going.

"Thanks, Dusty," I said.

He nodded quickly, then hurried out of the cabin. Donna sighed, looking after him.

"Do you like him?" I smiled in spite of myself.

Donna shrugged, then nodded. "Yeah. But I don't think he likes me."

Given what Dusty was involved in, I knew I had to be careful not to encourage Donna. However, I also needed to keep tabs on anybody Dusty was interested in.

"Why do you say that?" I asked.

"He'll talk to everyone but me." Donna sniffed. "Every time I was working up there, he'd be talking to the people in the rooms. He talked to the old man, to the lady in the next room over."

I quickly wracked my brain and came up with Ms. Sanchez in room 306.

"Everybody?"

"Yeah. It seems like." Donna frowned. "You know, he'll be walking around the common areas, and he'll see somebody, then go over and say hi or something. Me? He doesn't say a word."

"Hmm." I smiled at her again. "Well, I wouldn't get too wrapped up in it. You guys work together and that can make things really awkward when something blows up."

"You're right." Donna sniffed and blinked. "I'm not having a very good week."

"I know." I patted her arm. "But you'll get through it."

My walkie-talkie squawked.

"Lisa?" asked my father's voice in my ear. "Mrs. Mitchell is at the desk asking about her brother's computer."

Sighing, I clicked the talk button. "I'm on my way."

I suppose I could have just had my father hand the computer and Lipplinger's other belongings over to Hattie, since said items were stored in the locked closet in his private office. I, perhaps, should have. After I said hi to Hattie, who was standing at the front desk, I went to my father's office.

"Be right back," I told her.

"Take your time," she said, her voice tired and almost bored.

I was a little surprised. She'd seemed pretty worried about getting the plans that Lipplinger had the night before. Daddy was in the office, also looking harassed and a little tired.

"You okay?" I asked him.

"Well enough." He looked at me. "Where's that computer?"

"Oh, it's in your closet." I unlocked the door. "I thought it would be safer."

"So, why didn't you just tell me to give it to her?" His eyes narrowed.

I looked away and shrugged. I have a bit of a problem with getting things past my father. He's an insanely good poker player mostly because he can read people better than anybody I know. Worse yet, the only person who knows me better than Daddy does is Sid, and even Sid can't read my tells like my father can. The only reason the Ladies' Night Out women can read my tells better than Sid can is because we've been playing poker together once a month for over two years. And those women still can't read me like Daddy does.

"I wanted to say hi to Hattie," I said.

"That's right." Daddy nodded. "She's also one of those Travel Club friends of yours."

"Yeah." I smiled at him. "And Sid and I write for her magazines quite a bit."

"Hm." Daddy didn't say anything as I lugged the computer, the cords, and the box of floppy disks out of the closet, along with Lipplinger's suitcase and briefcase.

Cursing Dale O'Connor for landing me there every step of the way, I brought everything out to Hattie and dumped it all on a luggage cart that was at the end of the desk.

"Why don't I bring this up to your room," I said.

"Yes. That would be perfect." Hattie took a deep breath and turned toward the elevator.

I pulled the cart after us. Once in the room, Hattie looked around.

"Where, in Heaven's name, did he put the damned thing?" she asked, glaring at the computer. "That table won't support it. It looks like it wobbles."

"It does." I sighed. "He had us move the TV every morning so that he could put the computer on the dresser. Then had our guy come in the evening to put the TV back so that he could watch it."

Hattie rolled her eyes. "Oh, dear God. He didn't." She closed her eyes. "As I once told you, I'd apologize for his behavior, but there is no excuse for it."

"It's who he was."

Hattie squeezed her eyes shut and sniffed.

"I'm sorry," I said quietly. "I know you're grieving for him."

"Grieving." She looked blankly at the window, which still had the blackout curtains drawn. "I suppose." She suddenly looked at me. "Of course I am. He was my brother."

"It can't be easy for you." I smiled softly. "I mean, you've told me you don't have any other relatives except for your kids."

She went back to staring blankly at the window. "No, I don't."

"I'm willing to listen."

"I'm sure you are, darling." She smiled, then gently shook her head. "I just don't know if you'd understand."

"Do I need to?"

She winced. "Truth be told, I have no idea." She looked me over, her eyes penetrating. "Lisa, several years ago, I remember Sid telling me that you were a very different kind of bird. That you placed a high value on communication and relationship. That you chose to work on your relationships, even when others would not. I took that to mean that you came from a healthy family."

"Maybe." I shrugged. "I have my issues, like everyone else."

"Issues." Hattie snorted and shook her head. "You may have issues. But I, my darling, have full subscriptions."

I chuckled in spite of myself. "You've always seemed pretty together to me."

"And I have spent a great deal of time and money to get that way." Hattie blinked her eyes. "The point is, if you come from a loving family, it's very hard to understand what it's like when a family is… Shall we say, not so loving." She sighed. "As an adult, I avoided my mother. She was incredibly critical of me, wanted me to be like all the other girls. Thanks be, I met James."

"Your husband."

Hattie smiled sadly. "Yes. He was possibly the first person to be truly kind to me. He was the one who encouraged me to stay away from Mother and Miles. It was James who pointed out how dreadfully abusive they were."

"Your mother too?"

"Oh, yes. It wasn't the obvious kind of abuse, well, not beyond the constant criticism. But she idolized Miles. He could do no wrong. And when I protested the way he put me down or treated me with disdain, my mother usually blamed me for the way he treated me. Or she would excuse it. Finally, even she had to admit how horrid his behavior was and asked me to accept it to keep the peace." She shuddered. "I had a terrible time. I didn't want to believe that she was right, and mostly didn't, because the way Miles behaved was so unlike everything I read about how families were supposed to be. Not to mention how hurt I felt all the time. James and a lot of therapy finally helped me to understand that it wasn't my imagination, that my mother and Miles were behaving incredibly badly, and that it was not my fault."

"That sounds pretty awful."

"It was."

I sighed. "And I guess you have a point in that it's a little hard for me to understand. But I know it happens. I work with teens a lot, and yeah, a lot of what I hear is the usual adolescent angst. But there are those kids whose parents are genuinely terrible."

"One of the reasons Miles was so terrible was that he was bitterly disappointed that the rest of the world did not adore him the same way that Mother did."

"That makes sense."

Hattie pressed her lips together. "I hated him."

"Really?" I looked at her, puzzled. "You don't seem like your soul is that dark."

"It's not." Hattie sighed. "Not anymore. At least, I hope it's not. But there was definitely a time when I did hate my brother. Now, I like to think that I see him for the pathetic creature he really is." She stopped and swallowed. "Or was."

"I'm so sorry, Hattie."

She glanced at me, then blinked. "Well. That is enough whining for now. We have a job to get done."

"Okay. What, exactly, are we looking for? Papers? A microdot?"

"It should be either on his computer, itself, or on one of his floppy disks." She frowned at the small box that I put on the dresser. "There are two sets of plans, actually. One of my companies has the contract for a missile guidance system that will be used on submarines as part of the Strategic Defense Initiative."

"Star Wars?" I couldn't help chuckling. "I thought that was supposed to be lasers and decades away from happening, even if it can."

Hattie's smile was grim but there. "Which is precisely what we want everyone to believe, especially the Soviets. With all the chaos there, the last thing we need is for the wrong person to perceive us as a threat and use that as a rallying point. But there are other ways to shoot down ballistic missiles before they reach us than with lasers, and this new guidance system should help us do exactly that. The problem is, Dale made a set of the plans my company has developed and gave the set to Miles so that he could develop a dummy set that he would pass on to the young man who is supposed to be setting up the sting with the KGB agent making the tech buys from him. The young man is supposed to sell the dummy plans to the agent, thus misleading the Soviets."

"So, if I'm understanding you correctly, there are two sets of plans. One we don't want the Soviets to get and one we do." I frowned. "How am I going to know which is which?"

"That's why I'm here." Hattie didn't quite roll her eyes. "Shortly after you called about Miles, Dale called and asked me to take care of my brother's body and effects in person. I can, at least, read the two different sets of plans and tell which is the good one and which is the dummy. The problem is, we don't know how Miles hid the plans. Assuming he did."

I glared at the computer. "In other words, he may have assumed that no one would have the kind of computer that could use those floppy disks, let alone read what was on them."

"I'm afraid so." Hattie picked up the computer box and gingerly set it next to the TV.

"You know what?" I said. "I could try to get Dusty to fix that table. That might give you a chance to get to know him."

"You mean the target."

"Yep."

"That might be useful." Hattie shrugged. "In the meantime, I'll get the machine set up and see what I can do to read these disks."

"Okay." I turned and saw the closet. "Hattie, did your brother use cocaine at all?"

"Miles?" Hattie's eyebrows shot up, and she laughed. "Why do you ask?"

"I found some in the closet there. It had been taped to the underside of the shelf."

"Hm." Hattie looked thoughtfully at the closet as well. "As Miles always put it, alcohol was his preferred poison. On the other hand, he may have been keeping it to use as a weapon. You know, planting it on somebody, then calling the police. I don't know that he ever did that, but I wouldn't put it past him."

I checked my watch. "I didn't see anything in his stuff that could read a microdot, and as far as I know, he didn't leave the resort. We may have another agent onsite, but I don't know who it is. And that would be the only way your brother could have been making or reading a microdot."

"It's possible, I suppose." Hattie frowned. "It's more like Miles to use paper or a computer disk. He was prone to losing small items." She set the computer on its side next to the dresser, then picked up the briefcase. "Well, I'd best get to work." She smiled softly at me. "Thank you, Lisa. I truly appreciate the kind ear."

I went over and gave her a big hug. "You've been a very good friend to Sid and me. It's no trouble at all."

Hattie looked at me, completely puzzled. "And yet, you trust me around your husband."

I laughed. Well, Hattie was one of several women that I was still friends with, even though Sid had slept with them before he gave up sleeping around.

"I trust Sid," I said, grinning. "As long as you don't mind being a former lover, then I don't mind you being around."

"He was right. You are a very different kind of bird."

I left the room, not sure what to do next, so I went down toward the break room to see if the kitchen was slow enough for me to get some lunch. Which didn't happen. Irene Wu flagged me down from the front desk to ask me about the next day's check-ins and to generally complain about Lyle. Then Lourdes wanted to go over the next day's check-outs and room assignments because she didn't want Mira getting mad at her.

By the time I got down to the kitchen, lunch was almost over, Nick was off-duty and eating in the break room alongside Sid, who was also eating, although the two were not talking to each other and the atmosphere in the room was definitely cool.

That's when our pagers went off. Now, these were not connected to my walkie-talkie. These pagers were official Quickline equipment, and no one knew we had them because they vibrated silently. The three of us were wearing them because the pager we'd given to Dusty Simpson to summon him when his services were needed to fix something also had a tracer installed on it so that when he got within a few hundred feet of the resort's boundaries, Sid,

Nick, and I would get paged and one of us could follow him. After all, the job that no one was supposed to know about was to keep Dusty under surveillance, so that he didn't sell technology to the Soviets that he wasn't supposed to.

"I'll—" Sid started to get up.

Nick bounced up first.

"I'll go," he announced, running out of the room.

I sighed as he left.

"What happened now?" I asked Sid.

He sighed and shrugged. "I have no idea. I even complimented him today and told him he could learn to drive with your dad."

"He's still mostly talking to us." I winced. "Odds I can get some lunch?"

Sid smiled. "Sure. What do you want?"

To Breanna, 9/22/00

Topic of the Day: Write about a time you were angry with your parent(s)

Wow. First time we crack open that journaling book you bought, and we have to pick this question. Sorry. It's not an easy one for me, mostly because I am still so very pissed off at my first mother for a lot of reasons. Having to keep her leukemia a secret. Her leaving me alone so many times. And plenty of other reasons.

And it's not like I haven't gotten mad at Dad and Mom Two. But with them, well, it never really lasted. We'd fight, but we'd settle it, usually right away, and with the appropriate apologies, etc.

The big exception was the summer after I turned 15. Mom and Dad had to work a case on Grandpa Wycherly's resort, and Dad decided I should work as a busboy, since Dad was managing the wait staff in the resort restaurant. To be honest, it felt like I was mad at him for the entire summer. But even then, something happened that put a whole different perspective on the situation.

Grandpa used to hire a lot of college kids for the busy summer season. In fact, Uncle Neil used to work for him that way, and that's how he met Aunt Mae and Mom. Anyway, that summer of '88, there was this one kid, Dusty. He'd been set up to work there because that's what the case was about. Anytime he got close to leaving the resort, Mom, Dad, or I was supposed to tail him to see who he connected with.

So, this one day, I was really pissed at Dad, mostly because he was being so decent. I know. It doesn't make sense, but I guess I just wanted to be mad at him for making me work that summer, and he goes and lets me learn to drive with Grandpa and even tells me I'm doing a good job. Okay. It was that last bit that got me mad. I hated that job. It sucked. I didn't want to be good at it.

Anyway, the pager we had on Dusty goes off, and I jump on it. Sure enough, Dusty is headed into the woods around the place, and I follow along. I kept my distance, at first. It turned out he wasn't doing anything. Just walked around for a bit, sighed, then turned to go back to the resort. I made like I'd been out there doing the same thing and let him see me.

"Oh." Dusty looked at me and blinked. "Hi, Nick."

"Hi, Dusty. What are you doing out here?"

He made a face. "Just getting away from it all. You?"

"The same, I guess." I sighed. "Getting a little fed up with my dad."

"Why?" Dusty looked at me as if he really wanted to know.

I shrugged. "He wouldn't let me go to science camp this year because he needs me here, he says. But then he keeps trying to make it up to me, which really sucks, because if he really wanted to make it up to me, he'd let me go to science camp."

"That sucks." Dusty sighed, then shrugged. "At least your dad wants you around. Mine won't even support me. Says I'm a loser because I like computers and stuff, instead of making millions of dollars in real estate."

"Wow, that sucks even more."

"It's okay." Dusty's face got real hard. "I'll show him. Once I get some extra cash, I'm going to start my own company and make even more money than him. I just have to get my prototype built and tested, then get a venture capitalist, and, boom. I'll have more money than God."

"What are you making?"

Dusty shook his head real fast. "Can't tell you. I don't want to take a chance on someone beating me to it, you know?"

"Yeah."

We walked back to the resort in silence, but I couldn't help thinking about things. I didn't magically stop being mad at Dad. He had been pretty heavy-handed about me working that summer. But he'd done it because he needed me. He not only didn't think I was a loser, but he was trusting me with important parts of the operation.

Which is one more thing I'm mad at my first mom for. She would never have trusted me with anything like that. She wouldn't even let me have a skateboard because she didn't trust me not to kill myself.

July 23-24, 1988

Saturdays were my absolutely crazy day. The vast majority of rooms and cabins rented from Saturday to Saturday. With at least eighty percent turnover, we needed a full crew to make sure all the vacated rooms and cabins were cleaned even more thoroughly than normal days. What made it especially tricky was that the guests didn't always leave early. With check-out time at eleven, some of them took their time. And if they didn't, they'd often just leave the key in the room or cabin and take off, and we wouldn't know they were gone until after eleven, which meant we had less than three hours to get enough cabins and rooms ready for all the guests who would be arriving at 2 p.m. to check in.

The front desk was a zoo, with families checking out, paying bills, then trying to get shuttles or taxis to the airport, or packing their cars if they had them. Then around two, it would get just as crazy as families lined up to get checked in.

The morning rush in the restaurant was hectic with families trying to eat so that they could be packed and out of their rooms by eleven. But it slowed down after that, with next to no lunch guests. Dinner time varied. Some guests liked to eat at the resort restaurant their first night because they were still getting settled in. Others wanted to see as much of Tahoe as possible and headed out quickly. Still others had favorite places to eat away from the resort and visited those on their first night.

That Saturday, I was up at first light, ran and showered, and was ready to go by the time the first guests checked out at six-thirty. At seven, Lourdes handed out the room assignments. I wasn't doing any of the actual cleaning. My job was to do spot checks and to be available for the inevitable disasters.

It was barely eight when I got my first call on the walkie-talkie. A stuffed toy had been found in one of the main lodge rooms, and when I saw it, I knew it wasn't just any old toy. It was a rabbit that had once been white but was now gray. The plastic painted eyes were still there, but you could barely tell that they'd been blue once. Shredded formerly pink satin almost adorned the feet.

I grabbed the bunny and hurried downstairs.

"Who was in two-twelve?" I asked Irene.

Irene handed a guest a charge slip to sign, then shuddered when she saw what I had.

"The Emersons." Irene took the charge slip back and handed the card back to the guest.

"Did they drive or fly?"

Irene shrugged. I hurried into the reservation office and dug up the record.

It may not seem like that big a deal. Kids lose toys all the time, even ones as well-loved as that rabbit obviously had been. What is really aggravating is how often the parents blame us for the loss. I looked up the Emersons, found their home address and phone number. They'd entered a car license on their registration form, but they could have rented the car at the airport. I prayed they didn't have a plane to catch.

There wasn't much to be done, except note that the bunny was in our reservations office on the form, then call the home phone number. Fortunately, they had an answering machine, so I left the message.

I didn't get the call, but the family called around eleven and were told that Tina Bunny was in the office. They showed up just after two and were not happy. From the look on Mr. and Mrs. Emerson's faces, there had probably been a fight over driving back to Tahoe after more than a couple of hours on the road. The little girl, who had to have been around five, was snuffling and looked like she was about to start screaming, probably not for the first time that day.

As I brought the bunny out from the office, I saw another family checking in. Pedro and Lita Delgado both grinned at me, and I quickly shook my head. They got it. Lita got their three kids distracted so that they didn't say hi to Ms. Wycherly. The Delgado kids are remarkably well-trained, even at their young ages, and do what their parents tell them to do when they tell them to do it.

I restored Tina Bunny to the Emerson girl, who crowed with delight. Mrs. Emerson looked relieved, Mr. Emerson less so. The family left, and I noted that the Delgados had been placed in room two-twelve. I seriously doubted that would make much of a difference, but it was interesting.

From there, I went to the restaurant to warn both Sid and Nick not to acknowledge the Delgado family, and they agreed. They'd also seen Daddy looking at us funny a couple of times. I also called Hattie and warned her off.

Around four, I got a chance to go up to the Delgados' room and knocked on the door.

"Housekeeping," I called.

Pedro opened the door and let me in. The kids all gave me a quick hug, then I looked at them severely.

"You guys are going to have to pretend that you don't know me or Mr. Hackbirn, or Nick," I told them. "It's very important."

"Important means we do it," Pedro, Jr., age four, said solemnly.

"But why do we have to pretend?" Eight-year-old Teresa asked.

"Because we don't want anybody to know about the work we're doing here," I said. "There are a couple people here who are very bad, and they'll try to hurt us if they think that we're trying to find them."

Teresa nodded and grinned. Yeah, Lita's kids are very smart, and they get it, even if they don't know what, exactly, it is that their parents do.

"I'll take the kids down to the playground," Pedro, Sr., said.

The children cheered as I gave them directions, and they ran out of the room with their father on their heels.

"So, what's going on?" Lita asked as the door shut on her family.

I explained what Hattie had told me, and Lita cursed.

"So, that's what Dale is up to," she snarled.

She does not like Dale at all.

I shrugged. "At least, with me working housekeeping, it will be fairly easy to search rooms. What Sid and I need from you guys is to help us keep tabs on the target. His name is Dusty. He seems like a nice kid."

"Except that he's selling secrets to the Soviets."

"Who knows how that happened?" I winced. "It could even have been Dale's idea to get him to do it in the first place." I looked around the room. "Why don't I break this lamp? Then I can get Dusty up here to fix it, and you'll get to meet him."

"Here. I'll do it." Lita reached over and broke the bulb on the table lamp under the window.

The room was like most of the others, only with two beds. The window looked over the back side of the main lodge toward the cabins, the playground and the stables.

"But why pretend we don't know each other?" Lita asked.

"My dad. He was acting a little weird when Hattie talked to me yesterday." I made a face. "He knows Hattie is a friend of Sid's and mine. She has been for years. But with Dale pushing Sid on Daddy to work the restaurant this summer, then Lipplinger being Hattie's brother and him showing up here, Daddy seems to be wondering a little too much. And he's really sharp that way. The problem is, we need the extra help on the ground. Dusty doesn't have a car, thank God, but even with surveillance equipment, the three of us can't keep eyes on Dusty all the time. Plus, his contact is probably one of our guests, and we staffers can only get so friendly with them."

"Yeah, but other guests make friends all the time." Lita nodded. "It sounds pretty straightforward."

"We can but hope."

I gave her the frequency for the tracer on Dusty's pager, and she gave me the frequency for hers and Pedro's personal transmitters. I helped her put out super thin wires on the windows and room door so that they'd know if someone had broken into the room, and I got the code to disarm the wires if Sid or I had to go in for some reason.

A minute later, I called Ty Larson on the walkie-talkie and had him page Dusty with a light bulb to the room, then left.

The housekeeping staff was done by four, but I was not. Mr. Merle Wrightman had been less than thrilled the week before, when his family had checked in, that they had Cabin Twelve instead of Cabin Ten, which was the one they usually took. We didn't know what he had against Cabin Twelve – he refused to say why, but even after a week, he still wanted Cabin Ten, or even Cabin Eleven. However, Irene had put a small group of executives and their wives in Cabin Eleven for a corporate retreat that Lyle had neglected to put into the computer system months before and we'd only found the reservation because Irene had double checked everything the Monday before.

The Elizondos had already checked into Cabin Ten and were ecstatic. Well, their family members were getting older and some extra privacy was just the thing. The elder Mrs. Wrightman let her husband know that Cabin Twelve was just as good as their usual one. In fact, being just a hair larger, was better, as their family was also growing. Apparently, there were two new grandchildren that year. Mr. Wrightman was not entirely mollified, but went along with his wife.

I smiled and thanked her, but inside, I shuddered. I had no idea how well screaming infants were going to go over with the executives. Then again, I was praying that the executives wouldn't get too rowdy.

By dinnertime, I was pooped and working on a headache. Worse yet, Sid was still in the restaurant. Lee

Whitney, the dinner manager, had called in sick. Janine Fuentes, the assistant manager, was already there, but it was one of those weekends when everyone had decided to eat at the resort. Daddy took one look at me as I staggered into my parents' house and called the local pizza place.

Sid staggered into the house around eight-thirty.

"I'm letting Janine close tonight," he said. "It's been a day."

It was generally agreed that it had been.

The next day, I got up early enough to go to nine o'clock mass, riding to the church with Daddy, Janey, and Nick. Sid had other plans and had left a couple of hours earlier. Well, he wasn't going to church with us that summer, anyway. Sid is an atheist. He plays the organ for our choir back home, but that has more to do with our good friend Frank Lonnergan, who is the choir director.

After mass, I took Daddy, Janey and Nick to one of the casinos just over the state line to have brunch at one of the hotel buffets. We took our time and didn't get back to the house until just after noon. At twelve-thirty, Mama called from Florida. She and Daddy were talking almost every day, but on Sundays, Mama wanted to talk to the rest of us, too. So did my Grandma.

Now, I love Grandma Caulfield. We've always gotten along and ever since I married a man with money (Sid and I are wealthy), I've been her golden girl. But by that point, she was getting to be the last person on earth that I wanted to talk to.

I understand why she wanted to see me pregnant. She loved the idea of having yet another great-grandbaby. And she was brought up to believe that getting married and having children is what being a woman is all about. What we could not get her to understand is that Sid and I can't get pregnant.

Sid used to sleep around a lot. He was taught free love when he was a kid and saw no reason not to until he and I made our commitment to each other. But when he was 22, he couldn't imagine wanting to get married, let alone procreate (never mind that he had - he just didn't know he had until Nick was eleven). So, he'd gotten a vasectomy. Between how much time had passed by the time we got married and that fact that he'd had a few bouts with social disease, there was no hope of a reversal being successful.

Now, most of the time, I don't care that Sid and I can't have babies. Heck, that summer, I was getting out and out glad we couldn't, thanks to some of the kids I'd seen at the resort. But I do feel it sometimes, and Grandma being determined to see me reproduce, was not helping.

"Well?" Grandma demanded the second I got on the phone.

"Grandma, we've told you. The doctors say we can't."

"What do doctors know? Have you been drinking your mixture?"

"It's not going to help. Sid can't produce sperm—"

"I do not want to hear such filthy talk!"

"Well, if we're going to talk about having babies, Grandma, we're going to touch on some of how it happens."

Grandma humphed. "Be that as it may." She humphed. "You say it's Sid."

"Yes, Grandma."

"Maybe I'd better mix something up for him."

"It's not going to help, Grandma." My gut clenched, worried that it somehow could.

Yeah, I wouldn't mind having a baby with Sid and it does sometimes hurt that I can't. But if I'm honest, I'm perfectly happy that Nick is my only child.

Grandma finally left off, and we said goodbye. I hung up only to find out that Daddy and Nick were headed off to the local high school parking lot for Nick's first driving lesson. My gut clenched. I'd had that nightmare about Nick driving off a cliff the night before again, and it all came rushing back to me.

Sid's Voice -

When I was growing up, it was just Stella and me. My birth mother died when I was two and I had no father. It literally says "Unknown" on my birth certificate.

Raising a kid really made me appreciate my aunt in ways I would never have thought. Stella was a pretty darned good parent, for the most part. If things got rocky during my adolescence, a lot of that was the times. It was the 1960s, and not only was rebellion in style, that's what Stella had taught me. She just never expected me to rebel against her, and even then, it was more about me developing into my own person than butting up against her.

The bigger problem was that I often wondered if she'd really wanted me. She was not a very affectionate person. She did teach me kindness and respect for all human beings, and while she would snipe at me occasionally, she also made a point of praising me. But when she'd get annoyed with me, I kept getting the sense that I was a problem for her, a mess that she needed to clean up.

I later learned that it was a reflection of her own unhappy childhood and not me. But that was after we'd been estranged for sixteen years over me going into the Army when I'd gotten drafted, then my own terrible response when she'd tried to contact me after I got back from Vietnam.

I started thinking about Stella and my adolescence as I pulled away from the resort that Sunday morning, mostly because I was feeling guilty about taking off and leaving Lisa to deal with the craziness of working there. I don't feel guilty very often, and that morning I realized why. Stella had never played the guilt game with me.

Of course, the meeting I was going to also played a role in my thoughts as I drove toward San Francisco that morning. I was raised in The City, in Haight Ashbury, by a bunch of communists, beatniks, and later, hippies, which explains why I was so into sleeping around. It was just normal behavior among the people I grew up with. That there was any specific context for it was foreign to me until high school, and even then, I believed that was a crock.

I wasn't sure why Liz Warner had called my best buddy Tom Freeman and me, but the three of us had agreed that we wanted to meet at the same time. Liz and I were probably two of the most sexually active kids in our graduating class. That I was the stud and Liz was the slut was an incredibly gross injustice, but given the culture at the time, not surprising. Tom had slept with Liz, too, and we'd even done three-ways every so often.

The other thing about Liz was that Tom and I had considered her as much a friend as our other four buddies, possibly even more of one. Most of the other girls we jumped on (and, yeah, it was all about getting ourselves off) didn't really fall into that category. Still, Liz lost touch with me shortly after we graduated. Tom was better at hanging onto relationships, but had lost touch with her by the time I got back from Vietnam in '71.

Tom moved to L.A. in 1986. The weekend we met with Liz, he'd driven up to the Bay Area because it was cheaper than flying. That also meant he came up on Saturday and spent the night with his parents, who had moved out to Livermore sometime in 1972.

I called Tom on my car phone from the highway near Tracy. That way, he'd get to the BART station where we were meeting at about the same time. As I pulled into the parking lot of the Dublin/Pleasanton BART station, Tom was there.

"Thanks for calling me," Tom said as we quickly embraced, then headed up to the train into downtown San Francisco. "God, I needed to get out of there."

"Bad, huh?"

"God grant me the serenity to accept the things I cannot change." Tom shuddered. "How's it going at your father-in-law's?"

We chit-chatted on the train, got off at Powell and dodged the tourists in line for the cable cars, then walked to the restaurant where we were meeting. Liz had chosen the place and was waiting for us when we got there.

She was about average size and wearing a full-skirted blue shirtwaist dress with big padded shoulders. Her dark brown hair had been cut short and feathered. In fact, everything about her screamed money, and we'd all been dirt poor as kids.

"Hey, guys," she said, her smile just a touch wary. "I'm so glad you made it."

"I am, too," I said and grinned. "You look great, Liz."

Her smiled got tight. "Are you sure?"

"Absolutely," said Tom. "You look terrific."

Suddenly, I realized why she was hesitating and laughed.

"You got a boob reduction," I said.

"Holy crap, you did." Tom grinned. "It looks wonderful on you."

Her eyebrows lifted. "You're not disappointed?"

I shook my head. "I was never into over-large boobs, even then."

Which I wasn't.

"I was." Tom chuckled and rolled his eyes. "But I'd forgotten you had them. And I like to think I've outgrown that kind of thinking."

Liz suddenly relaxed and grinned. "I knew I was right to call you guys."

A minute later, we got settled at a table, perused the menus, and finally ordered. Liz asked Tom and me about our lives. I told her I'd gotten married two years before and that we had a 15-year-old kid, pointing out that Lisa is Nick's second mom.

"Second mom?" Liz asked.

"It's not a rating," I said. "It's when Lisa came into Nick's life. Nick's first mother passed three years ago, and Lisa adopted him."

Liz looked at Tom. "What about you?"

"Got married in seventy-two, got sober in nineteen-eighty and promptly got divorced," Tom shrugged. "I'd been teaching at our old school since I got out of college."

"You know, I'd heard that," Liz said with a smile. "Are you still there?"

Tom shook his head. "I'm down in L.A., now. Two years ago, I came down to go to Sid and Lisa's wedding, and at the rehearsal dinner, met their friend Angelique Carter, and Ange and I have been together ever since. What about you?"

Liz took a deep breath. "Well, it took Tom to get me into college." She smiled at him. "I still can't thank you enough for that. And, Sid, I know I didn't believe you when you kept saying that I was the smartest girl in school."

"Well, you were."

"It helped, though, more than you know." She blinked a little. "There was a reason I was so hyper-sexualized as a teen, and it wasn't just the boobs." She swallowed. "I was sexually abused by my father."

"Oh, Liz," Tom sighed. "I'm so sorry."

"I had no idea," I said. "That's terrible."

She shrugged lightly. "It's what happened. The good news is that you two believed in me, and that made a difference. I got my bachelors, got into protecting women's rights, and from there got a full ride to Berkeley Law."

Tom and I cheered.

"That is such good news," I said.

"Liz, I am so proud of you," Tom added.

She nodded. "I've been practicing law for the past twelve years. Started out with a major firm, then got my ass into trouble when I scored a major settlement for a client suing for sexual harassment."

"Wouldn't that have been a good thing for the firm?" Tom asked.

"Not when the CEO of the corporate defendant turned out to be a good buddy of one of our partners." Liz grinned. "And I may have put some pressure on by checking with other female employees of the company to try and build a class-action suit."

Tom and I laughed. Liz may have been easy in high school, but she could be a real ball-buster when provoked. One of the reasons why Tom and I had liked her so much. {Ball-buster? Seriously, darling, you know better than that. - LJW}

"Anyway," Liz continued. "The upshot is that I was able to feather my nest sufficiently to focus on more harassment cases, then offer pro-bono work to a couple shelters for domestic violence victims. Which is my real passion, I've discovered. I am very good at hiding women from their abusers."

I couldn't help grinning. "Liz, I always knew that you had way more on the ball than people were willing to give you credit for. But this is above and beyond. I, too, am so proud of you."

"Well, I am insanely lucky that I got the right kind of support," she said. "But you guys both played into that." She paused and swallowed. "Which is why when I got the invite to our twenty-year reunion, I decided to try and call you."

Tom and I looked at each other.

"I'm glad you did," Tom said, finally. "The committee was seriously after me to work with them since I'd worked there for so long. But I said no."

"Why?" Liz asked.

Tom shrugged. "Too many jokes from them about what a stoner and boozer I was. Which I was back then, and even for our ten-year reunion. I'd like to think that I've grown up since then. That I've actually achieved some real maturity. And I work with high school kids all day. I don't want to go back to my time in high school."

"What about you, Sid?" she asked. "Did you go to the ten-year?"

"Oh, hell no." I winced. "There were a few guys from our class who probably knew what I'd been through. But no one that I knew. Well, except Loser Renfrew, and he didn't make it back."

Liz gasped. "You got drafted."

I nodded. "Two of the worst years of my life and I do not talk about it."

"He really doesn't," said Tom, who also knew what I'd been like when I'd first gotten back.

What Tom didn't know - and couldn't - was that was also when I'd gotten pulled into intelligence work, and then not released from it when I'd finally gotten home.

I sighed. "Liz, you and I and Tom have been through some serious shit. The bottom line is, we all survived and somehow, I hope, came out of it as better people. That's what I hang onto. But at the same time, I do not see a lot of benefit in re-visiting that kind of hurt. Which is why I have zero interest in going to our high school reunion. According to Tom, Stan is doing his damnedest to totally fuck up his life."

"You can say that again," Tom grumbled.

"Loser is dead," I continued. "Bob and Wallace were never that close, anyway. In fact, the two people I would most want to see are already sitting at this table. I have nothing to gain by going."

Liz smiled. "Which is exactly how I feel."

We spent the rest of lunch talking about all sorts of stuff. Some reminiscing, such as the time Stella caught me and Liz doing it in our apartment, and I kept going while bitching at Stella about not having my own room. But most of it was about life, in general. The sorts of things real friends talk about when they get together because they have other stuff in common besides a past.

As we finished, I invited Liz down to mine and Lisa's place in Beverly Hills.

"I'd love for you to have a chance to meet Lisa," I told her.

"She's not going to be upset that you and I were lovers?" Liz frowned.

"She shouldn't be." I thought about it. "As long as you don't mind being a former lover, she's fine. Ange and I slept together fairly regularly, and Lisa's friends with her and always has been."

Tom suddenly groaned. Liz and I looked at him.

He sighed. "It has suddenly occurred to me that any woman I have had any significant interest in, Sid has slept with first."

"What?" My eyebrows rose. "I never slept with Beth." His ex-wife.

"And look at how well that one worked out." Tom shook his head. "You beat me to Liz. Remember Diane? You got to her first. Cheryl Nunes. You and Ange almost had something."

I laughed. "That was never going to happen."

We went on in that vein for some minutes more, then it was time to leave. On the train back to where we'd left our cars, Tom belabored our shared women for some time, only to conclude that it really didn't make any difference, which it didn't.

I got back to Tahoe in time for dinner, but just barely. Lisa had gotten it from the resort restaurant - she can cook but prefers not to. Nick was full of chatter about his driving lesson, and even Lisa smiled at him.

There wasn't much to be said about the case. Hattie was worried that the disks for her brother's computer did not have the plans for the guidance system on them. They had to be somewhere on the resort.

I didn't care and, later, focused on how much making my darling Lisa happy meant to me. And by that, I mean sex.

July 25, 1988

S id had been in quite the mood when he'd gotten back to the resort after his afternoon in San Francisco. It wasn't Liz, per se. It was the reminder of what I really meant to him. And that he wanted to make it up to me that he'd run off that day and I'd had to stay behind.

We cranked the television on rather loudly to cover up the noise we made. Our sex life is exuberant, and that can be embarrassing to my family members and anyone else on the other side of thin walls. Monday morning, both of us were happy, but a little bleary-eyed. Sid decided he could take a break from the breakfast rush and sleep in a little. It also gave us a chance to figure out what we were going to do next about the plans.

After running and showers, Sid hurried off to the restaurant. I put on my shorts and polo shirt, then turned on the walkie-talkie and checked in. Fortunately, things were quiet that morning. So, after eating some cereal at my parents' house, I got Motley, and we went back to the staff lodge. Half of the downstairs (the other half being the apartment Sid and I were staying in) and all of the upper floor had been divided into shared rooms with private bathrooms. The kids were all at work, and the lodge was deserted.

Even so, I didn't waste any time and went through each room, giving Motley a chance to find the floppy. He only alerted once, and that was in the room Marina shared with Donna. I found the package of what was most likely cocaine in Marina's purse, in a hidden pocket near the bottom of the brown leather bag. I debated taking it, but didn't want Marina to know that someone had been going through her stuff. Then I searched Dusty's room extra thoroughly and found nothing. There wasn't even anything in the downstairs common room, where the kids could hang out in the evenings, since they all worked days, when we needed the help more.

I was just putting the cushions back on the common room sofa when Dusty wandered in, wearing his bright yellow polo shirt and dirty jeans.

"Hi," I said, brightly.

He seemed startled, then shrugged. "Hi."

"Everything okay?" I asked.

"Fine. Fine," he said. "I just need my small screwdrivers. There's a kid whose toy broke, and I said I'd try to fix it."

"That's nice of you." I smiled at him. "Thanks."

"Yeah. Well." He scuttled off to his room and reappeared a minute later with a plastic, burgundy-colored, flat case I had not only just seen when I'd searched his room but knew for a fact contained only small screwdrivers.

I watched him leave, then debated what to do next. The common room looked like any other large living room, although there was a large rock fireplace on the back wall. The room was in the middle of the floor, with the bedrooms on one side and the apartment on the other. The apartment had the only kitchen because the kids either ate out of the restaurant, or off the resort, or had pizza delivered.

Actually, there was a lot of pizza delivered to the resort as a whole since we didn't have room service. A couple of other restaurants also offered delivery, but pizza seemed to be the most popular.

Motley whined a little, and I unlocked the door to the apartment and went in. A light flashed on the answering machine we'd installed at the beginning of the summer. We'd forwarded our business line to Neff and Mary's old number since Sid and I did have a freelance writing business to keep up. I checked the messages. Marge Benson had left one with a number local to the Tahoe area.

Marge was another Travel Club member. She lived in an RV that was parked most often in South Lake Tahoe and was one of Mama's friends. Mama, and I had reason to believe, Daddy didn't know about her connection to the Travel Club or the intelligence community, in general. Marge was technically retired from the CIA and had been for over ten years. But she'd remained part of the upper echelon of covert operatives, coordinating between a variety of agencies, both domestic and foreign.

Sid and I had decided while we were out running that morning to call her. Now that we knew the plans had arrived, and that they were missing, we decided we could use all the help we could get. And since Marge was one of my parents' friends, it wouldn't be odd for her to show up at the resort every so often.

I deduced that Sid hadn't been able to actually reach her, and dialed the number she'd left. Marge picked up right away.

"Good to hear from you," she told me. "What's up?"

"Were you updated on Dale's big plan to catch the operative buying our technology?" I asked.

"Hell, yes." Marge sighed. "I'm right here, aren't I? Well, I was going to be."

"What's going on?"

"Red Light. That long-haul courier on your line."

"What about him?" My tone may have been more than a little acerbic.

Red Light, whose real name was Scott Morgan, was a perpetual thorn in Sid's and my sides. He was an amazing tail, but we'd had more than a few problems with his attitude and tendency to assume he knew what he was doing.

Since Operation Quickline's primary mission was moving information around, each colored line had several stops that led to New York. The idea was that no two stops were more than a couple hours away from each other, allowing couriers the chance to lead seemingly normal lives. The stops were necessary to confuse enemy operatives who were trying to follow the information coming in from Europe and South America.

But there were things that were sometimes physically too big for couriers to handle, such as guns and some surveillance equipment, or that couldn't go by air for various reasons, but needed to go directly to Washington, DC. That's why we had Morgan working as a long-haul trucker serving all four of the different lines.

"I'll be taking his place for the time being," Marge growled, adding a couple extra curse words.

"Is he all right?" I asked.

"No." More cursing. "The idiot got his head blown off over the weekend. Got cocksure and walked right into a trap."

"Oh, no!"

"We told him to let you two handle the Soviet buyer. But no. He had a whole load of PCs and was using them as bait. Thank God, the buyer didn't get Red Light's truck."

"Oh, the poor guy," I said.

"Well, you don't live long being stupid in this business."

"Believe me, I know." I sighed. "I guess Sid and I had better find something else to do. We've got a lot of territory to cover here, and we have to be careful how we do it, especially now that Hattie's here. My father knows that she's part of the Travel Club, and he's beginning to get suspicious. You haven't told my folks that you're part of it, have you?"

"Hell, no." Okay. She didn't say hell. "Your dad is too damned smart to try and put something past him. I tried telling Dale that, but would he listen?"

"Of course not." I shut my eyes as my blood began boiling.

"Dale said, no. You two have worked around your father as yourselves before. You'd make it work." Marge cursed again. "He's got some plan for the two of you. I have no idea what it is, but he's been grooming Sid for years."

"You'd think Dale wouldn't want to blow that by messing up our covers," I grumbled.

"You'd think. I've got to give Dale a lot of credit. He is insanely good at managing all the chess pieces, if you know what I mean. But some days, I have to wonder about him."

I thanked Marge and went to put Motley back in the yard at my parents' house. After playing with Bowser puppy for a bit, I took him outside to do his business, then put him back in his crate.

I needed to talk to both Sid and Hattie and decided that since it was getting close to one in the afternoon at that point, it was time for lunch. So, I went to look for Sid, and instead found Bracha Solomon wandering the perimeter of the resort near the woods beyond the horse barn, where a small creek ran.

"Hey, Bracha," I called to her.

She was tall, with a solid build, black hair, and deep brown eyes. She was wearing a t-shirt and her checked chef's pants but hadn't put on the white coat she wore in the kitchen.

"Whatcha doing?" I asked as I walked up to her.

Her eyes flitted to the woods. I could have sworn I saw a bit of yellow flash between the trees.

"Oh, just getting some kinks out," she said, rolling her shoulders. "I worked breakfast this morning. I'm taking a split shift so that Felix can work dinner tomorrow for my night off."

That didn't quite compute to me, but I couldn't figure out why. I left her to her walk and headed back to the restaurant to find Sid.

He was in the kitchen, so I decided to get some lunch at the same time.

"What's the special?" I asked him as he filled salad plates for one of the waiters.

"You're going to love this." He shuddered. "Chili burgers with fries and coleslaw." He turned. "Marina!"

"Thanks, Sid." Marina rushed up and looked the plates over. "One was no carrot."

Sid pointed. "That one."

Marina quickly dressed the salads, then put them on a tray and rushed out.

"I'll have the special," I said, grinning. Chili burgers are one of my all-time favorite foods. "If this is a good time."

"As good a time as any." He put the order into the ordering computer.

I frowned. "I'm guessing the special isn't about doing something nice for me."

"It is, and it isn't." Sid rolled his eyes. "The kitchen inventory is a separate file on a separate computer than the ordering system. Which makes it really hard to coordinate what's being ordered with what's in the freezer." He sighed. "Bracha found a whole bunch of ground beef this morning just after our regular order had arrived." He smiled at me. "I did suggest the chili burgers on your behalf. But tomorrow, we're going to be doing sloppy joes. Your dad's idea. And we have a lot of extra cabbage because no one ordered cole slaw last week. So, there's going to be a lot of coleslaw on special." He shook his head. "This ordering system would work a lot better if it were integrated with the rest of the restaurant's computers. In fact, it would be nice to coordinate the restaurant's computers with the rest of the resort's systems so that we could get some data on which of the restaurant customers are staying here and who's coming in from the outside. The good news is your dad agrees. I told him I'd work on it."

My chili burger came up just then. Sid decided he could use a break and grabbed the plate, nodding toward the breakroom. I shut the door and got a tumbler from the cupboard and filled it with Dr. Pepper from the room's soda fountain.

"You want some?" I asked.

Sid loves Dr. Pepper but can't drink it too often because it upsets his stomach if he does.

He finished setting my place at the back table. "Oh, what the hell. Thanks."

I filled a second tumbler with the soda and brought it over. I smiled as I saw the place setting. Sid had even remembered to add my newest passion to the plate: a tiny cup of mayonnaise. Over the past couple years, we'd been to Europe several times on Quickline business. The Belgians and French rarely put ketchup on their fries. They put mayonnaise on them. I'd fallen in love with the practice.

"How did your search go this morning?" Sid asked as I dunked a fry and ate it.

"Fine, I guess." I got a big bite of my burger and sighed happily. "Oh, my god. This chili burger is fabulous."

"I'm glad." Sid grinned. He seems to think it's entertaining to watch me eat. [It's not just entertaining. It's incredibly arousing. - SEH]

"I didn't find the plans." I winced. "I found some cocaine hidden in Marina's purse. Or what looks like cocaine. It's a white powder, and it was in a hidden pocket."

"Could be heroin." Sid mused. "But coke seems to be the current favorite." He looked back at the kitchen. "Funny. Marina doesn't act like she's using anything."

"Could she be really good at covering it up?"

"It's possible." Sid thought it over as he sipped his soda. "On the other hand, I've been working with her for a couple weeks now. I find it a little hard to believe that I wouldn't have picked something up. I spotted Lee Whitney's problem almost immediately."

"Lee Whitney's on drugs?"

Sid nodded. "Marijuana. Well, I can't say for certain. I haven't smelled it on him or caught him stoned. But he sure acts like it."

"What are we going to do?" I looked at him, worried.

"There's nothing we can do until I actually catch him. It's not as though he's messing up on the job. He's not the greatest manager out there, but he knows what to do and gets it done."

"So, what do we do about Marina?" I fidgeted with one of my fries.

Sid sipped. "Probably nothing. I'll keep an eye on her, but let's face it, we're not looking for drugs. We're looking for plans."

"We probably should stay focused on that. Unless the drugs are where the plans are hiding."

Sid chuckled. We'd seen that before.

"I've got to bring Hattie up to date on this," I said, wiping my mouth. "Anything you want me to tell her?"

"Sounds like you've got it covered."

"Wait. I forgot something." I got up and got some more soda in my cup. "I saw Bracha walking around the edge of the resort. She said she was working a split shift so that Felix could cover her tomorrow."

"There was some sort of scheduling snafu." Sid shrugged. "I have to stay out of it because that's not my side of the business. Bracha told me when I came on this morning that she needs to stick around here more, anyway. Said having me around had made her lazy and she needs to stay on top of things better."

I also told him about the call with Marge. Sid took Red Light's death philosophically.

"You're right. It's sad," he said. "But it comes as no surprise."

"True." Then I told him about Dale's plans.

"Dale has plans for everybody." Sid chuckled. "It's not necessarily going to do him any good."

"He's not exactly somebody we can say no to."

Sid got up and stretched. "No, he's not. But at some point, he's going to have to face it that I'm not his long-lost son. In the meantime, I'm going to try not to think about his plans. We have plenty of other things to worry about right now."

"You're right. I'll go talk to Hattie."

"Thanks." He leaned over and gave me a very warm kiss.

"I'll see you later, sweetie."

"Hey." He smiled softly as I turned. "I love you."

"I love you, too, Sid."

Hattie was nonplussed about the situation with the plans, to say the least.

"Where, in Heaven's name, could they be?" she asked, pacing the room.

"Practically anywhere," I said. "We don't even know if your brother actually brought them with him."

"We should have at least found the dummy plans then."

"One would think." I sighed and shrugged. "He didn't tell Sid much about what he was doing, and nothing we didn't already know. If anything, he told Sid to stay out of the way."

Hattie groaned softly. "Is it possible for Miles to have been any more aggravating?"

"I don't know."

Hattie was about to say something else, but at that moment, my walkie-talkie squawked.

I was not happy about the summons to my father's office, but I couldn't refuse, either. I told Hattie that I had to run, and she let me go, shaking her head.

There were two detectives in my father's office waiting for me.

"Detectives, this is my daughter, Lisa Wycherly," Daddy said.

I couldn't help smiling briefly. Unlike a lot of people, my father hadn't changed my last name for me when I got married. Mama told me that Daddy had actually been rather proud that I'd kept my maiden name instead of taking Sid's. It did make things interesting when I adopted Nick, since he chose to keep his mother's last name and take Sid's and my last names as his middle names. Which means none of us has the same last name, and there are folks who do not get that.

"I'm Detective Olson," said the first guy, a medium-sized fellow in a tan suit. "This is Detective Pfizer."

The second guy was a little taller and considerably younger than Olson.

"May I see your IDs, please?" I asked with a smile.

Pfizer grinned as Olson sighed. Daddy just smiled. I looked at the IDs, then back at the two detectives.

"As we explained to your father," Olson said. "This is just routine. The coroner found a burn on the decedent's palm and we're trying to find out how it got there."

I'll admit I was not terribly comfortable with the way Daddy was watching me at that moment. Fortunately, I was genuinely puzzled.

"Honey, can you take these gentlemen to the facilities shed?" Daddy asked. "I told them about that TV that fell. Maybe that could help them figure it out."

"Sure. Happy to."

The facilities shed wasn't really a shed, just one more out-building on the resort. But it was Ty Larson's lair and where we stored most of the tools for things like basic plumbing problems, and other stuff on the resort that needed fixing. That Dusty and Ty had bonded did not surprise me in the least. The two were cut from the same cloth, both quiet and reclusive, both amazing at fixing things. The only difference between Dusty and Ty was that Dusty was young, and Ty was older than dirt.

I showed the two detectives to the shed. It was a one-room building which would have looked larger if it hadn't been crammed with tools and worktables. Ty had a desk in the back, but you really had to look for it to see it under all the papers and miscellaneous tools and parts.

Neither Ty nor Dusty was in the shed when we got there. It didn't matter. The TV from room 305 was the only television in there. It sat on a table near the door, its screen shattered. I tried to remember if it had been broken when I saw it, but then thought it had to have been. It had fallen off the dresser.

Pfizer looked at it, then Olson, and nudged his partner.

"He must have dropped it and that's how he got it," Pfizer said.

Olson glared briefly at his partner, then smiled at me.

"Yeah. That makes sense," he said after some consideration. "Thank you for your cooperation."

I walked the detectives back to the main lodge, feeling entirely unquiet, at best.

Honestly? If cops get sloppy, it's because ninety-nine times out of a hundred, they've already seen something more times than they can count and they have a pretty good idea of what they're dealing with. The stuff that Sid and I see? Well, that's pretty rare. So, you can't blame the cops if they don't pick up on it, and in this case, they couldn't know what might have happened.

Still, the detectives were wondering about a burn on Lipplinger's palm, and it sure sounded like they were thinking he'd been electrocuted. The problem was that I was pretty sure the TV had been unplugged before it had been dropped because the cable cord had already been disconnected. So, how could it have electrocuted Lipplinger?

Nor did I remember the screen being shattered. That didn't mean it hadn't been. I'd only been able to get a quick glance at the room before I had to bail to avoid barfing all over. There were two other people who had seen the room as well. Daddy, who I did not want to ask about it, and Mira.

I found Mira and Lourdes in the housekeeping office snarling at each other.

"What's going on?" I asked, far more brightly than I felt.

"Nothing!" snapped Lourdes.

She turned on her heel and all but stomped upstairs.

"She does not understand how to handle this place!" Mira groaned.

I sighed. "Yes, I know she can be difficult. But that's not why I'm here right now."

"It would be nice," Mira grumbled.

"Mira, I know it's hard dealing with her." I smiled even though I didn't feel it. "Right now, I've got a bigger problem. It's about last Thursday."

Mira made a face. "The dead guy?"

"Yeah. Do you remember the TV?"

"It was on the floor."

"But what shape was the screen in?"

Mira looked at me funny, then thought. "It was okay. I mean, the only reason you thought it was broken was because it fell."

"And it was unplugged."

"Oh, yeah. Both the cable and the electrical cord. What's going on?"

"That's the problem. I don't know."

I went back upstairs. Daddy was waiting for me.

"Well?" he asked.

"The screen was shattered, and the cops figured that's what did it," I said.

Daddy looked at me as if he didn't entirely buy my explanation.

"Are you sure about that?" he asked.

"Look, Daddy, if the cops are going to go with that, I'm fine." I sighed.

He frowned. "I suppose."

"I'll talk to Ty about the screen," I said. "Who knows?"

Daddy frowned at me again, but let it go and went back to his office. That's when it hit me that the TV was the one part of Lipplinger's room that I had not gone over with a fine-tooth comb.

Ty and Dusty were still elsewhere when I got to the facilities shed. I looked at the TV, then took the back off it. I suppose I could have gone through the screen, but there were several jagged shards of glass in the frame.

As I turned the box around, something sharp bit my hand. I looked more closely. A small copper wire protruded from the inside near the bottom of the box. I grabbed a screwdriver from another bench and got the back off relatively easily. I also found the wire from the outside of the box. The wire led inside the TV set to a small orange cylinder that had a wire protruding from either side and had been soldered to what had to be a circuit board. Just beyond that, on the floor of the box, I saw something glint.

It was a series of strips of black electrical tape stuck to the bottom of the box. I pulled them up to find the plastic casing of a three-and-a-half-inch floppy disk underneath. I got the disk unstuck and into my pocket. I hurried away from the shed feeling very unsettled and couldn't put my finger on why.

That evening, Sid made a cheeseburger casserole and coleslaw using some of the excess ground beef and cabbage from the restaurant. It was delicious, and I almost forgot about the floppy disk that I'd hidden under the pillow of our bed in the apartment. But it didn't last long. I got pensive while we cleaned up. I thought Daddy was going to say something, but before he could, Janey talked us all into watching the videotape of Roxanne that she'd pulled from the resort library that day.

Sid called me on my mood as we got ready for bed that night.

"What's going on?" he asked as he took his contact lenses out.

I winced. "I found something weird today."

I told him about the cops and going back to the shed, then showed him the floppy disk.

"Are those the plans?" he asked.

I groaned. "I have no way of knowing. But it is weird. Lipplinger had to have hidden the disk in the TV on purpose. The problem is why?"

"Have you talked to Hattie about it?"

"I wanted to talk to you about it first. There was that wire, too. I don't know why that's important, or even if it is. But it is an anomaly."

Sid frowned. "I'm sorry, my beloved, but I have no idea why that wire would make a difference, except that it probably shouldn't have been there."

"You're right." I bit my lip as I thought it over. "It shouldn't have been. Sid, I think Lipplinger may have been murdered."

July 26–27, 1988

The next morning, Tuesday, was Sid's and my day off. We'd debated what I'd found for some time but could come to no real conclusions about it. After all, the wire could have been deadly had the TV been plugged in, and it could have just been a loose wire. Not to mention that Lipplinger could have burned his hand some other way, and he'd died of a heart attack like we'd originally supposed. The one thing we decided was not to tell Hattie about the wire.

I took the floppy disk to Hattie's room as soon as I'd eaten breakfast.

Hattie pounced on the disk. But once she booted her brother's computer and opened the file from the disk, she groaned.

"These are the dummy plans."

I looked at the text on the screen.

"Right there." Hattie pointed. "That line of code in the notes section. It references the Valiant system, except that it's not spelled correctly."

She was right. The word on the screen was spelled "Valient."

"Are you sure it's not a typo?" I asked.

"That's the idea," she said. "Anyone knowing about the system, and there are good odds someone does, would look at this and just see a minor error. But Miles made it very clear that the dummy plans include this specific misspelling."

I made a face. "Okay. At least, we've found those. I guess it's still possible that your brother didn't bring the real plans with him."

Hattie sighed. "They're not where he was living. Marian called me yesterday, asking what to do with Miles' things. We sent him to London after that time you had him. I asked about anything like that, and Marian said that there was nothing in the files related to this project, and darned little related to any of the projects he may have been working on. Bloody inconvenient, she called it." Hattie squeezed her eyes shut. "She has no idea."

"I'm so sorry, Hattie."

Her smile was wan as she shook her head. "Lisa, darling, I appreciate that you're trying to be sympathetic. Sadly, sympathy will not get us those plans back in our safe-keeping, and that is our priority."

I sighed. "I'll keep searching as best I can."

"I know."

I left, sighing. I knew Hattie was worried, but she had to know that I couldn't just magically produce plans, especially if said plans had never come to the resort in the first place.

As I got to the bottom floor, I saw Judy Osbourne heading for the activities center and thought I'd say hello and maybe find out about the wire I'd seen on the TV from Lipplinger's room. I was about to go into the room when I heard Ms. Wannamaker's voice.

"The cops were here yesterday about it," the older woman said. "You know what that means. Something's up. It wasn't just a natural death."

I tried not to groan. That was the last thing the resort needed, let alone Sid's and my mission.

"Uh-huh," Judy grumbled.

"He was a professor, a Professor Lipplinger, they said," Ms. Wannamaker continued.

"Never heard of the guy." Judy's answer came much too quickly.

I went into the room. "Hey, guys. What's up?"

Judy looked at Ms. Wannamaker, then me, and gulped. "I've gotta get out of here."

She rushed from the room as I gaped after her.

"That's suspicious," said Ms. Wannamaker with a smirk.

"What are you talking about?" I growled.

"The cops were here yesterday. It had to be about the old man that died last week."

"Will you please?" I looked around. Fortunately, the hallway and the room were empty. "We don't want the guests freaking out."

"Oh! You're right." She giggled. "I'm sorry. It's just so interesting, though. I'm researching police procedure for my book."

"Book?"

"Yes. I'm writing a mystery novel."

I bit my tongue darned near in half. As much as the vision of smashing Wannamaker's head into a wall filled my brain, I really do prefer non-violence. A mystery novel? I shook my head to clear it and checked my watch.

It wasn't even ten a.m. on my day off. I had laundry to do, and I really wanted to get some sewing in. I make a lot of my clothes, and since Mama still had her sewing machine at her house, I'd brought up one of my machines and was taking advantage of it. Sewing is my therapy.

But that morning, I knew darned well I was going to be doing housekeeping spot checks in between loads of laundry. Housekeeping spot checks were my excuse for searching guests' rooms. It was necessary, but certainly not one of my favorite things to do. Then again, I needed to do the spot checks, anyway. It was part of the job.

I started on the third floor of the main lodge, Motley at my side. Neither of us found much, nor was I surprised. The rooms, thank God, were completely empty of people. I even searched 305, where Hattie was, and only found some of our normal equipment and a .45 automatic pistol.

However, I was almost done with room 306 when I heard the key in the lock. I quickly went back to wiping down the bathroom counter when Ms. Sanchez walked in.

"Hi," I told her. "I'm the housekeeping manager. I'm just checking the room to make sure that it was cleaned to our standards."

She smiled, then looked at Motley. "With a dog?"

I shrugged. "He's a great dog, and it makes the job a little easier."

She put her hand down for Motley to sniff. "Oh, he's very sweet."

Motley sat and looked up at her with his big brown eyes. She laughed and gave his head a good scratch.

"It looks like you're his new best friend," I said, smiling.

"I love dogs," Ms. Sanchez said, also smiling. "He is such a good boy."

Motley flopped down and rolled onto his back.

"Oh, my god," I laughed. "He does not do that for everyone."

Ms. Sanchez bent and scratched Motley's belly. His back paw pedaled in ecstasy.

"Well, who wouldn't want to scratch this sweet boy's tummy?"

I couldn't help chuckling, then headed out of the room, Motley trotting alongside me. A quick check of my watch told me that I also had a load of laundry to get out of the dryer if I wanted to finish that job before next year. Day off, my left foot. Even without the spot checks, I was working just as hard as if it were a regular workday.

I hurried across the resort to my parents' house, took Motley's leash off, then pulled the load of dark clothing from the dryer, set those aside and got the light clothing out of the washer and into the dryer. The next load in was the white clothing.

My next problem was figuring out whose underwear was whose. The polo shirts weren't that big an issue since we'd more or less assigned colors to each person, with me wearing green, Janey wearing pink, and so forth and so on. Nor was my dad's, my stuff, and Janey's such a problem. Sid's and Nick's underwear was. They both wore colorful silk boxer shorts of the same size. And both of them were somewhat grossed out by the idea of wearing the other's underwear, even Sid, who concedes his private parts have been some pretty interesting places. My problem was telling apart whose shorts were whose, because even if they were all different patterns, I could never remember if Sid had the turquoise paisley and the green window pane blocks or if Nick had them.

The khaki polished cotton slacks that both were wearing in the restaurant were also a problem. The only advantage I had there was that Nick's legs had gotten longer than Sid's. I had marked the insides of the waistbands with permanent marker, but that afternoon, I realized the marker hadn't been so permanent. So, I had to measure each pair of pants against the others to sort them out.

Early on that summer, I'd asked Conchetta Ramirez, our housekeeper back home, how she'd kept straight the undershorts, pants, and other clothes the guys wore. She told me that she washed Nick's and Sid's stuff separately, mixing those items in with mine, depending on how much there was to fill out a load.

Which goes to explain why I glared at my father when he wandered into the dining room where I was sorting laundry because the table there was big enough measure pant lengths and so on.

"What are you doing?" Daddy asked. "Today's your day off."

"Like that matters. These clothes aren't going to clean themselves," I grumbled.

"Not getting enough rest and burning yourself out isn't going to help, either." He looked closely at me. "I heard you were doing spot checks today."

"I have to." I kept my eyes focused on measuring pant legs. "Even if Lourdes does them, the rest of the crew knows she's not going to confront anybody, and they slough off. Beatrice does it all the time, and we even got a complaint last week about one of her rooms."

"Beatrice is doing just fine." Daddy folded his arms across his chest. "At least, Mira thinks so. And I do not want you working on your days off. It's not healthy."

It may not have been, but I couldn't tell him that you don't always get days off in the spy biz. I let Sid and Nick sort out their own undershorts, though. As I watched, I decided to stitch a ribbon marker into Sid's slacks, then realized I could do the same thing with his undershorts. Sid took one look at me and decided that would be fine.

Daddy took us all to dinner and to see Who Framed Roger Rabbit, which had come out the month before while Sid, Nick, and I were in Europe. I don't know why we hadn't gotten around to seeing it earlier that month. [We were too tired. - SEH]

It was a fun evening and just what we needed. But I didn't get any time to talk to Sid alone until it was time to go to bed. As we got undressed and under the covers, Sid asked me about my day, and I told him.

"I don't know what I'm going to do," I said as we cuddled. "Daddy doesn't want me doing spot checks on days off, and Hattie's worried sick about those missing plans."

"I know." Sid nuzzled my ear. "She said the same to me today. I had to explain to her that we could only do so much. We have our covers to keep intact. Besides, I'm not entirely sure that random searches are going to turn anything up. I mean, we've had a pretty solid turnover of guests since they went missing. Did you find anything?"

"Just some pot. I think it's the Winslow kid's. Her parents seem too uptight to be smoking it."

"Not sure who they are." Sid sighed. "I don't know that it's important." He suddenly frowned. "Unless she's Nick's current flame."

I shook my head. "No. She's a little too vague for him to be interested. That's the other reason I think it's hers. But we're getting off the subject. We've got a problem trying to get rooms searched. I'm the only one who can do it because I'm the one with the excuse to go in. But you're right about random searches. There's just too much ground to cover and there is no way to do spot checks on every room and cabin here in one week, even if I do them on my days off."

"We've got the Delgados, but they can't do room searches."

"Not easily."

Sid thought for a moment. "What if we could get some help doing background checks on the guests and maybe some of the employees? That might give us a better idea of whose room or cabin to search."

"Sounds good, but how?"

Sid smiled. "Getting the resort computers talking to each other and integrated. It's like I was telling you yesterday. Everything is on a different system, and it would work a lot better if it were all connected. So, if we can get a couple software specialists in to do that and they just happen to be experts at doing background checks, that would help, wouldn't it?"

"I can see that." I frowned. "Are you thinking Desmond Moore?"

"And Esther."

Esther Nguyen is one of Sid's and my dearest friends. Desmond isn't nearly as close, but still a friend. Both are part of our organization and insanely good at computers and software and even the hardware in Esther's case.

"That's an idea." I rolled onto my back and stretched my neck. "She's still looking for her great consumer application."

Esther worked as an engineer for a defense company and badly wanted out of that industry.

"I know." Sid kissed my shoulder. "Not to mention, trying to get this place wired will give her and Desmond an excuse to search places they otherwise couldn't."

I rolled back onto my side, facing him. "What about Frank?"

Frank Lonnergan is Esther's husband.

"He can help with tailing Dusty."

"That would be good." I stroked the scar on his left bicep where a bullet had grazed him back in 1983, then kissed it.

Sid kissed the scar over my eye that I'd gotten that same case. I smiled at him.

"What are you thinking about?" he asked.

"That big trip we took our first year together." I reached over and scratched his chin to appreciative purring. "I remember that first night having to share the bed. I couldn't have conceived of laying here like this next to you."

"I couldn't have, either. And yet, here we are."

"I'm really liking being married to you."

Sid laughed softly. "Really? Finally?"

"Well." I winced. The last thing I'd wanted to do with my life was get married, and I'd spent the first year after the wedding getting used to having done it. "It's just that this past year or so, I really haven't had time to think about our marriage or anything but grad school. I think that's one of the things that's got me off-kilter with this case. It's that I miss working with you. I know you're here and all, but we're each doing different things, not working together." I made a face. "I miss that."

"We worked that way in Kansas." That case had only happened the year before, in the winter of '87.

"Yeah. But I hadn't had an entire school year of being out of the house, going to classes, doing reading and papers, not being able to do any freelance writing." I sighed. "It's good that I went back to school. I've been wanting to get my doctorate for a lot of years and now's as good a time as any to do it. But I am feeling the separation, I guess. And working like we are now is only exacerbating it."

Sid chuckled. "I know what you're saying, and I suspect you have a point, my beloved. But I can't help it. One of the many things I love about you is the fact that you not only know how to use a word like exacerbate, but that you actually do in conversation."

"Hmph!"

If I snorted in response, it was that my extended vocabulary had become something of an issue at a Liturgy Committee meeting earlier that year. Some of the members had thought I was showing off by using some fancy words that I considered utterly normal. Apparently, according to one "nice" person, that wasn't in the least bit normal. I was shocked. I am a PhD candidate. Sid is a writer. We'd damn well better have good vocabularies and if it leaks into our spoken language that isn't a problem. It's just normal for us.

Sid laughed full out, and I laughed as well. The next thing I knew, he was kissing me full on. Yes, it was lovely being married to him.

The next morning, Sid and I took Nick and Janey with us to go running near the lake. When we got back, I hid out in my mother's sewing room and sewed labels into Sid's pants and undershorts, then put some time in on a blouse I was making from some gorgeous silk I'd gotten in Paris and a pattern from a German sewing magazine that had been translated to English. Sid popped in just long enough to tell me that he'd left lunch for me.

"Esther and Desmond are on board," he added. "But they want to know what is already here, so Daddy and I are going down to the main lodge to try to figure it out. Nick and Janey are already down there."

"Okay." I glared at the two pieces I was pinning together. "Oh, peewaddles."

Sid laughed and left.

Around one, I went and got my lunch, but then Daddy called from the main lodge to ask me to go down there and tell him what we could use on the housekeeping side of things.

"Take your time, honey," he said. "Eat your lunch first. We'll be in the office."

I rolled my eyes. My father was well aware that I was perfectly capable of taking care of myself, but he still tried to take care of me. And, I guess, I was possibly working too much. [You most certainly were. We both were that summer. - SEH]

I ate and washed my dish, leaving it in the drainboard, then got ready to leave the house by snapping a leash on Motley. Bowser wasn't in his crate, so I guessed that Nick and Janey had brought the puppy with them to the main lodge. Richmond snoozed on his pad next to the couch and Spot was outside somewhere. I put Richmond out just in case none of us got back to the house before Richmond had to go. Richmond curled up next to the picnic table and promptly went back to sleep.

I cut through the cabin paths and saw Lita on the edge of the playground watching her kids. She caught my eye and I sauntered around the edge of the playground as if I were going that way, anyway.

"You're one of the managers, aren't you?" Lita asked.

"Ms. Delgado, right?" I smiled. "How can I help you?"

Lita stepped a little closer. "I've got to tell you, this place is really great. The kids are having a blast." She bent to pet Motley, then lowered her voice. "I mean that."

"So, what's up?" I said softly.

"See the guy on the lounge at eleven o'clock your time? The one with all the papers in his lap?"

He had brown hair and a deep tan.

"I think that's Mr. DiNovo," I said.

Lita nodded. "His wife is Francine. He doesn't interact well with his kids and his wife practically ignores him."

"As in, they may not be a real family."

"Exactly." Lita petted Motley some more. "I don't think I've ever seen the two parents in the restaurant together, either, and we've eaten here the whole time."

I smiled broadly, then let my voice rise a little. "Well, thank you, Ms. Delgado. I appreciate your comments."

"More than happy to." She grinned as I moved on.

I went first to my father's office, but neither Sid nor he were there.

"I think they're in the restaurant," Irene told me.

"Thanks, Irene." I paused. "Oh. I almost forgot. I need to verify a room check on the DiNovo family."

Irene clicked keys on the computer in front of her. "Yeah. Here they are. Cabin Three."

"How long are they staying?"

"They're reserved through August thirteenth."

"Thanks."

I went through the front of the restaurant for some reason. Heading toward the back, I passed Ms. Sanchez eating by herself. The Deng family was at the next table, and their toddler suddenly started screaming. Ms. Sanchez smiled, then turned to the toddler.

"Why are you screaming, young lady?" the older woman asked.

Startled by a total stranger speaking to her, the toddler shut up.

"Is it naptime?" Ms. Sanchez asked the little girl. "I'll bet it is. You seem very tired."

"It is," said the child's mother, looking pretty tired herself. "I'm so sorry she disturbed you."

Ms. Sanchez laughed. "She didn't bother me in the least. I know how it goes on vacation. They just get so overwhelmed."

She made a funny face at the little girl, and Mr. and Ms. Deng both smiled in relief as the toddler laughed. I moved on.

Sid and Daddy were in the breakroom, huddled over a yellow legal pad.

"Well?" I asked.

They had me go over everything on the housekeeping end. Lourdes had offered some suggestions, and I had to agree that they were good ones. I had little more to offer, though, and took off to see where Nick and Janey were.

I found them in the activities center playing their guitars for a group of about ten kids of all ages. Bowser puppy lay at their feet, chewing on a chew toy. I thought I recognized the tune Nick and Janey were strumming, but couldn't quite place it.

"Here's a little song I wrote," Nick sang. "You might want to sing it note for note."

"Don't Worry. Be happy," Janey and the rest of the kids sang.

Now, I know that tune was recorded acapella, with Bobby McFerrin singing all of the parts on different tracks. Somehow, Nick had figured out a guitar part for it, and I was pretty sure it was Nick who had done it. He does stuff like that.

The odd thing is, Nick almost never plays his guitar except with our family or for himself. Janey is only slightly more likely to play for her friends. They don't see themselves as that good at playing music.

It's understandable. Both are surrounded by some talented musicians. Sid and Stella both teach classical piano to gifted students. Stella's lover, Sy Flournoy, is head of the strings department at Juilliard. My sister Mae, who is Janey's mother, is a very gifted singer and while she'd put that aside for a lot of years, she was getting back into it. Then there is Darby, Janey's older brother. He and Nick are the same age and best friends, too. Darby is also an exceptionally talented violinist, as in we fully expect him to become a professional performer.

I smiled as I watched my niece and son playing. Once the tune was finished, Ms. Wannamaker announced it was time for painting class, so Nick and Janey put their guitars away in cases. Janey went to help get the paints, brushes, and art pads distributed. Nick picked up his guitar case and Bowser's leash and came to the doorway.

"Hey, Mom."

"Hey, sweetie." I smiled as I brushed back the lock of hair that almost always fell over his forehead. "It looked like you were having a good time."

"I was." He shrugged and nodded toward the group of kids sliding into the hall. "They don't care if I'm not that good."

"You are that good, Nick," I said, holding his cleft chin. "Even your dad says that. You're just not a professional, nor should you be."

"That's what Darby says." Nick made a face. "It's more about having fun than it is about being good. Of course, that's easy for him to say."

I chuckled. "It is. But that doesn't mean you're not a good guitar player. In fact, you're a darned good guitar player. You're just not a whiz-bang, super-talented guitar player. On the other hand, you are a whiz-bang, super-talented chemist, and I'm very proud of you for that, too."

He shuffled a little. "Thanks, Mom."

I gave him a solid hug, and he hugged me back as only he can.

"Hey, guys." Sid came into the hall and walked up.

"We're doing a hug moment," I said, then looked at Nick. "Is it okay if he joins us?"

Nick smiled. "Sure."

The three of us did a group hug. Yeah, things were a little rocky between Sid and Nick. But ultimately, we all loved each other so very much and I knew that would eventually win out over the adolescent angst. I squeezed both my guys, utterly grateful that they were in my life.

July 28–29, 1988

"Where does your father think we're going to put them?" Irene groaned when I told her after the Thursday morning management meeting that some friends of Sid's and mine would arrive shortly. "Between it being summer and Lyle's overbooking mistakes, there isn't a bed to be had."

"We've got a convertible sofa in the apartment," I told her. "We can put Frank and Esther there."

Irene's eyebrows rose. "You sure they won't mind?"

She'd heard the comments about the occasional problems with the noise level in the apartment.

I sighed. "It's nothing Frank and Esther haven't heard before. I guess we'll just be playing the radio a lot. Anyway, Dusty doesn't have a roommate yet, so we'll put Desmond in with him."

"A new computer system, though." Irene shook her head. "This is not a good time of year to be putting something like that in."

"I know. And we will keep on using the old system for a month or so after everything is up and running. It's just that Desmond is between contracts right now and there's some big project coming up where Esther works and if she doesn't take off now, she won't be able to leave for another eight months or something like that." I smiled weakly at her. "In some ways, this is a really good time for them to begin the project. They'll see what the real-world demands are going to be on the new system."

"That makes a little sense." Irene glared at her computer monitor. "Maybe I can make this work."

I'm not sure what she did. We had a couple gaps in reservations, and she found a room for Frank and Esther. It had been Desmond's idea to room with Dusty to make it easier to keep tabs on the kid, which is why I told Irene not to worry about him. I also told Irene to put all three of them on Sid's and my tab, including their meals and any extras.

According to Sid, Hattie thought that having Frank and Esther and Desmond join us was an excellent idea and told him it would be no problem using their real names. Apparently, there was a plan in place for them. Sid and I had a bad feeling we knew what that meant, but like so many things in Quickline, there wasn't much we could do about it.

Desmond showed first, around three that afternoon. He'd flown in from Phoenix, which is where he's stationed.

"Are you sure you're okay with sleeping with the summer staff?" I asked, pulling his suitcase on the bag cart behind me.

Desmond is a Black man with solid shoulders and dark skin. His hair tends to change, and he had it in short braids that month.

"If what Sid told me is true, the kid is a total nerd." Desmond laughed.

"He totally is."

"Then we should get along like a house on fire."

I'd paged Dusty to his room when Desmond arrived, and he was waiting for us. I introduced the two, and Dusty grabbed Desmond's suitcase off the cart.

"Thank you for letting Desmond room with you," I told Dusty. "There just wasn't anyplace else to put him while he's working here."

Dusty's eyes lit up. "The new computer system."

"Yeah," said Desmond, and started talking about interfaces and writing code, and a second later, he and Dusty were deep in conversation in a language that only vaguely resembled English to me.

"I'll leave you guys to get to know each other then," I said, and pulled the bag cart back to the main lodge.

After getting the cart put back where it belonged, I went to find Sid. Daddy told me Sid and Nick were in his office and, from the look on Daddy's face, I got the feeling that things were not going well in that department. Sure enough, I heard Nick's voice raised.

"I'm not doing anything!"

"I'm not saying you were." Sid's voice was equally angry.

"Well, it would be nice if you trusted me."

"You, I trust. It's about her father. If he thinks you are, then it doesn't matter that you're not doing anything. Believe me, I know how that works."

"You don't want me to do anything!"

Nick burst out of the office and rushed off somewhere. Sid came to the office door, breathing heavily and a worried frown on his face.

"Damn it!" Sid snapped.

"What's going on?" I asked.

"Nick's latest girlfriend." Sid shuddered. "I caught her father giving Nick the evil eye this afternoon."

"But I thought you said you trusted Nick not to do anything."

"I do! That's not going to help." Sid added a few epithets. "He's a jealous, over-protective father. He's going to assume the absolute worst in Nick, and I can't get Nick to see that. I don't even want to think about the trouble this could cause your father."

"Daddy didn't worry about the guests when I was dating the boys."

"Oh, he worried about the boys, I'm sure." Sid began pacing. "But he didn't have to worry about their fathers suing the snot out of him because he didn't keep you away from their sons. It's different with Nick because he's a boy, and that makes him dangerous to the honor of a sweet, young girl. And I didn't say that Nick had to stay away from the girl. I just suggested that he be a little more discreet about it, and he went off, screaming that I didn't trust him and that I don't want him to have any fun."

"Do you want me to talk to him?"

"For all the good it will do." Sid sighed deeply. "Actually, you know who would be good would be your father. I just wish I didn't feel like I was abdicating my responsibilities by letting him handle all this stuff."

"Letting me handle what?" Daddy said, coming up behind me.

"Nick and I just had a fight, is all," Sid said. "Mr. Jolna is not happy with Nick dating his daughter."

Daddy nodded. "Cabin Four, right? I had a feeling. I'll go talk to the fellow. And don't worry about Nick. I know he's behaving himself."

"I trust him." Sid sighed. "It won't matter if the old man decides Nick isn't."

Daddy laughed full out. "And I know how that works. I'll take care of Jolna, and talk to Nick, too." He reached out and patted Sid's shoulder. "That's what grandparents are for, Sid. Trust me, the only reason Mae survived her teens was that we shipped her off to my Aunt Aggie's every summer until she was seventeen."

Sid frowned. "I thought she and Neil met here when he came in as a summer worker."

"They met." Daddy nodded. "Neil would get here before she left, and then she'd come home a couple weeks before he left to go home. And those first couple years, she didn't really notice him. He'd noticed her, damn him."

I couldn't help giggling. Daddy was, and in some ways still is, a very jealous and over-protective father, never mind that he's come to love Neil and Sid very much.

"Anyway," Daddy continued. "When Mae was seventeen, she flat out refused to go because she wanted to see Neil. Turned out the two had been writing letters to each other during the school year, when Neil was in college at Sac State." Daddy looked at me. "I just wish Aunt Aggie had been alive when Lisle turned into a teen. It would have made those years a lot easier."

Sid looked at me. "You didn't go to your grandparents?"

"I spent a couple weeks with Grandma Caulfield when I was fourteen." I made a face. "It was fun, but I hated being around my cousins, and they were always around."

"And my mama wasn't going to take her," Daddy said, laughing. "She'd had a bad enough time with Lisle when she was ten and Mama had to babysit while Althea, her mama, and I were in San Francisco getting Althea's breast cancer treated."

I quietly crossed myself. Grandma Wycherly had died that spring.

Daddy shrugged. "When are your other friends getting in?"

"I'm not sure," I said, checking my watch. It was a little before four. "They're driving up. With luck, they'll be here for dinner."

To Breanna, 7/7/00
Topic of the Day: My Most Embarrassing Moment
Okay. I get that this is one of those, yeah, we'll really get to know each other kinds of questions. But come on. The whole reason people don't talk about their most embarrassing moments is that they're embarrassing.

Then there's the way you were fussing the other day about how horny young teen boys are - with good reason. But while I agree with you that our sex-obsessed culture sets it up, having been a horny 15-year-old boy, I have to say some of it has got to be biological.

Seriously. I was determined not to be like my dad. I mean, I get why he was so into sleeping around. But with the AIDS thing going on and Dad's own brush with it, I did not want to go down that garden path. Yeah, I was assuming the worst, yet again.

But then the summer after I turned 15, I went to work at Grandpa Wycherly's resort. The good thing about that summer is that I got to be really close to Grandpa. I also got to date a lot of different girls. This wasn't one month and done. It was one week and done because that's how long the girls were staying at the resort.

There was this one girl that I met near the beginning of that summer. Tiffany. She was really cute, with long blonde hair and dark brown eyes, and really smart, too. Grandpa noticed right away that I was interested, and we had this really intense talk about appropriate behavior. The thing that surprised me was that Grandpa was cool about a little necking, but he got me to promise that I'd keep my hands outside any clothing at all times, and no touching anything a bathing suit would cover.

Okay. I broke the promise, at least about the bathing suit part. Tiffany and I got going one evening, and I got a hold of her breasts. Outside of her t-shirt, but, oh, man!!!

She got all excited and so did I, and the next thing I knew, I'd come in my pants. I don't think she knew what had happened, but I was utterly mortified.

I did talk to Dad about it. I mean, I was terrified that something was horribly wrong with me. He laughed and reassured me that it was completely normal. It had happened to him plenty of times, even as an adult.

It was one of the few times in my life that he did not get where I was coming from. I was not just humiliated, I was traumatized. Seriously. I did not touch another boob until I was eighteen. Which is probably why it took me so long to lose my virginity - I waited until the summer I graduated from high school.

Esther and Frank arrived somewhere around five-thirty. Irene, who was working the front desk at that moment, paged me the second they showed, and I paged Sid. By the time the two had their luggage on the bag cart, Sid and I were there, and we took them up to 302.

Hugs were distributed. Frank and Esther may be part of our team, but they ended up that way because they were good friends with Sid and me long before they got recruited into Quickline.

"Oh, this is nice," Esther said, poking around the room. She's fairly short, with a round face and black hair that's usually cut haphazardly at best. "That table's a little small, though."

"And rickety," I said, rolling my eyes. "It's getting to be quite the popular complaint this summer."

"We need to talk some strategy," Sid said. "So, why don't you guys get settled, then meet us down at the restaurant? We'll have dinner, then go over to the apartment where we're staying."

"Sure," said Frank, who is tall, with dark hair and fair skin. "But we've got big news for you guys."

I looked at them, then gaped happily. "Esther, are you...?"

"Am I what?" Esther looked puzzled. "Oh. No. I'm not pregnant yet. We're still trying." They'd been trying for the past year or so. "But it may be just as well that I'm not. Last week, I told Ross Sorensen to do something obscene to himself."

[She told him to go fuck himself. - SEH]

"Finally?" Sid laughed.

"Yeah. I walked." Esther giggled and added other expletives. Her command of American profanity is... um, quite extensive, and English is not her first language. "I'd totally had it, and I don't need to be there anymore. I found my business. Security equipment for homes and businesses. I've already gotten a contract to help an armed-response company improve their technology and two other clients. Kathy's helping me with the business part of it, too."

"I'm so happy for you!" I gave Esther a huge hug as Frank grinned proudly at his wife.

"It's about time," Sid said as I let Esther go. He, too, hugged her. "You deserve it."

"And we'll be okay financially," Frank said. "Between the money we get from the side business and our savings, we can put the money from the security business right back into that business for a while."

"Are you going to be able to finish grad school?" I asked him.

Frank was getting his master's degree in choral music.

"Oh, yeah." Frank grinned. "I've even got a nice part-time job at church. Now that Mrs. Koch had to go into that home, Father John hired me on as music director on the condition that I finish my degree. So, the money from that will help pay my school fees for the year, and then I'm done."

"Besides, knowing how to make security technology will help us defeat it when we have to." Esther giggled again.

Sid and I laughed, then we left to let them get settled. They met us in the restaurant, where Sid and I casually pointed out the Delgados. Frank and Esther had already met Hattie at our wedding two years before, and as soon as Frank saw her at a table not far from ours, I could tell he realized Hattie was part of the team. Frank's good that way.

"We've got one other agent stationed here," Sid told them after dinner, as we relaxed in the living room of the apartment. "But we don't know who."

"The biggest problem we're having is keeping our covers intact around my dad," I grumbled, shaking my head. "He's been asking questions and I can tell he's not entirely buying my answers."

"Well, that makes sense," said Esther. "He's the one who taught you how to play poker, and he's really good at reading people."

"I know," said Sid. He has lost a fair amount of change to my father, as have all of us.

I also booted up the computer that we'd put in the apartment and showed Esther the copy of the dummy plans that Hattie had made and put on a floppy disk my computer could read.

"We're looking for the ones that have Valiant spelled correctly," I explained to her.

"Hmm." She was lost in reading the file.

Desmond came in from Dusty's room, and the five of us went over everything. Esther pulled out the guest list from the week before, when Lipplinger was killed, but shook her head.

"I didn't find much," she said. "I was only able to do a cursory search. Just FBI database and CIA. Kathy is looking up Social Security numbers, but when you've only got names, it's hard to tell who's who. There must be, like, forty-thousand Maria Sanchezes in the U.S., and don't even talk to me about Brian Lanes or Jim Winslows. I found something in the FBI database on..." She dove for her briefcase, which she'd brought with her to the apartment, and pulled out a yellow legal pad. "You called me about him yesterday morning. Here it is. Avery DiNovo. It's just the standard background check they do on U.S. employees working in potentially compromised areas. Di-

Novo was in Saudi Arabia for a long time, working for an oil company. The report says he's clean, but being in that part of the world doesn't mean he was."

"That's why there are FBI files on people like that." Sid shook his head. "It seldom means they're operatives for either side."

"It's still something worth checking out," I said. "I'll see if I can talk to him in the morning."

"And there's something else." Esther cleared her throat as she pulled a printout from the briefcase. "It was in the FBI database. I was searching on anything connected to your parents' resort and found out that they have B-one clearances."

"B-ones?" Sid took the printout from Esther and began flipping through it. B-1 isn't a top-level clearance, but it's pretty high up, usually used for safe houses and other administrative personnel.

I looked over Sid's shoulder. "That's weird. They got them in October '82. That's right after I was adopted."

"That probably explains it," said Sid. "We'll have to see what clearance Stella has."

"I wonder if my father has one," Esther said. "Frank's brother is a B-one, but he's with the FBI."

I shrugged, then looked at the others. "Tomorrow won't be such a bad day in terms of resort work, but you guys may as well plan on just hanging out on Saturday or working with Sid. Saturday is when we get our big turnover on the guests, and it is crazy."

The others nodded, and they left shortly afterward.

The next morning, it seemed like every time I tried to catch Mr. DiNovo, he went someplace else. I finally found his wife, Francine DiNovo, watching the kids at the playground from the lounge chairs scattered around. I made like I was tidying, then smiled at her. She barely lifted her eyes from the book she was reading. It had a burgundy cover with no paper cover and was a good three inches thick.

"How are you today?" I asked, straightening the chair.

"Fine. Thanks." She glanced up at where her three kids were scrambling over the climbing bars, then returned to her book.

"Is there anything I can get you?"

"I'm fine." Her voice was firm. "Thank you."

Lita was not far away, sitting in a similar lounge chair, sipping from a glass of what looked like a nice, icy cola. I kept straightening until I was next to her.

"And how are you today, Mrs. Delgado?"

"Perfectly lovely." Lita grinned and got a sip of her soda. There was a wheel of lime floating in the top.

"And what are you drinking?" I asked, softly.

"To Cuba Libre." She laughed. In other words, a rum and cola, which I'd figured. There was no bar service on the resort except at dinner in the restaurant. But that wouldn't have stopped Lita. She tended to carry her own rum with her, as she claimed you can't get decent rum outside of black-market sources in Miami. "I saw you trying to talk to Mrs. DiNovo."

"Didn't get very far."

"Nobody does. They are an odd pair, all right. She's good with the kids, though."

"That's interesting." I lowered my voice still further. "Her husband worked in Saudi Arabia up until this past year. No mention of whether or not she was with him."

"That is also interesting." Lita smiled at me. "Thanks. Oh, Nina found a transponder this morning. She said it was behind the horse barn. Pedro is checking it out, but it looks like it might be KGB equipment. It's definitely not ours."

I shrugged. "Well, we know they've got a mole around here someplace. Thanks for letting me know."

I nodded at her, then looked over the lounge chairs as if I was satisfied with my work. I debated checking out the transponder, but if Pedro was already doing it, then I really didn't need to.

I went back to the apartment, checked the messages, and sighed deeply. The department secretary at my school's English department wanted me to set up an appointment with the department head.

Clarissa, the secretary, didn't tell me what was up when I called back, only that Dr. Stevenson was meeting with each of the PhD candidates. I set the appointment up for one o'clock, August nine, which was a week and a half away, feeling more annoyed than panicky.

Given Dr. Barber, I should have been terrified that I was about to get the boot. But I wasn't. I almost didn't care one way or the other, and I couldn't figure out why. My PhD was my dream. And yet it seemed so... inconsequential at that moment. Certainly not worth dealing with all the political nonsense involved.

My stomach gurgled. It was time for lunch. All the food that we made was in my parents' house. If Sid or I were cooking, it was to feed Nick, Daddy, and Janey, too, so it didn't make sense to stock anything in the apartment. For some reason, I did not feel like going down to the restaurant.

I wandered down to the house. Bowser wasn't in his crate, which was odd, but then I went into the kitchen and Daddy was there, finishing a sandwich, Bowser at his feet.

"Hey, Daddy," I said. I went over and kissed his cheek.

"Hey, sweetheart." He looked at me. "You seem a little off."

"The department head at my university wants a meeting with me." I pulled some of the whole wheat bread out of the bread box, then went to the fridge to see what I could put on it.

"It isn't about bad news, is it?"

"I don't think so." I pulled out some ham and a bit of lettuce. "At least, I hope it isn't about getting booted out of the program."

"Would that be so bad?"

"I don't know." I frowned. "It's just that I've wanted to be a college professor my entire life."

Daddy chuckled. "Not your entire life. As I recall, you started out wanting to be a superhero, then a knight in shining armor a little after that."

"I wanted to be a smoke jumper."

"Nope." Daddy grinned as he shook his head. "Smoke jumper was when you were five and a half. We had that bad year with fires."

"That I remember." I dug four slices of bread out of the bag.

"Before that, when you were four, you were going to be SuperWoman." Daddy laughed at the memory. "At first, you said Superman, but then Mae said you actually had to be a man to be Superman, and that you were a woman. So you became SuperWoman and told everyone that's what you were going to be when you grew up."

"I don't remember that." I laughed a little.

"I sure do." Daddy laughed again. "We had a dickens of a time getting you to leave your cape at home when you went to nursery school or church. Then that spring you turned five, and got sick like you did every year, your mama read to you about King Arthur and you wanted to be Sir Lunkalot. Remember all those magic capes you made when your mama first taught you to sew?"

"Yeah. I wish I'd saved one of them."

Daddy nodded. "You kept wearing them out. But even with the smoke jumping, you still wanted to be a superhero or a knight until you were almost out of elementary school. You didn't start talking about getting your PhD until you were well into high school, and even then, you were still thinking about firefighting."

"The most viable of my career aspirations." I rolled my eyes as I put mayonnaise and mustard on the bread, then assembled a couple sandwiches. "I guess it's a good thing Mama wanted me to go to college. That's really when I fell in love with academia. I don't think I could have before that."

"Maybe." Daddy smiled and got up. "Which reminds me. I was cleaning out our personal storage shed this morning. Your mama said last night that we'll be needing some space when she and your grandmother get back. Anyway, I found something."

He went to the back door of the kitchen and got something from the small porch there.

"Here. Remember this?" He smiled as he handed me the small wooden sword.

"How could I forget?" The electrical tape on the handle had gotten a little sticky, but, grinning, I brandished the sword anyway.

Neil had made the sword for me. The "blade" was a little over a foot long and cut from a plank. Neil had added a small bit of wood for the hilt and wrapped the handle.

"Did Mama save this?" I asked.

"No. I did." Daddy smiled and shook his head a little. "Your mama used to get so mad at me for encouraging you to be a tomboy. Funny thing was, she was just as likely to."

"I didn't get that."

"Honey, she wanted you to be happy, and you were happiest when you were saving the world or slaying dragons or putting out wildfires. She got a little worried when you announced you were going to be a college professor. She thought that might be a little too settled in for you. But then you said you were going to specialize in Shakespeare, and I told your mama that made sense."

I chuckled. "I could still be a knight or a witch or a king."

My walkie-talkie squawked. Sid wanted to know where Daddy was, so I sent my father back to the main lodge and finished my lunch.

Nick showed up shortly after that - he could only work part time, being so young. He found me in the living room, looking through an old photo album.

"I thought you didn't like looking at your old pictures." Nick said, scooping up Bowser and cuddling him.

"I don't usually." I touched the photo I'd found. "But I wanted to look at this one."

It was a picture from when I was eight years old of Neil giving me a piggy-back ride. I had the current magic cape on, a beat-up steel colander on my head, and I brandished my new sword in my hand, calling the charge to my valiant steed.

"That's you and Uncle Neil!" Nick laughed. "Woh. He looks a lot like Darby."

"He does, doesn't he?" I laughed.

"How old were you guys?"

"Neil was sixteen." I smiled at the memory. "It was his first summer at the resort. It's kind of funny how things worked out with him and Mae because he was my best buddy at first. Daddy thought Neil was making moves on Mae almost from the start. I mean, they liked each other in a kind of vague way. But Neil didn't really get interested in your Aunt Mae until she came back from Great-Aunt Aggie's that summer when she was sixteen."

"But I thought Uncle Neil went to Sacramento State to be near Aunt Mae."

"He did, sort of. But it wasn't just Mae. Neil wanted to be near all of us." I winced a little. "It's complicated, Nick. You know Neil's father and mine are best friends, right?"

"Yeah." Nick put Bowser down on the floor.

"Mr. O'Malley has always been a nice guy," I said. "But he does drink too much. And he and Mrs. O'Malley don't have a very good marriage. They'd been high school sweethearts, then got married within a month of Mr. O'Malley graduating from college. The problem was Mr. O'Malley had gotten more liberal while in college and Mrs. O'Malley, who didn't go to college, got more conservative. Mama told me once that they might have broken up, but Mrs. O'Malley got pregnant with Uncle Neil, and they had to get married. Then they had Neil's two sisters and after that, they were going to stay together come hell or high water. Neil has a decent relationship with them, but they're not happy people. Which is why Neil is so unflappable. It was his defense mechanism." I put the photo album back on the shelf. "Anyway, he realized his second summer here, right before he had to apply to go to college, that he was happy whenever he was here and that was because we were mostly happy people, and he wanted to be near that. Of course, I didn't know that when I was a kid. I just knew that he was a lot of fun to play with." I smiled at Nick. "That's how the picture happened. I had just made my latest superhero cape and was wearing it, but only had a pine twig for a sword. Neil came up and asked me what I was playing, and I got a little annoyed and said I was slaying dragons and I practically dared him to tell me that little girls don't go around slaying dragons. But he just smiled and said that I needed a better sword if I was going to do that kind of heavy work. The next day, he gave me the sword in the picture. Daddy had let him use the power tools that evening and found some scrap for him. Then Neil gave me the old colander he'd found, dubbed me Sir Lisa, and volunteered to be my valiant steed. We were running around the yard when Mama grabbed the camera and took the photo."

Nick looked down, stopped Bowser from chewing on his shoe, then laughed.

"Is that the sword?" he asked, picking it up from where I'd set it next to the couch.

"That's it. Daddy found it this morning."

Nick brandished it as well. "That is a cool sword."

"It's mine." I grinned and held out my hand. "And you can't have it."

"Wanna fight me for it?" Nick grinned.

"Do you really want to try that?"

Nick feinted and the two of us started sparring. Since we need to keep up our hand-to-hand combat skills, it wasn't an unusual family activity. Nick had his larger size on me – he'd just recently gotten a little taller than Sid. But I had a few years more practice, and I've gotten pretty good at martial arts. I had Nick pinned on the living room floor in no time and took my sword back. We'd knocked over the coffee table, but thank God, it hadn't broken, nor had Bowser gotten trampled.

I bowed to Nick, then sauntered back to the apartment, the sword resting on my shoulder.

July 30, 1988

I was in such a good mood that Friday night, I almost hated to go to bed. Of course, me being in a good mood meant that Sid was in a good mood, which probably led to some complaints and raucous joking about the noise levels in the staff lodge, but that night I did not care.

Alas, Saturday morning arrived all too soon. I was barely dressed and hadn't even had time to get breakfast when the walkie-talkie started squawking. Lourdes and Mira were squabbling again over room assignments, and I had to go sort them out. Nor did things let up.

I handled the next two issues in the break room while munching on bacon, hash browns, and scrambled eggs from the restaurant. We found three lost toys and the shredded remains of someone's blankie. Irene nearly pounded Esther for getting in the way and asking questions during checkouts that morning.

"Is it always this crazy?" Esther asked me as I double-checked something in the reservations book in the front office.

"On Saturdays? Yes," I said, flipping pages on the printout and praying we didn't have another double-booking problem.

"Can't you assign check-in and check-out times?"

"No." I tried not to glare at her. "People want to leave when they want to leave and arrive when they want to arrive. Plus, flights get delayed and canceled. Cars break down or lunch stops take longer than planned. We've got three kids in Cabin Five who spent the night throwing up and they want a late check-out so the kids can get some rest before heading home." I shuddered, glad that I didn't have to clean that cabin.

"Oh. Hm." Esther was thinking and started to open her mouth.

"Esther, can you do me a favor, please?" I cut in before she could ask. "Can you just take notes today and ask your questions later? I don't need you practicing your hand-to-hand to keep Irene from strangling you."

"Okay."

"Thank you, Jesus!" I'd found what I wanted on the printout and sighed in relief. There wasn't a double-booking after all.

The walkie-talkie squawked again, and I was off and running, pausing just long enough to let Irene know we were okay. Then I had to go assess the damage in Cabin Eleven, thanks to the executive retreat. I brought Motley with me for that one. Sure enough, they hadn't been there to build better connections on the executive team. Or, rather, their idea of building better connections involved doing lines of coke, drinking to excess, and probably wife-swapping. Motley found traces of white powder all over the cabin. Empty liquor bottles abounded. The place reeked of marijuana and stale booze, and I found several sex toys in the common area of the cabin. I called Irene to let her know that we'd be charging a cleaning fee and to hold the cabin as long as she could.

Later that afternoon, as I was rushing through the lobby of the main lodge, I saw something that put my heart in my throat.

A small party of an older couple and three young children stood at the front desk, checking in. I recognized the couple. Clint and Dierdre Foster were members of the Travel Club. He was average size, with a bald spot and neatly trimmed brown hair. She was equally nondescript. He was the CIA liaison, specializing in covert operations in South America. She was a cover member. I wasn't sure who the kids were but knew that the Fosters had three grandchildren.

I ran to the kitchen.

"Clint and Dierdre Foster are checking in," I gasped at Sid.

Sid cursed. "What the hell are they doing here?"

"I have no idea and no time to call Dale about it."

"I'll call Dale." Sid looked around the kitchen. Things seemed relatively quiet since it was the end of an almost non-existent lunch rush. "Can you talk to Hattie?"

I nodded, then flew up the service stairs to the third floor.

"What's the matter?" Hattie asked as she admitted me to her room.

I explained about Clint and Dierdre being there.

"Why are they here?" Hattie began pacing as well.

"I have no idea!" I snapped. "Sid's calling Dale. Or he's going to try to. I don't even know if any of them know we're here, and I've gotta find some way to warn the Fosters about the Delgados and my dad and keep the Delgados away from them."

"A good thing, but inconvenient, at best." Hattie shook her head. "Do you know which room the Fosters are in?"

"Not yet."

"Why don't I go downstairs and see if I can talk to them?"

"Just don't let Daddy see you do it. He's been asking too many questions as it is, and he knows about our connection. If he sees you talking to Clint, he'll figure out about him as well."

"It is a visible way of knowing each other." Hattie patted my shoulder. "We'll find a way around it. In the meantime, I'll go talk to Clint. I'll page you when we need to talk."

My walkie-talkie squawked again, and I left Hattie as I answered the call. It was some minor matter, but I was needed to deal with it.

After that, I headed back to the kitchen to update Sid. He had not been able to reach Dale, which did not surprise me. That's when Hattie paged both of us.

Sid shook his head. "You'll have to take it without me. Lee's late for work and we're already booked solid for dinner, so I've got to stay until he shows."

I hurried out and found Hattie in Room 209. Clint paced the larger space with the two beds. Dierdre had taken the kids to the playground, and every time Clint wandered past the window overlooking the back of the lodge and the cabins, he looked outside and half-smiled.

"Crap. What are you doing here?" Clint growled.

Hattie rolled her eyes before I could bite his head off. "Honestly, Clint. Her name? This is her father's resort?"

"That doesn't mean she'd be here." He glared at me. "Is your husband on site too?"

"Yes. We're both working here for the summer."

"And we've got the Delgados nosing their way into this." Clint had apparently been told that they were here. He looked out at the playground, half-smiled, then snorted. "Whose bright idea was all of this?"

"Dale O'Connor's," Hattie said. "He says he knows what he's doing."

"We don't need the backup," Clint snarled. "We've got it under control."

"Are you sure?" asked Hattie.

Clint snorted. "That we're all here together, along with the Delgados. Well, why not? We're friends."

"We haven't told anyone that we know the Delgados, and we'd better not." I sighed. "I suppose it will be okay if we know you and Dierdre. The hard part is that Daddy is really good at spotting fibs, and he can read me like a picture book."

"You'll be fine, Lisa," Hattie said.

Clint looked at my shirt and my walkie-talkie. "So, you're working here?"

"Yes. Assistant manager and head of housekeeping," I said. "Why?"

"Perfect. You can get intel to the Delgados and Hattie. You'll be our hub."

"Of course." I pressed my lips together and did not tell him that I was already the hub and that Sid and I were supposedly running the operation.

"Why don't you two clear out?" Clint said. "We'll go to dinner tonight. You got that restaurant here, right?"

"Not tonight, I won't," I said. "I've been eating with the rest of my family and the last place we'll want to be is that restaurant. We'll connect later."

"Same here," said Hattie. "In fact, I've already got plans to have dinner with Marge Benson tonight before she leaves, and we're going to someplace in town."

Clint shrugged and Hattie and I left, heading for the elevator.

I sighed. "We do not need this."

"We most certainly do not." She pressed the call button, then looked at me. "Any hope of finding those plans?"

"The only thing I can think of is that the target is keeping them on him. I've searched everywhere that I can think of. Did Sid tell you about the background checks we're doing?"

"It's as good an idea as any." Hattie blinked. "Of all the times."

"I know."

It was getting near dinner time and the worst of the check-in rush was over. So I went to the kitchen to see where Sid was.

He was working the wait station.

"What's going on?"

"I had to send Whitney home," Sid said. "He seemed sober enough, but he reeked of pot. We can't have that."

"No, we can't."

"I told him he can come back if he can pass the smell test." Sid shook his head. "It's not looking good for him."

"Why don't I try talking to him on Monday?"

"That would be great. Thanks." He sighed. "Apart from Whitney, this place is running pretty good. I may even take off early. Janine is up to it."

"Okay. We'll wait to have dinner until you know what you're doing."

Fortunately, Sid took off early enough to get dinner with the rest of our family at the Mexican food place. They were kind enough to bring a churro with a candle in it for Janey's birthday that day. Sid and I went back to the apartment early. We were going to have to be up extra early to get to the airport. The five of us were flying down to Burbank to spend the day with the rest of Janey's family to celebrate her birthday.

Sid's Voice -

I was having a good time that summer. I like restaurant work and always have. Well, except for the low wages. I never liked that, but I had always made it up in tips when I waited tables.

Being a consultant, that was fun for me. It was a challenge, especially physically. I'd forgotten how exhausting it can be to be on your feet all day, and I make a point of keeping myself up.

However, I had two flies in my personal ointment that summer. The first was Nick, who was being a pain in the ass in general. But we were still talking for the most part, and while he wasn't happy with me that summer, he didn't hate me, either. So I had to figure most of it was typical adolescent behavior. I'd certainly been nastier to my aunt when I was growing up.

But then there was Lisa. She'd had a difficult time that first year we were married, although it wasn't our relationship. It was that she'd never wanted to be married, never wanted to be a parent. It's a testament to how much she loves Nick and me that she became the last thing she wanted - a wife and mother.

That's why I had encouraged her to go back to her original plan of becoming a college professor. I'd seen her teach. We'd had that case in Wisconsin, where she'd gone undercover at a small arts college, and she'd gone above and beyond, really working to teach her students basic writing skills, rather than sliding through. Better yet, she enjoyed it.

Her first semester as a doctoral candidate did not go well. As she's already noted, she'd been bored out of her mind and couldn't figure out why. She loves Shakespeare, quotes the Bard even more often than she quotes the Bible, and doesn't mind reading scholarly journals on the topic.

Then came the class with Dr. Barber. It was bad enough that he was a sexist prick. Most of her classmates were, too, and it really didn't help when Lisa's essay from the previous semester on keeping Shakespeare relevant by re-thinking the female roles got published by one of the more distinguished journals in her field.

By the time that late July rolled around, Lisa was fed up to her back teeth with the resort work, and knowing her, was probably just as worried about disappointing her father, even if she wasn't admitting that to herself. I felt almost as frustrated as she did with the way the case was breaking. But she wasn't happy, and that really bothered me.

The Saturday of Janey's birthday had been a relatively shitty day, too. I'd covered the morning and lunch rush for Amelia Petrossian, the daytime manager. She'd had a kid get sick. Then it had been more nuts than usual at lunch, with several guests deciding to not only eat there, but one table that was not satisfied with anything.

Then Lisa told me about the Fosters, which was bad enough. After Lisa left to talk with Hattie and Clint, Lee Whitney showed, and I damned near got a contact high off his clothes. His eyes were clear, but there was no way he could work smelling like he did.

I had talked to Daddy about Lee, and Daddy wanted me to give him every chance as long as Lee didn't come to work stoned. Daddy was good at giving people in trouble a chance. It explained Lisa's tendency to forgive others. That woman will find a way to forgive Hitler.

I did not want to work that night, but we were fully booked out on reservations and when that happened, we needed both a manager and an assistant. So, I stayed, but only for the first hour of dinner rush. Lee returned odor-free, finally, and the rest of the family was waiting for me to go to dinner.

By the time Lisa and I got back to the apartment, I was bushed. Lisa told me what Clint and Hattie had said, and I was not happy. But there wasn't much we could do about it, no matter how fed up we were getting.

"Well, it could be a hell of a lot worse," I told her as we cuddled after lovemaking.

"I suppose," she sighed.

It wasn't like her to be that pessimistic. I held her close to me and kissed the scar on her temple.

"We're both alive. The kid's alive. And if your dad is onto us, he's not doing anything about it." I nuzzled her ear. She really likes that, and I really like doing it. "We've got a long day tomorrow, too. Why don't we try to get some sleep?"

It wasn't even eleven at that point. I know because there was a soft beeping sound and a red light blinked next to the clock radio on the bedside table.

"Shit." I squinted at the clock and got out of bed.

"Odds?" Lisa asked, her voice thick with sleep.

"Probably one of the kids tripping it. I'll check."

"Shorts."

I sighed. "Right."

I grabbed the pair of running shorts on the dresser and quickly got them on.

There was a distinct problem we were having with securing Dusty's room in the staff lodge. Dusty's pager was set so that it didn't trip the wires on his room, and we'd set up a pager for Desmond the same way. However, the summer help, made up of college kids, was very prone to wandering in and out of each other's rooms at all hours of the night, sometimes for sex, sometimes just to talk. Dusty was not the most sociable kid, but he'd made a couple friends, and Donna Mars had a serious crush on him. So, it was not unusual for one of the other kids to go into Dusty's room to see if he was there.

The problem was that wandering in and out of the room triggered alarms. Lisa and I had realized the first night someone had visited Dusty in the wee hours of the morning that showing up with guns aimed and no clothes (we sleep in the raw) was not the best way to deal with it. On the other hand, we couldn't assume that because an alarm had been triggered that it was just one of the kids doing what they do.

As I left the bedroom, Lisa pulled a small automatic out of her bedside table and grabbed her terry robe from the hook on the closet door.

I slid out of the apartment. I knew Lisa was behind me, but her job was to hang back in case it was one of the kids. The big common area was empty. I looked down the hall toward the rooms on the other side of the common area. The hall was completely dark, and I went on alert. If it had been one of the usual wanderings, I would have either seen the kid who'd triggered the alarm or a light under Dusty's door.

I listened first at the door. There was definitely someone on the other side. I eased the door open and looked. A form about the same height as me, wearing black and an all-over ski mask, looked up from the trunk at the end of Dusty's bed.

A second later, he sprang. I blocked a couple punches, but the guy was good, and I was barefoot. He got in a quick kick that grazed my nuts. There are few things that hurt like that does, and I sank to my knees. The dark form grabbed my neck and tried to get behind me. I knew the move and as soon as he'd thrown his arm around my neck to attempt to break it. I popped my knuckles into his biceps. He cursed softly, but didn't entirely let go.

Lisa screamed and flipped on the lights. A second later, the dark form dropped me and knocked Lisa over as he scrambled away. Lisa and I hurried to our feet, but the intruder had disappeared through the front door of the staff lodge, which hung open. Lisa, having put on some flip-flops, ran ahead, but came back shaking her head.

"He's gone," she said. She looked at me. "You okay?"

"Singing soprano."

"Oh, no!"

"It was only a light graze, but it did enough."

Lisa looked out the front. "It's funny, Sid. When I flipped on the lights, I saw him look down and that's when he dropped you."

"As in, I wasn't his target."

We didn't get any time to debate the issue, though. Dusty and Desmond walked into the lodge from the front.

"What you guys doing up?" Dusty asked us.

"We thought we heard something funny," I said. "Where were you guys?"

"We went to the movies," Desmond said as Dusty hurried off to his room. Desmond lowered his voice. "What happened?"

"Intruder," Lisa said. "Did you see anything outside?"

"No." Desmond frowned.

"Someone's been going through my stuff!" Dusty yelped.

Lisa went to talk to him. I held Desmond back.

"Have you found anything?" I asked.

He shook his head. "He's not even carrying anything on him. I've checked his clothes when he was wearing his skivvies and watched him get ready for the shower. So, unless those plans were small enough to swallow, he hasn't got them."

"Shit."

Still, it was Lisa who found the ray of hope.

"The intruder was looking for something," she told me a bit later as we returned to bed. "And it sounds terrible, but you and Dusty are about the same height. In the dark, the intruder might have mistaken you."

"Which means he was trying to kill Dusty."

"And he must have been looking for the plans, which also means that he doesn't have them."

July 31–August 1, 1988

I hate getting up early in the morning. Sid is a morning person and seldom sleeps past six a.m. Me? If I can stay in bed until noon, I will happily.

But there wasn't much I could do about the early morning flight out of the South Lake Tahoe airport to Burbank. The only later flight didn't leave until after three that afternoon, and we wanted to be at Mae and Neil's for as much of that Sunday as possible.

It was Janey's birthday, and the Whole Fam-Damily, except for Mama, was there. The Whole Fam-Damily was a joke Darby had made the year before and he'd thought he was really getting away with something. Except that the phrase stuck. It consists of my parents, Mae, Neil, and their six kids, Sid, me, Nick, Sy and Stella.

Mae, Neil, and the kids might have come up to the resort that Sunday, but between the fact that there was no place to put them and that it was too expensive to fly in for the day, Daddy and Sid had agreed for them, me, and Janey to fly down to the Burbank airport, then get a shuttle to Pasadena where the O'Malleys live.

Also, both Mae and Darby were performing in a community theatre production of Fiddler on the Roof. An arts group in the city of Pasadena was putting it on. The summer before, Darby had joined the little community orchestra, which got Mae trying out for that year's production of Kiss Me Kate. Mae got the lead, Lilli Vanessi, and Darby had played second chair violin.

This summer, Mae had tried out again and won the role of Golde in Fiddler. The conductor and the director had thought it would be fun if the Fiddler could really play and got Darby to do it. It wouldn't premiere until later in August. But the rehearsal schedule meant that driving up to the resort would have been really difficult, even if there had been some place to shoehorn the family in.

We spent a pleasant day with everyone, then Neil drove us to the airport for that evening's flight back to Tahoe. But as the five of us waited for our flight, I noticed Nick was sulking.

"You okay, honey?" I asked, playing with the lock of hair that had, again, fallen over his forehead.

He made a face. "I just don't want to go back. I mean, Darby got to go to music camp. He gets to do the show. It's not fair."

"You got to do a play," I said.

We couldn't say so, but Nick and I had gotten involved in a production of Richard III during the Kansas case eighteen months before.

"Yeah."

"I thought you said you didn't want to do it again."

"I don't." Nick frowned. "It's just that Darby gets to do all the fun stuff. I have to work. I hate that job."

Sighing, I put my arm around his shoulders. "I know. I'm not liking the work, either. But it is helping your grandfather, and you are learning to drive. Darby isn't yet."

"I know." Nick huffed.

They called our flight and Nick went to get on the plane.

Thanks to the noise of the plane, Sid and I were able to make a plan for the next couple of days. Sid had called Esther at the resort before we took off and had found out that things had been quiet. Desmond would continue to keep an eye on Dusty where he could. Frank would hang out and do perimeter checks while Desmond and Esther were working. He was also making friends with Pedro Delgado, and the two had done a couple searches, but had found nothing beyond the transponder behind the horse barn that had already been found. Pedro had yet to get any information on the equipment's origins. Esther had seen it and didn't recognize where it had been made, either.

The problem was, neither of us was sure what to do about the attack on Dusty, or even if it was an attack on Dusty and not just someone surprising a burglar. It had certainly seemed like Dusty was the intended victim, but since we weren't even sure that Lipplinger had been murdered, we couldn't say whether the two events were connected.

So, the first thing I did Monday morning was print out a list of the guests who were at the resort when Lipplinger was killed and another list of the guests who were there that Saturday when Dusty's room had been broken into. That didn't mean that the attacker hadn't come onto the resort from someplace else, but it was a place to start.

I also messed up my back a few minutes later. The really annoying part of it was that I wasn't doing anything that should have popped it out, like landing really hard on my backside. I simply twisted wrong, but the pain was incredibly intense and there wasn't much I could do about it.

I had another errand to run. It was Lee Whitney's day off and I had promised Sid that I'd talk to the errant manager. I eased myself into Sid's Beemer and took off. Whitney lived in a small apartment to the north of the town. The thin young man with brown hair and eyes blinked at me sleepily when he opened the door to his place.

"Come on in," he grumbled.

He was dressed, but in a dirty t-shirt and rumpled jeans. I wondered if he'd been sleeping in his clothes. A ratty couch sat in the center of the room, facing a new TV on a battered table. The place reeked, and a thin mist of smoke permeated the room. How much of that was pot and how much was incense, I couldn't say. I can't always tell when it's marijuana that I'm smelling or someone's cigar, I don't care how distinctive people say the smell of pot is.

"Lee, you know why I'm here, don't you?" I asked.

"Not really." He shrugged sadly. "Sort of." He blinked. "Is Sid still mad at me?"

"I don't think he's mad, but he is worried about you."

"I don't go to work stoned."

"Yeah, but you called in sick the week before last and you came in stinking of marijuana the other night."

"It's just weed. Who cares?"

"Well, I do, for starters." I frowned at him. "I thought you liked working the restaurant."

He shrugged and flopped down on the sagging couch. "It's as good as anything, I guess."

"Is there something else you'd rather be doing?" I sat down next to him, trying not to choke on the fumes.

"I don't know." He took a deep breath, then looked over at the small counter in front of the kitchen. A thin stream of smoke wafted up from an ashtray. Next to it, a stick of incense glowed.

"Well, what did you want to be when you were a kid?"

"A grown up." He blinked at me. "Honestly, Lisa. I have no idea. I just wanted to get through high school and be on my own." He took a deep breath. "I figured I'd find something sooner or later. But I didn't. I liked waiting tables. It was easy, and I didn't have to think too much. And being manager was kinda cool. But it's kinda like is this all there is?" He sighed. "My dad keeps yelling at me that I need some direction for my life."

"Well, you're not going to get it smoking weed."

"I suppose." He blinked. "And some days, it totally sucks. But most days I'm cool with waiting tables and smoking on my days off."

"Except that Saturday night, when we needed you, you came in smelling like a stoner."

"I wasn't stoned."

"You're getting awfully close to it." I got up. "And if you do come in stoned, you will get fired." I went to the door. "I hope that doesn't happen. You don't deserve that."

He shrugged. "Okay."

I left the apartment and blinked. The weird thing was that I felt dizzy and shook my head to clear it. It didn't entirely help. I managed to drive back to the resort without mishap, but couldn't figure out how I'd done it. I found Sid in my parents' kitchen, making lunch.

"Oh, man, I feel weird," I told him. "But I messed up my back this morning, and it doesn't hurt now."

Sid got a good snort of my clothes. "I'm guessing you got a solid contact high."

"If this is being high, then I don't like it." My stomach gurgled. "And I'm starving, too. Any chips around?"

Sid laughed and got me some Cheet-ohs. I plowed through the bag.

"Someone's got the munchies," Sid said, handing me a ham sandwich.

I ate three more sandwiches, then went to rest in our room.

Sid's Voice -

Poor Lisa was a mess, but I appreciated the way she'd talked to Lee. It was even more interesting that the contact high had taken the edge off her back pain. I was a little concerned about Whitney, but he was merely an annoyance. Clint Foster was a full-on problem and, thanks to the contact high, Lisa was in no shape to hear what had happened that morning.

Things were running smoothly at the restaurant by the time the breakfast rush eased, so I focused on working with Esther and Desmond on the new computer system. Clint somehow found us in the main office and insisted on talking to me. I took him into Daddy's office and locked the door.

"What the fuck is going on here?" Clint demanded. "I was called in to pull a simple sting on the kid selling the tech to the Russians, and now Hattie's telling me that he's being set up to give them a set of dummy plans."

"Hattie told us the same thing."

"And what the hell are you doing here?" Clint's face was just starting to get red.

I folded my arms across my chest. "Lisa and I are here to make sure our Soviet mole gets the dummy plans."

Clint got in my face. "Whose fucking idea was that?"

"How about your good buddy Dale O'Connor?"

"He called me in on this."

"I can't help that." I spread my hands. "This little clusterfuck was not my idea and I don't like you getting all over my ass just because Dale got turned around. Not to mention the fact that yelling at me is not going to help this mission succeed."

"This is why we have the Travel Club." Clint started pacing. "You should have said something."

"Oh, for fucking Christ's sake! A- you could have said something and B- that's assuming either of us were told the other had Need to Know on our respective operations."

"We clearly had Need to Know."

"No shit. But neither of us knew that, did we? You want to bitch about it? Go talk to Dale. In the meantime, we should probably figure out a way to verify the objective, then see what we can do to make it happen."

Clint got back in my face. "Do not tell me how to run an operation. I've been in this business since before you popped your cherry."

I couldn't help chuckling. "I wouldn't put any money on that. I lost it pretty early." I held up my hands. "Look, can we find a way to work together on this? It doesn't matter who fucked up."

"I'll talk to Dale." Clint moved away. "In the meantime, you stand down and stay out of my way."

"Fine."

I shook my head as Clint left the office. There was a reason Lisa and I pretty much hated The Company.

Lisa's Voice -

When I woke up that afternoon, I still felt pretty dragged out, but at least my head wasn't spinning and while my back still hurt, it still felt better than it had. I also wondered about Marina and that stash of cocaine I'd found in her purse. She'd worked with Lee in the afternoons. I believed Sid when he'd said that he didn't think Marina was using. But I began to think that it was possible that Marina was dealing. The question was how to ask her about it.

I was about to go up to her room when she came into the staff lodge from the front and flopped onto a couch.

"How's it going?" I asked her.

She yawned. "Okay. I can't wait 'til Wednesday, though."

"Day off, right?"

"Yeah." She grinned and wriggled her shoulders. "I'm going to sleep in until mid-afternoon."

I plopped into a nearby easy chair. "Um. Maybe you can help me. I've been hearing some rumors about drugs in the restaurant."

Marina's face went pale. "It's not me."

"Marina?" I looked at her. "What's going on?"

"Nothing!"

"I'm not thinking you're involved."

Marina burst into tears. "Tommy thinks I am, and it's all the fault of those stupid executives on the retreat. But I didn't do anything. I swear."

Tommy was another college kid who was waiting tables during the day.

"What happened?" I moved over next to her and put my arms around her shoulders.

Marina shook her head. "I swear. I didn't do anything."

"I'm sure you didn't. But you're obviously upset. Why don't you tell me what happened?"

"Tommy." Marina sniffed. "We were joking about where those executives were getting their coke and Tommy said that I was selling it to them!" She sobbed. "I didn't sell anybody anything. I really didn't."

"Then why would anybody think you had?"

"Oh, lord. This is so awful." Marina blinked and tried to get a hold of herself. "It's one of the guys I go to school with at Sac State. I'm a computer science major. Anyway, the guys there are always giving me a hard time. Except Doug. I mean, he's not a friend. He's kinda mean. But he found out about my job up here, and he's working up here, too, at one of the casinos across the state line." She meant in Nevada, which we're literally right on top of in Tahoe. "So, he gives me this book to hold for him. And I think, no big deal. It would be nice to get one of those guys on my side. So, I take the book. Only there was this little plastic thing of white powder inside. I mean, it has to be coke. Doug gets too wired, you know? So, he calls me and lets me know that if I get rid of the book, he will come after me. That's when I looked at the book and found the powder. I can't get rid of it. Doug will come after me. But I can't let anybody find it, either." The tears started flowing again. "Only Tommy must have. I mean, I thought it was hidden really well."

"It probably is," I said softly, knowing full well that it was. "Tommy was just making an insensitive joke."

"You don't think I'm dealing?"

I chuckled. "Marina, it's a lot easier to tell when someone is dealing than you might think."

That wasn't entirely true, but unless Marina was one hell of a lot better an actress than I thought, then it was pretty unlikely that she was dealing.

"But what am I going to do?" She caught her breath as she began to hyperventilate. "I can't get rid of it. Doug will hurt me. And if someone else finds it, I'll be screwed."

"I understand." I smiled at her. "But it will be alright. Why don't you give it to me? If your friend Doug comes after it, I'll find a way to protect you. And if I have it, there's no way that Tommy or anyone else can find it on you."

"You can protect me?"

I shrugged. "I deal with all sorts of cranky, nasty people. I can handle it."

Whether she believed me, I didn't know, but she did eventually lead me up to her room and dug the packet of white powder out of her purse. I could see her shoulders relaxing as she gave it to me. I wished I could have felt as relieved.

I kept the packet in my pocket as my pager vibrated. Hattie wanted to ask me something and I couldn't really ignore it.

I made my way to the main lodge and upstairs, feeling nettled. It wasn't as though I didn't have plenty of other things to take care of and I really resented being on Hattie's leash, as it were. I was surprised to see Sid in the room with Hattie.

"What's going on?" I asked.

"Clint wants us to stand down," Sid said. "He thinks Dale brought him in to set up the sting on Dusty."

"What does Dale say?" I asked.

Hattie's eyes rolled. "Who knows? He is not returning any of our calls and he is not in Washington or here."

"So, do we stand down or what?" Sid asked.

"We still have those plans to find," Hattie said. "Especially now that we know someone else is looking for them. Until we get our hands on them, they are not safe."

Sid sighed. "Would it make sense to focus on that and let Clint worry about any sting operations for the time being?"

"It does to me." I watched Hattie carefully.

She groaned in frustration. "I swear, I would dearly love to electrocute Clint. And Dale, too."

She spoke with such venom it startled me. Sid looked over at me.

"Alright," he said slowly. "We'll work on that."

Hattie nodded, and Sid and I left the room.

"Let's talk in the apartment," I muttered.

Which is where we went.

"What are you thinking?" Sid asked as I checked the messages on the answering machine.

"Sid, do you think Hattie knows that her brother was electrocuted?"

"We don't know for sure that her brother was electrocuted."

"True. But it seems really odd that she put it that way about Clint." I frowned. "And she was so angry, too. That's not like her."

"No, it's not." Sid frowned. "Wait. There is a perfectly innocent reason why she might know and it's that, as next of kin, she probably has access to the coroner's report."

"Still." I began pacing. "She got here awfully fast that day. You know as well as I do how hard it is to get a connecting flight here. How did she do it?"

"Hard to say. But you called her in Washington."

I looked at the phone and answering machine. "No. I called her home phone number. That doesn't mean she was actually in Washington."

"How would you have reached her, then?"

"The same way people are reaching us. Our phone number has been forwarded to this phone." I shook my head. "She could have forwarded her number to almost anywhere and we wouldn't necessarily know. You can hear it switch sometimes when it's forwarded, but if you're not paying attention, you'll miss the sound."

Sid winced. "Okay. I'll have to buy that possibility. But we still don't know for sure how Lipplinger died, and if he was electrocuted, how that could have happened? The TV was unplugged."

"I have no idea." I got the two print outs I'd made earlier that morning. "Maybe if we look at who was here when Lipplinger died and who was here this past Saturday, that will help."

There were five spaces that had not vacated that Saturday, with only three that had been at the resort both when Lipplinger died and when the attack had occurred. The Winslows were staying the entire summer and were in Cabin Eight. The DiNovo Family, in Cabin Three, were reserved through the middle of August. Maria Sanchez had extended her reservation the week before.

"Ms. Sanchez is in the room next to Lipplinger's," I told Sid. "But if she's hiding that she's a Soviet spy, then she is doing a masterful job of it. She's incredibly nice."

"Could she be about my size?" Sid asked.

"She's closer to my height," I said. "Plus, she's got some decided curves. On the other hand, it was dark." I looked at the paper again. "I'd think the DiNovos are more likely, but they're not wandering around a lot. He mostly works and she spends all her time reading and sometimes keeping an eye on her kids."

"There's also the Winslows." Sid shook his head. "He's not that tall, and the girls are pretty much oblivious."

"Yeah, but they're regulars. They've been spending the summer here since…" I frowned. "Come to think of it, he used to come with his family when he was a kid, and I possibly had my weekly fling with him. I don't think so, but we might have." I sent Sid a mock glare as he chuckled. "For crying out loud. There's no reason I should remember the guy, and you can't possibly remember every woman you slept with."

He laughed. "Not if I have to come up with a list of names. But when I see someone I slept with, I generally remember." He thought about it. "Although high school was twenty years ago. It's entirely possible that I wouldn't be able to place some of the girls I knew back then."

"And it's been well over ten years back for me." I leaned into him.

He nuzzled my ear. It was so tempting, but then the walkie-talkie squawked, and I had to go running.

August 2-3, 1988

I slept in the next morning, then took Janey with me to go running by the lake. It was so nice to not think about missing plans and room cleaning and everything else.

The only problem was that when I got back, Lita paged me. I met her at the paddock next to the horse barn.

"What's up?" I asked, scooping up a bit of hay for one of the mares.

"It's Maria Sanchez," she said. "She came over to the table where we were having dinner last night to say hi. She recognized us as Cuban."

"As in, she is, too." I smiled as the mare nibbled delicately from my hand.

"Yeah." Lita shrugged. "It doesn't necessarily mean anything."

"Except that we have intel that there might be a Cuban operative around."

"I know. She seems like just a nice lady."

"That's what I thought." I grinned at Lita. "But you seem like just a nice lady, too."

Lita laughed. People frequently underestimate her and her partner, Barb Wasserman. It's not a healthy thing to do.

"The funny thing is," Lita continued. "Barb said right before we left that she'd heard that the Cuban operatives had given up." She shook her head. "That doesn't make sense, but it could be. They don't have a lot of resources to spare."

"And Ms. Sanchez does." I looked back at the lodge thoughtfully. "Well, thanks for the update. You've seen the Fosters, right?"

"Oh, yeah. Dierdre and I are making friends with each other." Lita sniggered. "She is pissed to hell at Clint for dragging the grandkids out while he's working. Apparently, he didn't tell her they were coming here for an operation."

"My poor heart just bleeds for him." I rolled my eyes, then patted the mare on the nose. "You know, I think I'm going to go for a ride."

Lita put her hands up. "All yours. They're pretty to look at, but I'm not going to mess with one."

The time on horseback did me a world of good. I came back right before lunch and joined Sid, Nick, Janey, and Daddy in my parents' kitchen. Sid said I smelled like horse, but he was smiling.

I got a quick shower before heading out to run an errand. Not only had the ride helped me relax a little, it got me thinking about that TV in Lipplinger's room. So, I called Judy Osbourne and told her I'd bring in the broken television to see if she could fix it or use it for parts.

I liked Judy's shop. It was in a strip center that held the local supermarket. The shop had a lighted sign over it that read, "Video Stop. Rentals. Repairs." You went inside and it was almost dark, with all four walls lined with videotapes. Worn and sometimes yellowed labels identified the different genres, and chest-high shelving units filled the floors. Judy provided videotapes for a lot of places in the area. Her own interests were eclectic as all get out, and the wall behind the glass case with the register held laser discs, Betamax tapes, and a host of foreign films in VHS, as well as some movie memorabilia.

The back was equally full, but exceedingly neat. Metal shelves along one wall held televisions and VCRs, most of them either waiting to be repaired or waiting to be picked up by their owners. A large table stood in the center of the room with a large white fluorescent fixture overhead, flooding the table with light.

Judy had me set the broken TV on the table, then turned it around.

"Well?" I asked.

She shook her head. "It's worse than that. It's dead, Jim."

"What?"

"Oh." She smiled and shrugged. "It's a Star Trek tune on the Dr. Demento show."

"You mean the radio program?" I nodded. "Nick has been getting into that."

Judy laughed full out. "You realize that means your kid is turning into a massive nerd, don't you?"

"Not turning into," I replied grinning. "He's always been one. He'd rather spout batting averages than try to hit a ball. He can recite the entire Periodic Table. The only reason people don't figure it out right away is that he takes after his father in the looks department and doesn't dress funny."

I couldn't tell her how good he was getting at explosives.

"I knew there was a reason I liked him." Judy smiled softly, then turned to the TV. "Anyway, there's no point in fixing this. The parts would cost more than a new television."

She shifted the set around, then yelped.

"What's the matter?"

"There's a loose wire here." She pushed the TV onto its back, then looked at me. "How long has thing been unplugged?"

"Over a week. Why?"

Judy sighed in relief. "TVs can be kinda dangerous. They have these parts called capacitors that hold a lot of electricity. Now, normally, when something is turned off or unplugged, that electricity dissipates within a few minutes. But the capacitors in televisions hold on to their charge, and a lot of it, for up to twenty-four hours after the box has been unplugged."

She pulled out a flashlight and shone it through the broken screen into the set's insides.

"You mean a TV can be unplugged and still electrocute somebody?"

"Exactly." She suddenly cursed. "And this one may have done just that." She looked at me, her eyes filled with worry. "Lisa, this looks like it may have been set up as a trap. Look here." She pointed with the beam of the flashlight. "There's that loose wire that bit me just now. And see? It's wired to that capacitor near the back."

"And if somebody picked that up, even if it was unplugged, he'd get zapped." I bit my lip.

"Like Dr. Lipplinger." She gasped and squeezed her eyes shut.

"You know his name."

Judy nodded. "He ruined my life." She sank onto a nearby metal stool. "Okay. I mean, it wasn't just him. You know I got accepted to Georgetown right out of high school."

"No, I didn't." I bit my lip. Lipplinger had been teaching at Georgetown when Sid and I had first known him. "You went?"

"Yeah. But I couldn't hack it. I was so far away from my family and friends." She blinked back tears, but they fell anyway. "I took beginning physics with him. I was going to be an engineer."

"I remember that." I looked at her. "You were one of the smartest kids in school."

Judy snorted. "A lot of good that did me. Lipplinger had it in for me. We'd get quizzes back, and the one guy I was friends with would get a better grade than I would with the same answer. I went to Lipplinger for help, and he said that I was wasting my time. That I'd never understand physics, and I might as well go home, get married, and have babies."

"That sounds like something you could have sued over." It also sounded a lot like something Lipplinger would have said.

"I was eighteen. You think I thought of that? No. I believed the bastard. And I got an A in physics in high school." She shook her head. "I went home for Christmas and couldn't get myself to go back. My confidence was shot. I was miserable and lonely. I tried going to Sac State, but I spent so much time doubting myself that I failed again. So, I gave up. I learned how to fix TVs and then VCRs and built this business from the ground up. Anyway, a couple of weeks ago, when I was delivering tapes, I saw Lipplinger checking into your dad's place. I nearly died. I'm pretty sure he didn't see me." She shuddered and sniffed. "I never wanted to see that bastard again."

"I can imagine."

She suddenly sat up straight. "I didn't rig this."

"Why would you have told me about it if you had? Besides, when would you have had the opportunity?"

She nodded. "That's right. We should probably notify the police."

"Not a bad idea. Can I look at the inside again?"

She got out her flashlight and showed me the wire and the insides of the TV. It was as I'd remembered it, except for the tape and floppy disk that I'd removed. I thanked her and rushed back to the resort.

I was so lost in thought as I hurried into the main lodge that I almost ran over Brian Lane.

"I'm so sorry!" I yelped. "Back with us again?"

"Yeah. I like it here." He smiled. "Beats the corporate-owned cookie cutter rooms."

"I'm glad." I looked around and saw Ms. Wannamaker slinking along the hall to the playground and indoor pool. "Excuse me, will you?"

I tried following her, but was interrupted by loud voices coming from the stairs to the basement.

"You have to write her up!" Mira yelled. "She's just going to keep walking all over you."

"I don't need you to tell me what to do," Lourdes snapped back. "I know what I'm doing."

I hurried downstairs. "Ladies? We can hear you upstairs."

Lourdes glared at Mira. "See? This is your fault. Now, leave me alone!"

Lourdes stomped upstairs. I looked at Mira.

"Beatrice again," Mira grumbled.

"Daddy said that you thought she was okay."

Mira rolled her eyes. "Yeah. When I'm in charge."

"Well, maybe Lourdes is trying a gentler approach."

"That's fine." Mira snorted. "I totally agree with being gentle. But you also have to follow through with consequences. Lourdes does not get that and Beatrice is taking advantage of her to goof off."

"Do you want me to talk to Beatrice?" I sighed.

"No. I want you to get Lourdes out of here. She's a disaster."

"I'll try to think of something."

I went back upstairs, shaking my head. Lourdes wasn't a disaster, but she was awfully close to being one. Once up the stairs, I headed toward the pool area, but didn't see Ms. Wannamaker. I found her in the activities center.

"Hi!" I said as brightly as I could.

"Oh, hello, Lisa."

"How has your afternoon been?"

Her eyes narrowed as she looked me over. "It's been fine. We had fifteen kids in for the open crafts period, another seven for drawing. Twenty-three video tapes went out, fourteen were returned. We also checked out twelve books from the grown-ups library."

"Sounds like a normal day." I smiled. "It's just that I saw you a bit ago, heading toward the pool. I almost thought you were sneaking out to get a smoke."

Ms. Wannamaker held herself up in high dudgeon. "I do not smoke, and I have been here the entire afternoon."

"Must have been the lighting in the main lobby." I smiled at her.

It wasn't, but I knew darned well that Ms. Wannamaker snuck out to go to the bathroom several times a day. The only problem was that there was a bathroom much closer to the activities center than the one near the pool.

I slid through the back of the lodge to head up to the apartment. Nick came running up.

"Mom!"

"What's up, sweetie?"

"Dusty's pager went off." Nick grinned. "It was my turn to tail him, so I did. I think I know why he's spending so much time in the woods near here."

"Oh?"

"Yeah. He met up with Donna. You know, the maid?" Nick looked around, then leaned closer to me. "They were necking."

I pulled back. "That doesn't make sense."

"Why not?" Nick's eyes rolled like the reels on a slot machine. "He's totally gone on her and she likes him, too."

"You're right about that, sweetie." I frowned. "But why go out to the woods? Half the college staff is sleeping with each other and no one cares."

Nick glared at me. "Well, if you're not going to believe me..."

"I do believe you." I smiled at him. "You did a good job. Thank you. I'll see you back at your grandpa's for dinner."

Instead of huffing off, however, Nick hung his head and wandered away. I sighed inside. As if I needed yet another mystery to decipher.

Sid was reading in the apartment.

"Well, we've got a new development," I told him as he put his book down.

I told him about my conversation with Judy.

"That's interesting." Sid frowned. "I know she's your friend, but do you think she wired the TV?"

I made a face. "Actually, I don't." It suddenly hit me why I didn't. "She had it in for Lipplinger, but why would she have set a trap in the TV? It doesn't seem like she'd have known that he wanted the TV moved every day. People don't do things like that. And everyone on the floor knew that it was Dusty who was moving the TV, not Lipplinger."

"That is an excellent point." Sid mused. "But Dusty was off that Thursday. Wouldn't someone have figured that out?"

"You'd think, but no." I shuddered. "Even Lipplinger hadn't. He'd called down that morning demanding to know where Dusty was."

"He did." Sid got up and began pacing. "And if I recall correctly, Ms. Sanchez is in the room next to where Lipplinger was."

I groaned. "I hope not her. She is really nice."

"So are several people we know who are pretty deadly when push comes to shove." Sid paused. "Honey, is it possible that Dusty set the trap for Lipplinger?"

I thought about that. "Given what a pain in the backside Lipplinger was, I'd almost have to say that it's not just possible, it may even be likely." I stopped. "No. There was no reason to believe that Lipplinger would move the TV himself. He'd been pretty adamant about having someone else do it, and there was no way Dusty could have known who the old man would get to do it."

"So then we have to believe that Dusty was the actual target of the trap." Sid sighed.

"Yeah. I know."

Sid got up and paced. "How likely is it that our mole is someone on the staff?"

"You mean one of the college kids?" I asked.

"Possibly, but it could also be someone else." Sid had a pained look on his face. "I know most of them have been here for years, but it is possible that the Soviets got control of one of them."

"Like who?" I thought over the staff members. "Maybe Lee Whitney. Come to think of it, he hasn't been here that long. Um. Mira?" I frowned. "Lyle has been a problem, but that's the computer, not Soviet control."

"Irene is pretty good with computers," Sid said. "In fact, she and Esther have been talking a lot, and Irene obviously gets what Esther's saying about data collection and inputs. She might be able to look at that floppy disk and recognize it as something Lipplinger might have had."

"That also makes sense." I shook my head. "We don't have any actual evidence, though."

"I'll get Esther to question Irene a little more closely." He paused. "You know who else is very new here compared to everyone else and is also a foreign national. Bracha Solomon."

My eyebrows rose. "You know. You're right. I saw her wandering the perimeter of the resort last week, too, and she brushed it off to getting the kinks out. And she was not on her usual schedule. But would she have the tech savvy to wire that TV, and if she did, when did she?"

"Both excellent questions." Sid smiled. "I'll make a point of talking to her about her background, and leave Mira and Lyle to you."

I sighed. "Thanks."

Sid turned, and he got that hot little smile on his face that means he's thinking about us making each other happy. I went for it. Hey, it was our day off.

The next day was also supposedly a day off. Shortly after breakfast, I helped Irene work around another over-booking that Lyle had made.

"Daddy, we have to do something about him," I told my father a bit later in his office.

"I know." Daddy looked over some papers on his desk.

"Can't you talk him into retiring? It's not like he isn't old enough."

"I've already tried." Daddy shook his head. "Lisle, the poor fellow doesn't have anything else in his life. All his friends are here. He has no interest in traveling or anything else. I can sometimes get him out to go fishing, but even then, he won't go on his own. He goes home and watches TV, and that's all he does. His life is at this resort and that's it."

I winced. "That's kinda sad."

"Well, it's his life." Daddy sighed. "And I let Neff work until he dropped."

"But Neff was still competent and was even able to handle the new reservation system."

"I am well aware of that, Lisle." Daddy shook his head. "I'll figure something out. I'll take any suggestions you have, but you don't need to worry about Lyle. That's for me to."

I left the office just tense enough that I headed for the horse barn. Even if I couldn't get a ride in, being around the horses would make me feel better.

I found Sid and Bracha on the grass behind the barn. Bracha came after him, throwing several punches. Sid blocked them, but Bracha pushed him back. She didn't seem to have a weapon on her, but I couldn't count on that. Sid and I hadn't been able to carry our guns while working, so I was pretty sure Sid was mostly unarmed.

Sid pushed back on Bracha, but she deflected his blows expertly. My heart in my throat, I ran and jumped on Bracha's back.

Bracha yelped as Sid fell back even further. Bracha tried flipping me, but I hung on and tried to hook one of my legs around hers. She punched my right bicep as I kicked her calf. She staggered, and I rolled off and then, keeping low, tackled her. We both fell, me on top of her, and Bracha stopped struggling.

Laughing like a maniac, Sid came over and helped me up.

"It's okay, sweetheart," he said, then held out a hand for Bracha. "We were just sparring."

"What?" I looked at the two of them.

Bracha got up, laughing as well. "Why not?"

"What?" I repeated.

"Bracha's teaching me some krav maga," Sid said. "It's the Israeli army martial art."

"Okay," I said weakly, then bent over and stretched just in case. "Crap, you guys scared me."

Sid pulled me into his arms and kissed the side of my head. "Sorry, lover. I suppose it would look pretty bad if you didn't know."

Bracha laughed again. "Sid's pretty good at it."

"We have to be," Sid said. I looked at him in alarm. "It's okay. She's Dale's extra mole."

I gaped. "You're with the Mossad."

"Unfortunately." Bracha shrugged her shoulders. "I'd really rather be just a chef. But it's the same in our business as yours. Once you're in, that's it. You're in for life."

"Pedro got the intel on the transponder back here," Sid said. "It's Israeli. So, I came to check it out, and it's hers. I caught her red-handed."

"I'm the coordinator between my government and yours," Bracha said. "My job is to feed your government what my government wants you to know, and feed my government what your government wants us to know. Dale's my primary contact, and when he found out your dad was looking for someone who could run a restaurant, he sent me here."

I looked at Sid, who rolled his eyes.

"We can bounce Dale on his ear some other time," Sid said.

Bracha looked at us curiously.

"I'm sorry, honey," I said. "I am getting really fed up with him just deciding he can play around with my family's lives."

"Dale knows what he's doing," Bracha said. "I've had to trust him with my life more than once, and he's not going to risk killing a bunch of kids. But he needs somebody here in Tahoe. There's a KGB operative in town. I've seen him around. Bumped into him at the Video Stop last week. His name is Yuri Voskoff, and he's a known operative and doesn't care."

I swallowed. Both the CIA and the KGB had operatives that the other side knew about, which generally meant they weren't that effective. But then there were the ones that everyone knew about who didn't care that everyone knew about them. That's because their job was not to ferret out secrets, but kill people.

"I don't know who his target is," Bracha said. "My guess would be Dale. It might be worth it to the KGB to take him out."

I glanced over at Sid. "On the other hand, someone wired a trap that could have taken out our target for the tech sale. It's just how and when?"

"It wouldn't have been that hard for Yuri." Bracha made a face. "He's really, really good. One of the best around. He can break in anywhere, and he's even defeated a few alarm systems."

"But how would he have known about Lipplinger wanting the TV moved twice a day?" Sid asked.

"Unless Lipplinger was the intended target." I made a face. "But again, how would Yuri have known to set the trap on the TV?"

"Maybe he had Lipplinger bugged," Bracha said. "I don't know how. I've checked this place out regularly since I got here and haven't found any. Or maybe he's working with somebody on the inside to tell him what's going on."

"Any thoughts on who?"

Bracha frowned. "Maybe Lyle. I know he doesn't have much of a life outside this place, and it could be because he doesn't have any money to speak of."

I shook my head. "Daddy's got a pretty good pension plan in place, so unless Lyle is spending a lot of money on something that doesn't show, it's not likely. And Lyle doesn't gamble as far as I know."

"How about Lee Whitney?" Sid asked. "He's got that pot problem. That would make it easy to control him, and he needs money for his drugs."

Bracha rolled her eyes. "I'll keep an eye out for him."

"You know, it could also be Mira or Lourdes," I said. "Lourdes could be worrying about losing her job, and both of them would have known about Lipplinger and the TV." I made a face. "And this Yuri guy wouldn't have had to bribe them to get the information. He could have just made friends with them and listened to them gripe."

"I think I know who they are," Bracha said. "They live off the resort, don't they?"

"Yes. Mira and her family live just south of here and Lourdes and her husband live on the north side of town."

"Can you give us a description of Yuri?" Sid asked.

"I'd say around one-point-seven-five meters, dark hair and eyes," Bracha said. "Probably looks older than he is, but he's got a solid build, and like I said, he's darned good at what he does."

Sid was doing some math in his head. "In other words, he's about my size. You know. I think he was here last Saturday night. Almost got me."

"Hm." Bracha nodded. "Well, why don't we find some time to spar again? Either you or Lisa." Bracha grinned. "Lisa, you're pretty good, too. It would be fun."

"I suppose."

Sid laughed again and he and I headed back to my parents' house for lunch. What we found there did not help my mood any, although when Sid saw the bottle that had come in the mail for him, he laughed even harder than he had when I'd tackled Bracha.

"It's to help with my potency," he said, reading the note my grandmother had packed with it.

"Oh, for crying out loud." I grabbed the note and read it myself. "I told her that wasn't the problem."

Sid grabbed me around the waist and licked the back of my neck. "Wanna see if it helps?"

"Sid Hackbirn, the last thing you need is help performing." I gulped. "What if it works? I mean, not with the performance, but with the sperm?"

"And?" Sid chuckled as he began running his hands all over me. "Do you really want to disappoint your poor, aging grandmother?"

I pulled away. "Sid!"

"I'm sorry." He softened. "I was just teasing. I don't want another kid any more than you do, and whatever is in that bottle is not going to override a v-sect and several cases of gonorrhea." He looked at me and his eyes grew a little worried. "You okay?"

"I don't know." I smiled softly at him. "I guess I'm just feeling frustrated. We've got lots of possible leads, no real direction on what we're supposed to be finding out, and if we don't take care of things fast enough, it could really hurt somebody we care about."

"And you're not having a very good time here, are you?"

I shrugged. "I had a good time in Kansas and you didn't. It's only fair that we get a case where I'm chronically annoyed and you're having all the fun."

"I'm not having all the fun, but I get what you're saying." He smiled and pulled me close to him. "Come on. Let's get some lunch made, and then maybe just the two of us can take off for a while."

Sid made a point of emptying the bottle Grandma had sent. Nick, Janey, and Daddy joined us for the sandwiches and cole slaw that Sid and I put together. Sid pulled me away the second we'd finished, leaving the others to clean up.

In the car, Sid and I spent a few minutes talking about the coke Marina had given me (no conclusions to be made about that), and what Nick had said about Dusty and Donna necking. It was possible that Donna was secretly working with Dusty, but she hadn't acted like it before. Sid promised to tell Bracha so that she could also be on the lookout, while I would brief the rest of the team. Then Sid put his foot down and tabled any more talk about the case or the resort.

We went to see A Fish Called Wanda, then went to dinner just the two of us, still giggling over the movie. Later that night, Sid talked to me in Italian and Russian (one of the jokes from the film). Neither language got me all that excited, but I did laugh hard, which I sorely, sorely needed.

August 4, 1988

S id's Voice -

I should have seen it sooner, but being worried about Lisa, I missed it until that Thursday morning. Nick showed up on time for work and he didn't slack off. I have to say, as much as he hated that job, he didn't use that as an excuse to be sloppy about it. In fact, he was one of the best bussers we had.

Still, the boy wasn't smiling, and I could see that something had him down, and that's when I realized what day it was. I waited until he came off duty at two, then pulled him away to the apartment. He went reluctantly, but he went.

"It's the anniversary, isn't it?" I said softly, once I'd shut the door.

"I'll be fine," he grumbled.

"I know. But it's only been three years since your first mom died. That's not an easy loss to deal with."

"I'll be okay!" He glared at me for a moment, then sighed. "I'm sorry. I don't mean to be so grumpy."

"I understand."

"Do you?" He did not use a defensive tone, and I could tell that he was really wondering if I did.

"I admit, I don't remember my mother." My mother had been killed when I was two. "But I have lost people I care about. And even if they weren't as close as your mom was to you, I still think about them when the anniversary of their deaths rolls around. It doesn't surprise me that you're feeling down about your mother."

The truth was, Lisa and I had always known that Nick had some very conflicted feelings about his first mother. It would have been hard to imagine that he didn't. Rachel... Well, she had been pretty shitty about how she handled him. She was distant, letting her mother mostly raise Nick, and we'd heard from one of Rachel's friends that Rachel and Nick hadn't gotten along that well. She lied to him that I had run out on her when I'd found out she was pregnant. I had no idea she'd gotten pregnant, let alone by me, until she dropped Nick on Lisa's and my doorstep when the boy was eleven. Then, when her mother died, Rachel left Nick alone a lot while she worked as an emergency room doctor. When Rachel was diagnosed with leukemia (which was why she brought him to meet me), she forced Nick to keep it a secret, especially from me and Lisa. Nick did, but it had been a hell of a burden for the boy to carry.

At the same time, Nick had deeply loved her. She was his mother. She had loved her son, as well, no matter how badly she'd sucked at the parenting thing. Lisa and I had agreed very early on that we had no right to put Rachel down in front of Nick or otherwise question his love for her. Which was why we had both decided that we'd let Nick decide when to talk to us about any conflicted feelings.

"I don't want to be," he said softly. "I mean, come on. It's been three years."

"It's how you feel."

He made a face. "It's okay to be really mad at someone you love, right?"

"Of course it is."

I pulled him into my arms and just held him. He held me back and sniffed a little. That's when I realized that he hadn't been talking about being mad at me, and if he didn't want to talk to Lisa or me about being angry at his first mother, it was because he didn't want to admit to himself that he was.

Lisa's Voice -

The Thursday management meeting started out smoothly. Then Irene brought up that there had been a problem the previous Saturday because some of the cabins and rooms hadn't been cleaned in time for the first check-ins. Before I could point out that there had been a problem with Cabin Eleven, thanks to the executives, and the one late check-out with the sick kids, Lourdes took offense and snapped that she knew what she was doing.

Daddy pointed out the problems with the check-outs and that mollified Lourdes somewhat, but the meeting remained tense. I wanted to be anywhere but there. Dusty's pager had shown him leaving the resort while Sid and I were out the day before. Lita had done the tailing, and I wanted to know if she'd found anything.

Not that Lita had anything for me when I finally got a chance to talk to her. Dusty had just wandered around, looking morose. I thanked Lita and moved on.

It looked like it was going to be yet another frustrating day. I winced. I had also remembered that it was the anniversary of the death of Nick's mother. That had always been a difficult day for him, but he was still at work in the restaurant.

I went back to the main lodge, hoping to find a minute of peace in the office behind the front desk. I did not get my minute. Shortly after I settled into the desk chair at the reservations desk, I heard voices floating in from the front desk.

"I just don't get any respect," Lourdes said to somebody.

"It's the same with me," Lyle replied.

Their voices were not all that loud, and when I got up and peeked out to the front, they were standing near the door. The lobby was empty of people.

"I have been here for more than forty years," Lyle continued. "I know how to take care of guests. They put that new computer in and now Irene treats me like a two-year-old."

"And computers are confusing, too. My son got me one, and I was completely lost at first."

"You know how to work one of them things?"

Lourdes snorted. "Yes. And I'll bet Mira doesn't know how. But she sure knows how to boss people around."

"And you can make a computer work?" Lyle sighed deeply. "Maybe I am too old."

"Lyle. Don't. My son taught me about the computer. And I still need him to program my VCR. My son keeps telling me that computers aren't that hard. They're confusing. Very confusing. But see, it's like what my son says. Computers are pretty stupid. They can only do what you tell them to do, which isn't the same thing as what you want them to do all the time. That's why you have to do things in just the right way, or they can't understand. It's like when you check somebody in, you can see if the person who took the reservation spelled something wrong. You just re-write it and go. Computers have to have the name match perfectly or they can't find the name."

Lyle snorted. "Well, no wonder things are so messed up since that damn thing got put in."

"I'll bet I can help you make it work. Come here."

I looked out the door. Lyle and Lourdes were focused on the front desk computer. Irene came up from the other side of the lobby. She looked over at Lourdes and Lyle, then at me. I put my finger to my lips.

A minute later, Irene and I watched as Lourdes checked a young couple in. She looked happy and confident. Lyle smiled at her.

Irene and I slid back into the office and shut the door.

"I think we may have solved the front desk problem," I said.

"Who would have thought Lourdes could make the computer work?" Irene gaped happily. "And she knows how to work with Lyle."

"Yeah, she's helping him learn the system." I looked back at the door. "Actually, it's not that surprising. She's the one who came up with putting all the time sheets on the new system, along with personnel notes and performance scores."

Irene bit her lip. "Will she consider moving to the front desk a promotion?"

"We can make her an assistant manager, can't we?"

"That would probably work, since moving from house-keeping to the front desk is a promotion in and of itself. But what do we do about Lyle?"

I opened the door and peeked out. Lyle, with Lourdes behind him, was writing on one of the paper maps of the area that we kept for guests, directing Mr. Lane some-where. I pulled back and looked at Irene.

"What are the odds that Lyle scored some good tickets for one of the shows across the line?" I asked.

"Better than good." Irene grinned. "That's one of the reasons the guests love him so much. Honestly, Lisa, no-body knows this area like he does, and he can get any show at any time. At a discount." She laughed. "If Lyle doesn't want to work on the computer, why don't we make him our concierge? He mostly does that now, and that's what he's really good at."

"With Lourdes as the front desk manager." I grinned. "Do you want me to talk to Daddy?"

"Let's both do it." Irene went straight to Daddy's office.

The door was closed, and Daddy looked entirely ex-hausted, but perked up considerably when he heard Irene's idea for Lourdes and Lyle.

He smiled at me. "That means you're going to have to find and train a new housekeeping manager."

I grimaced, then went to talk to Mira. She was ecstatic.

"I am so happy for Lourdes," she crowed. "That's per-fect. She totally deserves it. And Lyle will be right there to help her manage the other clerks. Maybe she'll grow a backbone."

"Well, I do have to let the others know that there's an opening for the housekeeping manager. It's only fair if someone else wants a shot at the job, too." I patted Mira on the back. "And if you get the job, then we'll have to work on training and you'll have to find an assistant manager to run things on your days off."

"Beatrice." Mira grinned.

"But I thought..."

"I know! Beatrice goofed off when Lourdes was running things because she felt like Lourdes didn't appreciate her. She knows I do, and she's good. Plus, she's been around longer than the others."

"Well, we'll see. And please don't say anything to Beatrice or the others until everything is official."

"Of course not." Mira was almost dancing, she was so happy. "And don't worry about Lourdes as a manager up front. She won't have as many people to supervise, and she'll be able to grow into the job with Lyle there. While your mother was here and before that, Mary, Lourdes didn't have to do that much. They ran the department. Then when your mother left, Lourdes got tossed into the deep end, and she was not ready for it."

"Yeah, I know." I couldn't help grinning, myself.

Mira would be great at the job, which meant I would not be stuck running things, nor would my mother. I couldn't wait to go home.

My elation was, however, to run a very short course. As I walked past the horse barn on the way to my parents' place, I saw Janey feeding one of the horses in the paddock. She looked so sad and so listless, which was completely unlike her. I went over.

"Janey?" I asked softly.

She patted the horse's nose one last time, then looked up.

"Oh. Hi, Aunt Lisa."

"You seem really upset."

She made a face. "Yeah." She took a deep breath. "It's nothing I can do anything about. It just sucks is all."

"You want to tell me about it?"

"Sure." She frowned. "It was this afternoon in the activities center. Krystal Washington? She's one of the kids here, and she's a really good artist. So, today, Ms. Wannamaker said so and that she should become a professional one. Which Krystal totally wants to do. And everybody was encouraging her. I don't want her not to be. She deserves the encouragement." She sighed. "It's just that no one is going to encourage me to be what I want when I grow up."

"Why not?"

Janey looked at me and hesitated. "I want to be a priest."

"Oh." My heart sank. "Yeah, that one is going to be pretty difficult. I suppose it is possible that they'll change things by the time you get to be a grown-up."

"Uh-huh." Janey looked away sadly. "I suppose. Sister Casey at church? She doesn't think that will happen any too soon. But she did say that I could be a pastoral associate. With all the priest shortages, they're going to need them. It's almost there, but not quite the same thing."

"No. It's not." I reached over and pulled her into my arms. "For what it's worth, I think you'd make a terrific priest."

"Thanks, Aunt Lisa." She hugged me tighter. "It doesn't usually get to me. I mean, it's not like I've ever thought it would be possible."

"Yeah. Kinda like me wanting to be a superhero when I grew up. Your grandpa and I were talking about that last week. He figures I went into English Literature because I could still pretend to be one."

Janey laughed a little. We went back to the house for lunch. Daddy was there and the three of us had a lovely time, even if Janey was still feeling sad about her career prospects. Daddy told me that Lourdes was thrilled with moving to the front desk, and was not only picking it up very quickly, she'd helped Irene resolve Lyle's latest over-booking goof. Lyle had been bemused by the fancy title of concierge, but loved the idea of doing that as his job and not having to worry about reservations. I told Daddy that I'd get a notice up in the housekeeping office right after lunch just in case somebody wanted Lourdes' job, but that I really wanted Mira for it.

I got the notice up and talked to most of the staff as they came in at the end of their shifts. It was actually reassuring that nobody really wanted the manager job. Well, Donna told me that she might.

"Why?" I asked.

She frowned. "I'm thinking about dropping out of school. It just, like, feels like a big waste of time."

"What are you majoring in?"

"Business. It's really boring."

I looked at her. "What do you like doing?"

"Partying." She shrugged.

"That's a hard way to make a living."

"Yeah, I know." She cocked her head. "But the thing is, all I need is a living. It doesn't matter what I do to get it. Get my money, then go party at night. That's what's fun. Working here full-time would get me that."

"Maybe. But the first time you come into work hung-over, you'll get your backside fired."

"Oh, I don't drink that much and I don't do drugs. I just like being at parties."

"Well, I'll think it over."

I was so glad to finally be at the end of my day. I turned the walkie-talkie off and went to find Nick. He was at my parents' house, reading in the living room.

"You doing okay, my sweet guy?" I asked, sitting next to where he was sprawled on the couch. I ran my fingers through the lock on his forehead.

"Okay enough." He winced. "I mean, I'm sad, and that's just the way it's going to be at this time of year. It's like Dad said earlier. It's okay to be sad, and I just have to get through it. Talking about it helps a little, but it doesn't change things, and that's what I'm sad about."

"I get that. I'm here and I'll always be here, one way or another."

He smiled softly. "Thanks, Mom."

We got in a solid hug, then Daddy came in and asked about dinner. Sid was already in the kitchen working on it.

After dinner, Janey and I did the cleanup. Nick said that he wanted to go for a walk, and got Bowser out of his crate. Darkness finally settled on the resort. The smell of pork ribs filled the air, as Daddy and Bracha checked the BBQ rig for the next night's picnic and outdoor movie. Sid and I walked slowly to the staff lodge.

Gunfire erupted near the playground. Sid and I ran as fast as we could, never mind that we didn't have any guns on us. We couldn't. Shooting at a bad guy would immediately peg us as operatives. We had them back at the staff lodge, but it would have taken too long to get them.

Dusty stumbled out of the trees as the echo from the shots faded away.

"Someone shooting at me," he squeaked, and sank to the ground.

"Are you alright?" Sid asked.

Dusty nodded. "Not hit. Scared."

"Where's Nick?" I shrieked.

Nick, breathing heavily, came out of the trees, holding Bowser.

"He got loose," Nick said, setting the puppy on the ground. "He ran at the person with the gun. Probably saved Dusty's life. Dusty saw the man and ran."

"Did you see him?" Sid asked.

Nick shook his head. "Only sort of. He was wearing a mask. But he was maybe a little taller than you? Not sure."

Sirens wailed in the distance, and several people came out of their cabins.

"What's going on?" Mr. Winslow demanded from outside his cabin door.

"It's alright," Daddy hollered back. I was a little surprised that he was almost on top of us. "Looks like everyone is fine. Lisle, you and Sid check the outside buildings, make sure nothing went through a window. Nick? Dusty? You two come with me."

It took a while to canvas the outsides, but there didn't appear to be any bullet holes anywhere. The police arrived, took a bunch of statements, somehow missing Dusty and Nick, and came to the conclusion that it was some idiot hunting out of season or drunk and shooting for the fun of it. That sort of thing happened in the area, but had never happened at the resort.

Worse yet, the gunman had fired from off the resort, according to the officers who found some casings, as in we couldn't have done anything regarding signage. Not that it would have helped if there really had been some drunk idiot with a gun shooting for the fun of it.

Several families gathered in the dark at the playground, waiting to talk to the cops. That's when the woman screamed.

Two bullets had pierced the playground slide.

August 5, 1988

S id and I did not get a lot of sleep that night. By the time Friday had dawned, we were bleary-eyed. We ate breakfast in the apartment after running down the local road.

"Alright," said Sid. He pulled out a legal pad and one of his Mont Blanc fountain pens, then sat back down at the small kitchen table. "I think it's time to lay out every possible scenario and suspect and see if we can't figure out where this is coming from."

I winced. "Should we even? What if it was Clint doing the shooting for some reason? We don't know where he's at on his little sting operation."

"For that matter, it could have been our mole." Sid scribbled on the pad. "Have you seen Clint doing anything since he checked in last week?"

"No." I thought about it. "I haven't. I've seen Dierdre and the kids around occasionally, but him? No. I wonder where he's been."

"That is a good question." Sid sighed. "And there's Hattie to consider, too."

"Why would she be shooting at Dusty? She needs him to set up the phony plans." I got up and began pacing.

"Which we still have, but not the real ones." Sid twirled the pen in his fingers.

"Honey, if Dusty doesn't have them, and Desmond is pretty sure he doesn't, could it be that's why Dusty got shot at?"

"Then the person doing the shooting has to be the mole we're looking for." Sid frowned. "But who could it be?"

"There's that Yuri Voskoff guy, but if he's an assassin, he wouldn't be interested in buying illegal technology, would he?"

"I suppose it's possible. Just because our side knows about him, that doesn't mean he's that easily recognizable. Not to mention the shooter was wearing a mask."

I sighed. "I wonder if Judy Osbourne was involved. Bracha said that she'd seen Voskoff in the Video Stop last week, and Judy's the one who showed me the trap. She could have wired it or told Voskoff about the TV being moved. She'd probably heard about it while delivering tapes."

"Okay." Sid wrote that down. "But she's only one more possible suspect."

"Then we have the guests." I bit my lip. "Brian Lane was checking out when Lipplinger was killed, but could have set the trap. Plus, he heard Lipplinger going on about moving the TV, so he would have known to set it for Dusty. But he wasn't at the resort, or even in town as far as I know for when Dusty's room got broken into."

"We also have Ms. Sanchez in the room on the other side of Lipplinger's, and she's been at the resort this whole time." Sid scribbled again. "In terms of body-size, she could fit, except that she does have some rolls on her.

We also know that she's from Cuba, which might mean that she's working with the Soviets. It might not."

"What about Avery DiNovo?" I went back to pacing. "He and his family have been here the whole time. He and his wife are practically strangers, nor does he interact well with their kids. I can't remember how big he is, though."

"He also could be connected to the Soviets through his time in Saudi Arabia. Or it could be his wife."

"That's a possibility, too." I paused. "I'd suggest the Winslows, but they're ongoing regulars. On the other hand, they've been here the whole summer, and their daughter may have a pot problem."

"And if there is a connection to drugs, then we have to consider Marina, who had some hidden on her." Sid looked up at me. "You said you got them from her. Do you still have them?"

"Somewhere. It tested positive for cocaine. What about Donna? She would have known about the TV."

"Apparently, she and Dusty have a bit of a thing for each other."

"Possibly." I frowned. "She likes to party, though, and she is thinking about leaving school."

"Any other possibles on the staff?"

"Lee Whitney, although with his pot habit, it doesn't seem like he'd be that effective."

Sid nodded. "We can suspect everybody. The problem is we have no way of figuring out who was where last night."

"Wouldn't Lee have been at the restaurant?" I flopped into the kitchen chair. "The shooting happened before nine, and they were still serving, weren't they?"

"Something to consider." Sid sat back. "Okay. Why don't you see what you can find out from the DiNovos,

Sanchez, Donna, Lane, and... Hattie? I'll take the rest of these, including the Fosters."

"Sounds good."

My walkie-talkie squawked and Mira wanted to talk to me in the housekeeping office.

"I'll be right there." I sighed, then bent and kissed Sid. "I don't know when I'll be back."

I saw Dierdre Foster lounging near the playground, while her grandkids played on the swings, and was grateful. Lita and Pedro were sunning themselves while their kids played as well. But they were about the only ones doing so. I was shocked to see the line at the front desk. Families were everywhere, trying to leave.

"It's not safe here!" snapped an indignant woman as Lyle scrambled to get her paid up.

"Ma'am, I have been here for forty years, and this is the first time something like this has happened." Lyle smiled, but the woman was not satisfied.

I hurried downstairs.

"We've lost half our occupancy," Mira told me. "Do I have permission to call some of the others in?"

"Half?" I groaned. "Yeah. Get them here pronto, and let's go over the room assignments, too. At least we're only losing one night."

That's what I'd thought. Turned out we'd gotten a few cancelations that morning. How people coming in had heard about the shooting, I do not know, but that was why they'd canceled. I tried not to fret about it as I helped with the check-outs and did spot checks on the freshly emptied rooms. I was so busy, I didn't realize that I'd missed lunch. In fact, I was eating a hamburger and fries with Sid watching me in the break room at close to two p.m. when Hattie and Clint came in with Dale O'Connor.

Sid and I were on our feet in a second.

"What are you guys doing here?" Sid asked.

"Dale finally called back." Hattie glared. "He came over and asked your father for someplace he could have a small conference. Your father sent us here."

"Damn skippy, I did," said Daddy, coming in from the kitchen and shutting that door. "Why don't we get settled and have ourselves a little chat?"

He was really mad. I swallowed.

"Anybody want any soda?" Sid asked, getting the tumblers from the cupboard. "Coffee?"

Daddy poured himself some coffee as the others made their requests. Sid had the tumblers and mugs filled and distributed within a minute, and everyone settled into chairs around the table. I stuffed some more French fries into my mouth.

"Now, O'Connor," Daddy growled. "I want you to explain to me what the fuck you've got going on at my resort."

I gaped. I knew Daddy's language got a little coarser when my mama wasn't around. Mama really hates foul language. But I had never heard him use that word before in my life.

"It's nothing to worry about, Bill." Dale smiled expansively. "I've got it under control."

"Like hell you have!" Daddy snapped. "I just had an employee get shot at last night, and now half my occupancy is running like scared chickens because there were two bullet holes in the playground slide. And Nick told his parents that the shooter was wearing a mask. You've got something going on involving your little so-called travel club, and damn it, you're going to tell me what it is."

Dale took it calmly. "I have an operation going. It's critical to our national defense."

"It's a simple sting operation," Clint said, then glared at Hattie. "We just have to figure out who our target is and how it's going down."

Dale looked confused for a second. "You know who the target is. That's why we have the fake plans."

Clint glared at him. "You didn't tell me."

"Yeah, I did. In June."

"That is neither here nor there!" Daddy snapped.

Dale shrugged. "This seemed to be the safest place to stage it. You're well covered here."

"Which is why you wanted my daughter and son-in-law here this summer." Daddy shot daggers at Sid.

"They are two of our best operatives, Bill."

"No!" I yelped, leaping to my feet. "Dale, you can't tell him that."

"Honey?" Daddy asked.

"Daddy, if you know about us, then you're part of it." I furiously blinked, trying not to cry, then turned on Dale. "You can't recruit my father! You leave him alone!"

Dale smiled smugly. "He's already been recruited."

"The B-one clearances," Sid grumbled.

"What?" I gaped at Dale.

Daddy also gaped. "What the hell are you talking about, O'Connor?"

"You've been doing favors for me for years, Bill." Dale took a sip of soda, then leaned back in his chair.

I looked at Hattie and Clint.

"I've used this place as a safe house," Clint said, for a change, looking rather abashed. "I didn't know it was without your permission, though, Mr. Wycherly."

"It's like this." Chuckling, Dale leaned forward. "When Sid picked up Lisa and recruited her in September, nineteen eighty-two, it was my job to check out her parents. Adrienne and I got a room here, and I almost got caught, Bill, when I was searching your office. That's when I knew Sid had hit the jackpot for us with Lisa. I was retiring from the army. We needed a new congressional liaison on the House committee, and the rep here at the time was running for re-election that year, promising that if elected, it would be his last term. We could have found another way to ease him out, but it worked out. I needed a place to settle, and it had to be someplace where I could legitimately get elected to Congress. There were a couple other guys doing the same thing. I'm the one who won in eighty-four. That's why I got Lisa's clearance on a rush that fall of eighty-two."

"Henry told me that went through very quickly," Hattie said.

"It sure didn't seem like it," Sid said.

Hattie chuckled. "It usually takes months."

Daddy turned his glare back on Dale. "So, those folks you asked me to put up were in hiding or something?"

"They were." Dale grinned. "And in eighty-three. Remember the drug ring funneling their product through your store? They were using several stores, but I knew what I had in Lisa as an asset and wanted to see what I had in you. So, I got Fletcher Haddock to investigate the drug ring and told him to let you help him."

"That was you?" I snarled.

"Yeah. That's why I called you and Sid in." Dale got another sip of his soda. "Fletcher's our DEA liaison. He'd discovered that someone was also shipping secrets along with the drugs."

"It would have been nice to know that." Sid folded his arms across his chest.

"You figured it out on your own and without alerting Fletcher in the process." Dale smiled at my dad. "I told you, they're good. And so are you, Bill. Fletcher really liked working with you."

"It doesn't matter." Daddy got up slowly, then leaned on the table over Dale. "I am not doing another favor for you, Dale O'Connor. You got that? I can't stop you from sending a guest my way, but I'd better not know about it and I am damned well not paying for it."

"Bill..." Dale leaned back and, for the first time, looked nervous.

Daddy shook his head. "You have no right to use me and my business any old way you please. I've had five cancelations this morning. Do you have any idea what that is going to do to my bottom line? I need my summer traffic to keep this place profitable. I have spent almost thirty years building this business, bit by bit. I have worked my ass off, building a reputation in this community as an honest and solid businessman, and among my guests as a good host. You cannot come in here and put all of that at risk, not to mention the families that come here! Now, you get your ass off my property and do not come on it again, or I will get my shotgun. You probably know what a dead-eye my little girl is. Well, I taught her."

Daddy pulled back just enough to let Dale get up.

"I guess it's time to leave, then." Dale smiled, then hurried out.

"I'm sorry, Mr. Wycherly," Hattie said. "I had no idea how far out of the loop you were. I only knew that Lisa was worried about her cover, which made sense. You are only a B-one, and that's not usually high enough to know much of the personnel." She looked at me and Sid. "We still have a job to do. I can work it off-site, if you'd rather."

"Don't bother," Daddy said, sinking into his chair. "It's too late now."

"I'll be standing down," Clint grumbled. "But I'll have to stick around. Dierdre wants another week here with the kids, and it looks like we'll have it." He put his hand up. "I'm paying for it, Mr. Wycherly."

"Can't say no to that." Daddy shook his head, defeated.

Hattie and Clint left. I fell into my chair and let the tears I'd been holding onto fall. Sid patted my arm.

"I'm so sorry, Daddy," I sobbed. "I really didn't know that he'd gotten you into this. I really didn't."

Dad glared at Sid. "I knew you were trouble."

"I'm sorry, Daddy." Sid shook his head. He looked as miserable as I felt. "The problem is, when I recruited Lisa, I had no way of knowing what that would mean for her family. And I had no idea that Dale was behind any of this. I hadn't seen him or heard from him in years."

"You knew him?" Daddy asked.

"Not as Dale O'Connor, but, yeah. He was the SOB that roped me into intelligence when I was in the army." Sid didn't say SOB.

"Daddy, you don't hate Sid again, do you?"

"I never hated Sid and still don't." Daddy sighed, then looked at us. "But I am pretty pissed at you two. Couldn't you have told Dale no?"

"I tried to," I said, sniffing. "But he'd already set everything up. He is one of our bosses."

"And we can't quit," Sid said. "Once you're in this business, you're in it for life." He looked up at Daddy. "I have no idea what that means for you."

Daddy shrugged. "We'll make the best of it. Somehow. What about Dusty?"

"He's in his room for the time being," Sid said. "It's his day off, anyway." Sid glanced up at Daddy, then sighed. "And it's being monitored, so he's more or less safe. However, whatever our next steps are, I think Lisa and I had better figure that one out on our own. I realize what the stakes are for you, Daddy, but you don't really have the clearance."

Sid began cleaning up the tumblers while I took my lunch plate back to the kitchen. Daddy was still there when I returned.

"I shouldn't have made that crack about you being trouble," he was saying to Sid. "What I was trying to say was that I was on to you all along. That first Christmas you joined us, I'd catch you and Lisa looking at each other, and I knew something was up. It wasn't just where Lisa was living, either."

One of the conditions Sid had placed on my coming to work for him had been that I live at his house. However, for a lot of reasons, I couldn't tell my parents where I was, some of which involved Daddy being incredibly jealous of Sid and worried about him, too.

Daddy looked over at me. "Then that fall and the drug thing, and Fletcher made a crack about you being a spy, that's when I figured it out."

"You said it was ridiculous," I said.

"I know, and your mother still thinks it is. But then I realized that didn't mean it wasn't true. And as the years passed, I could see more and more signs that you had a secret that you were keeping."

I sniffed. "I didn't want to hide it from you, Daddy, but it was safer for you not to know anything."

He smiled softly. "I understand. I trust you, Lisle, baby. I wasn't happy about it in some ways. Had to figure it was dangerous. Every time you or Sid got hurt, I couldn't help worrying about the two of you."

Sid shook his head softly. "Daddy, we've survived because we're good at what we do."

"That I believe, son." Daddy patted his back.

"Daddy..." Sid took a deep breath. "I realize that there have been serious consequences for you and the family because I took Lisa in. But I've got to be honest. I do not regret that I did for one second. Because of Lisa, I have my son. Because of Lisa, I reconciled with my aunt and not only have her, but Sy, as well. But most of all, because of Lisa, I have become a part of your family. I can't tell you what that has meant to me. I love your daughter more than I have loved anybody in my entire life, and along with her, Nick. And I am so grateful that includes loving you."

Daddy wrapped his arms around Sid and held him. "I love you, too, son."

My tears started falling again. Daddy and Sid pulled apart, both sniffing. Daddy wrapped me in another hug and just held me for several minutes. Then Sid and I had to leave.

[When your mother first insisted that I call her and your father Mama and Daddy, I did because, well, it was your mother being who she was. But it didn't feel natural to me, and I always got the feeling from your father that he was a little uncomfortable with it, too. That afternoon at the resort, it finally felt natural. Not having a father, I've had many father figures in my life, including Sy. But that day, I finally had a real father in yours, and I still can't say what that means to me. - SEH]

I turned off my walkie-talkie as Sid and I hurried back to the apartment. Sid double-checked his bug finder, just in case. Desmond and Esther were working in the common room as we came in with Frank hanging out next to them, softly playing his guitar.

"How's he doing?" Sid asked, nodding in the direction of Dusty's room.

"He's fine," said Desmond. "Shook, but fine. You two look like you've had a shock."

"Yeah," I said. "I don't expect him to say anything, but be extra careful around my father, please."

Esther guffawed. "He figured you guys out, didn't he?"

"I do not want to talk about it," I said, flopping onto the couch.

"Esther, have you found anything on a Yuri Voskoff?" Sid asked, pacing.

"Oh…" Esther shook her head as she picked up her legal pad. "He's not a very nice fellow."

"You have to expect that from a KGB assassin," Frank said, chuckling.

"However astute that assessment is," said Sid. "It's not a help at the moment."

"Too bad we don't have a fax machine," Esther said. "We could get a photo of this guy."

I shook my head. "We have one in the resort office, but it's not a secure line and I don't want anything connected to this case going through there anyway." I bit my thumbnail. "Our first objective is to keep Dusty safe, and hopefully, by extension of that, keep the guests safe and unaware of any potential danger."

Frank grinned. "Kathy and Jesse wanted to come up for the fun of it. Why don't we call them in? Kathy will be able to use the modem on the computer in our room and Jesse can help with surveillance."

"Sounds good," I said. I looked at Sid.

"I agree." Sid thought for a minute. "We'll do that. I also think Lisa should talk to Dusty. It shouldn't blow our cover. After all, he told us that there was someone shooting at him."

"I'll take care of it now." I got up.

The door to Dusty's room was shut. I knew he was in there because none of the trip wires had been tripped. Even Sid and I couldn't get past that kind of setup, so we doubted Voskoff could. I knocked, and Dusty's response was almost too soft to be heard.

"Can I come in?" I asked.

"Sure." A moment later, the door opened.

"How are you doing?" I asked, going into the room.

The window had been blacked out. A lone lamp shone on the desk, and the monitor glowed with orange type. Dusty offered me the desk chair and slumped onto the side of his bed.

"You're here to fire me, aren't you?"

I sighed. "It's not up to me."

"Oh, come on. You can't have someone shooting at me here. There's kids. They'll get hurt!"

"We probably need to do something to make sure you're safe. If you're safe, then the kids will be safe, don't you think?" I paused, but he didn't say anything. "Dusty, do you know why somebody was shooting at you?"

He swallowed. "I can't say. It's just bad, you know?"

"Okay." I frowned. "Do you have any place you can hide?"

"Not really." He sniffed.

"Alright." I reached over and patted his arm. "Let me see what we can do."

Somehow, I was not surprised to see my father in the common room, chatting with Desmond and Esther about their progress on the new computer system. As soon as I came into the room, though, he smiled at the two of them, then nodded at the apartment. Sid was already there.

"I just thought," Daddy said, settling onto the couch. "If that kid Dusty was the target for that gunman, we probably need a way to hide him." He looked at Sid and me. "I'm guessing he's part of this whole thing you're working on."

"Yeah," said Sid. "We're trying to work that out now."

I shrugged. "It's not like Dusty has anywhere he can go. Where he's at is currently the easiest to monitor. The problem is, the gunman knows which room he's in."

Daddy nodded. "One of the advantages to having Dusty at the house is that it's not as likely to affect the rest of the resort as much."

"What about Nick and Janey?" Sid asked.

"Maybe we can move them over here, and your friend Desmond can stay at the house with me and Dusty."

"You figured him out, too," I grumbled.

Daddy chuckled. "He used to tend bar at the Keno lounge at Harrah's. I'd seen him plenty of times when Dale would invite your mother and me to drinks at the casino. He turns up here as your friend? Had to figure there was a connection."

Sid cursed. "Daddy, you are too damned good at this. Now, if you can hold off speculating about the rest of our friends, that would help."

So, we spent the rest of the evening getting everybody moved around. Janey ended up in the apartment, sleeping on the front room couch. We left Dusty's room empty and put Nick upstairs in an empty room next to some of the older college girls. I prayed the girls would behave and that Nick wouldn't take after his father that way.

August 6–7, 1988

Lourdes had her first Saturday on the front desk that week. I was profoundly grateful that it wasn't as crazy as usual. There were still a lot of families vacating, but that had more to do with their reservations being up. Several of them were kind enough to let us know that they'd be back the following year.

There hadn't been that many cancelations, thank God. Enough to worry about, but the larger portion of the guests coming in had no idea that there had been a shooting. They weren't likely to find out, either. Daddy had found somebody to rip out the playground slide on Friday, and while the replacement slide hadn't shown up yet, a missing slide was more of a nuisance than a slide with bullet holes in it.

I watched Lourdes working with a feeling of deep satisfaction. Even better, as she finished with one family, they asked her a question and she turned them right over to Lyle at his new position on the desk. She then greeted the next guests as Lyle talked to the family with the question. I grinned. Not only was Lyle settled, with him answering questions while Lourdes checked families in, checking in moved a lot more quickly.

Lourdes had even arranged for the crib to be set up in Kathy and Jesse's room when they arrived with their 11-month-old son, Keshon. Lyle teased the little guy, and Keshon shrieked with joy.

I embraced them warmly as they turned from the desk.

"I'm so glad to see you!" I grabbed the luggage. "Come on. I'll take you upstairs."

I also paged Sid, and he was waiting at the room door on the third floor when we got there.

Jesse grabbed Sid and hugged him. "Good to see you, dude!"

Jesse is a little taller than Sid, with mahogany skin. He was wearing his hair clipped close to his head that summer.

Kathy, who is slender and tall, with rich chocolate skin, had her hair in tiny braids. Keshon, it turned out, was already walking.

"So, how bad is it?" Kathy asked as Jesse got their suitcases into the closet.

I winced. "It's been pretty intense."

Fortunately, Kathy had a couple of reports for us, but as she was about to tell us, there was a knock on the door.

"It's us!" Frank hollered.

We let them in. There were more hugs because Frank and Esther are just as close to Kathy and Jesse as Sid and I are, and Sid and I were close friends with Kathy and Jesse long before they got recruited into our business.

"Kathy has a report," I told the others after the hugs.

"It's not much," Kathy sighed. "I haven't been able to isolate a lot of the names that came up in the Social Security search. I did find Francine DiNovo, though, and she looks very clean. Not much of a work record at all, which leads me to believe that she's been a housewife for a very long time. I checked a few other of my databases and finally isolated which Maria Sanchez we wanted. She, also, is very clean. Does human resources consulting." Kathy handed me a printout. "Here's her company's information. She works mostly in the hospitality industry."

"I suppose we should be encouraged that she's coming here," I said, flipping through the pages.

"And I found something today," Esther said. "It's your reservations manager Irene? Turns out she doesn't know what a three and a half floppy is."

"What's a three and a half floppy?" Sid asked.

I groaned. "That's the disk that Lipplinger was using, honey. They're much smaller than the usual, and they have these hard plastic cases."

"In other words, that's what we're looking for." Sid sighed.

"Exactly." I shut my eyes. "There are too many things going on."

"Which is kind of the problem," Frank said. "Irene wouldn't have to know what the type of disk is, just that she's supposed to pass it on to the Soviets."

"Although, I don't think she's behind this," Esther said, then sighed. "It's just a feeling, which I know isn't evidence, but it might be something to go on."

"Something," Sid sighed.

He looked at me and shook his head. We warned Kathy and Jesse about my father, then eventually took off. Nick volunteered to babysit Keshon that night, and all six of us went to dinner at the restaurant, where we talked about anything but the case.

Sid's Voice -

Lisa, Nick, Janey, and Daddy had just left for mass the next morning when I got a page from Lillian Ward. She's the head of Quickline. I called her right back.

"I heard from Hattie that you had a bit of a blow up out there yesterday," Lillian said.

"We did."

"Oh, dear. Marian was right. We're going to have to do more to keep Dale in line. But that's our job, not yours. I'm sorry. I had no idea he was using your father-in-law's resort. Lisa must be furious."

"She is. We both are."

"I can imagine." Lillian sighed deeply. "Just please be careful with Dale. He's always said he has a plan for you, and I must say, it's worked very well so far. That is part of Dale's genius. He used to be a chess champion when he was in high school. I'm not sure what happened, but he went into the Army instead of college, although he managed to get an undergraduate and a law degree while serving. And he is incredibly good at seeing the big picture." She paused. "I suppose I shouldn't say this, but he is carrying around a deep sadness of some sort. Perhaps it's a shattered dream. I don't know. It's not something he's going to talk about, but I do believe it's why he's always trying to run people's lives. He wants to make them happier than he is. I was so glad when he and Adrienne found each other and she decided to retire."

"From modeling?"

Lillian chuckled. "No. From intelligence work. She may not look like it, but she was an incredible spy. The intel she got out of Europe in the seventies... She ran a production company, making films, and no one caught on."

"That's interesting." I thought for a moment. "I'm afraid it's time for me to have a talk with Dale. I know you said keeping him in line is your job, and I'll mostly leave that to you. But there's also his plan for me." I winced. "I've got a bad feeling there's something personal driving it, something about me, and I'm the only one who can get through on that level."

"You've got an excellent point. Alright. Just keep me posted, please."

"I will."

I hung up, not happy, but knowing what I had to do. I drove to Dale's home at the north end of town. It was a huge Swiss-style chalet. Dale answered the door when I rang, then led me into the cavernous living room in front.

"Let me guess," he said, still standing. "You're here about the other day."

"You threatened my family, Dale," I said quietly.

He gazed out the huge front picture window. "I do what I have to do."

"I get it." I took a deep breath. "The problem is you don't let anyone else in on it and the wrong people are getting hurt."

"I'm not the one who's prone to gross insubordination." Dale turned on me. "If I could count on you to follow orders, we wouldn't have this problem."

"Bullshit. This isn't about insubordination. It's about you deciding that you know what's best for me better than I do."

"Maybe I do, Sid." He held my eyes.

I looked right back. "Not always. And did it ever occur to you that you might get better cooperation if you worked with me instead of manipulating me into everything you wanted me to do?"

"You were up against rape charges, son. Two weeks into boot camp."

"And you know damned well I didn't rape her. That the base commander was calling it rape in revenge for me staining his precious little girl. That's why you were able to get me off." I looked away. "And, okay. You might have been right about pushing me into intelligence. But you didn't give me much of a choice."

"You still could have chosen to go into the stockade."

"Maybe. But you didn't give me a choice when I got out. Dale, I don't get what this paternal thing you have toward me is, but it's really fucking things up."

"Paternal?" Dale winced. "It's like I told you three years ago, Sid. You reminded me of myself when I was your age. Young, lost, utterly alone in the world. I didn't get to go to college. I had a chess scholarship, but it wasn't enough and I didn't have anyone to pay for the rest. So I went into the army and it saved my life."

"You were alone?"

Dale looked away and sighed. "I don't have a family, Sid. I was raised in an orphanage."

"That sucks."

"A lot of life does, son."

"That still doesn't give you the right to decide what's best for me."

"I know what I'm doing."

"Yeah, but I don't." I held him with my glare. "That's the problem. It's like the shit you pulled with Bill Wycherly. He didn't know he was being used, and when he found out, guess what? You lost him. If you'd been up front with him, you might still have a damn good asset on your side. And I can promise you, Dale, if you keep this up, one of these days, you're going to go too far and you're going to lose me, too."

"I need you, Sid," Dale gasped.

"I don't give a fuck. I don't know what this big plan of yours is for me, but if I don't like it, I'm not playing."

"You don't get it." Dale turned on me. "You're the only person who can do what I do. You're the first person I've met who can see the whole board."

The light dawned. "You want me to replace you?"

"Eventually."

I shook my head. "I'm not going into politics. Sorry."

Dale laughed in spite of himself. "That's the least of what I do, and, yeah, being on top of the House Committee helps. But you don't need to be in Congress, and frankly, you'd suck at it."

"At least you have some faith in me."

"I have a lot of faith in you, Sid." Dale looked away again and sighed. "There's a lot I can't tell you right now. It's how things work at the top regarding the intelligence units. But the reason I am where I am is because I can play all the pieces. I can see the moves coming. So can you. That's one of the reasons you're still alive. You're damn good at it. Nobody would have thought Lisa Wycherly would make a great spy. You spotted that. When we had the leak on the Yellow Line, you got ahead of that and caught them."

I shook my head. "I got captured. It was Lisa who led Lillian and the others to the whorehouse."

"You trained her, and, yeah, the two of you together are incredibly effective that way. But it starts up here." Dale tapped his temple. "Being able to look at a situation and see all the vantage points, all the places an enemy can come from. You've always been able to do that. I've never met anyone else who could. That's why I have plans for you and why I work around you. I can't afford to lose you. This country can't afford to lose you."

"This country." I snorted. "I'm not indispensable, however good I may be. And like I said, it's not that you want me to do things. It's that you don't give me the chance to make the decision myself. I can't work that way." I looked at him and sighed. "We may have more in common than I like to admit. But I'm not a chess piece and I don't like being moved around, and if you keep it up, then you're going to regret it."

"I'll see what I can do." He looked away.

I sighed, but pressing it further would not do anything. Dale manipulated and kept his plans to himself because that was how he operated, and if I'm honest, probably how he'd survived.

I left and went to meet Lisa and the others at the casino buffet, not sure what all I would tell Lisa about our conversation.

Lisa's Voice -

Sid seemed pretty bemused when he caught up with us at the buffet where we went after mass. I've always had a feeling that Janey is onto us, but she's never said anything, so we're not going to. Daddy was also looking at Sid as if he was wondering, but wasn't going to say anything, either. Janey hung close to Sid, as she always does when he's bugged.

It was a pleasant afternoon, and we returned to the staff lodge just in time for all hell to break loose.

The screaming had already started as Sid and I approached the outside door from the porch. Thank God it wasn't loud enough to attract attention from the guests. We burst inside to find a young man, about average height with long, straggly brown hair, wrestling with Donna, while Marina screamed near the door to the stairs.

"What the hell?" Daddy yelped from behind me.

Sid was already on top of the young man while I pulled Donna away. The new kid came back at Sid, throwing punches wildly, but Sid just dodged him, tripped the kid, and had him down and a knee in his back in record time.

"What's going on?" Daddy asked again, more softly.

I looked at Marina, who was crying now.

"I didn't know I had it until later," she sobbed. "He gave me a book to hold, and it had something in it."

"It's mine, dammit!" the kid screamed. "It's mine, and you got no right to keep it."

"Time to call the cops?" Daddy asked as Sid bucked and held firm.

"That would be nice," Sid said.

I followed Daddy into the apartment. Daddy went to the phone and requested a little discretion, which the police understood. I found the bit of cocaine that Marina had given me. Daddy looked at me.

"It's a long story," I said. "But she did hand it over without me having to push and I'm pretty sure she's on the level."

Daddy nodded. The police arrived in an unmarked car, found the little packet of white powder in the kid's pants where I'd put it, and were happy to slap the cuffs on and take him out the back door.

"You okay, Donna?" I asked.

She was crying and had a bloody nose. "Yeah. My face hurts, though."

Sid fetched the ice pack while I got her settled on the couch.

"I took self-defense last semester," she said. "I thought it would help."

"It looks like it did," I said, smiling. "But it helps to practice and keep studying."

She smiled weakly.

Things quieted down in time for dinner. Donna didn't seem like she had a concussion, but Marina took her to the hospital just in case. Sid, Nick, Janey, Daddy, and I all went to my parents' house and amused ourselves playing poker with Dusty and Desmond. Nick was thrilled when he won several hands. It's not easy beating Daddy, Janey, or me at poker. We also ate dinner there, then Sid, Nick, Janey, and I headed back to the apartment.

Donna was back - there was no fracture or concussion, but her nose and cheeks had a spectacular bruise on them. The other kids prevailed on Donna and Nick to tell them what had happened, then they all decided to watch a movie on the common room TV.

I took Sid back to the apartment.

"It's been a day," I said.

Sid snorted. "More than." He looked at the door to the common room. "Donna did pretty good getting that kid down today."

"Yeah." I frowned. "A lot better than I would have thought. She's always seemed so mousy."

"Just like someone else I know." Sid flashed me a fond half-smile.

"I wonder what that means in terms of Dusty," I said, thinking hard. "I don't quite see her as a KGB assassin, and if she is, it doesn't account for Yuri Voskoff being in town. Still, she could have had that gun and some other connection to the Soviets."

"We should probably have Esther or Kathy pull her school records." Sid shrugged. "She's at Sac State, right?"

"Yeah." I looked at him. "Where were you this morning while we were at church?"

Sid took a deep breath. "I went to have a talk with Dale O'Connor."

I watched him carefully, and he chuckled softly.

"Truth be told, I don't know how much of our conversation needs to stay between us. He didn't really specify." Sid looked at me. "It's something Lillian told me this morning. He's got some deep sadness within him. He told me he was an orphan. That's why he was so interested in me. I didn't have any family to speak of, either." Sid looked at me, then took a deep breath. "When I first got busted for sleeping with the base commander's daughter, Dale - as Colonel Landry - got assigned my case as the judge advocate. That's why he was able to talk the base commander out of accusing me of rape and how he got me hooked into intelligence." He sighed. "I had it out with him for using me the way he does, and he told me that he needs me to replace him eventually."

"In Congress?" I made a face.

Sid laughed and shook his head. "No. Not in Congress. I'm not sure what, exactly, Dale's position is, but he's in some sort of supervisory role and needs to keep tabs on all the players and pieces. He says I have the same skill."

I thought about it. "You know, you do."

Sid shrugged. "It was just weird, is all. I don't know if I got through to him. He's been operating this way for a very long time." He looked at me sadly. "You've always liked our side business."

"Yeah." I shrugged. "I haven't liked the barriers it's created between me and my family. I don't like worrying about you or Nick or any of our friends getting hurt or killed. But it is kind of fun and it does make us special."

He smiled softly at me. "As if you weren't already so incredibly special."

"Okay. You're looking pensive again."

"Something Dale said. I spotted you as a potentially good spy. I never really thought about it that way, but, yeah, I did. And I was right."

We got cozy for a little bit, but then Janey came in after the movie and Sid and I had to move to the bedroom and keep the noise down.

[I was a little worried about how much to tell you, but I shouldn't have been. I knew I would. It's who you are and what I still love about you. - SEH]

August 8-9, 1988

Monday morning arrived, and I was not interested in getting out of bed. Sid wanted to work the morning shift at the restaurant, so he was long up before I was. I still dragged myself up and out for a run, then showered and ate breakfast in the apartment.

It was a quiet morning. Mira seemed to have the housekeeping staff well in hand, but I figured I'd better do a few spot checks and while I was at it, search a few rooms.

I saw my first chance when Avery DiNovo drove off in his car, leaving his wife watching the kids at the playground.

I knocked on the door of Cabin Three. "Housekeeping."

Dead silence. I used my passkey and entered the cabin. Mira's crew had already been through, and it looked perfect from that perspective. Well, mostly perfect. I made a note on my clipboard, then got to work, searching drawers, under the beds and mattresses, in the closets and the kitchenette.

There were piles of papers on the little dining table next to the kitchenette, but they all seemed to be geological reports. I shot pictures of a few of them just in case.

Books littered one of the dressers, all of them very thick and various books on legal theory and cases. I couldn't help thinking about how dry were the books I'd been reading the previous school year.

I did not find any floppy disks or anything computer-related at all, nor did I find any weapons or drugs. In fact, apart from their behavior, the DiNovo family seemed pretty clean.

I did a final check on my clipboard, then headed out.

I debated where to head next, but then saw Ms. Sanchez sitting by the playground, watching the children with obvious pleasure. I made like I was tidying the lounge chairs and worked my way around to her.

"How are you doing today, Ms. Sanchez?" I asked pleasantly.

"Enjoying a day off," she said. She was wearing shorts and a short-sleeved button-front white blouse, and rolled her shoulders back, lifting her face to the sun. "I cannot tell you how restful this place is."

I chuckled. "It hasn't felt like it lately."

"Yes. I heard about the problem Thursday night." She shook her head. "I was working with my client, and they'd heard about it from the police. As I understand it, the gunman wasn't even on your property."

"That's what the cops said." I smiled nervously at her.

"That is the problem with the hospitality business. Guests don't think." She paused and smiled, slightly embarrassed. "I'm here as a consultant for a couple of the hotels across the state line. Mostly on building housekeeping teams."

I couldn't help a snort. "I could have used you here this past week."

"You fixed it." She chuckled. "It was kind of hard to miss the chatter, but then that's my job."

"I'm sorry."

"Don't be. It's like all those idiots leaving last Friday and blaming the resort management because of something you could not have expected, let alone been responsible for. I didn't leave because I knew you were handling it as well as anyone could and taking steps to keep everyone safe. But then, I work in this industry, so I hear and see things most people don't." She stretched again and smiled. "I promise you, even with personnel problems and kids screaming all over the place, it is so much nicer to stay here than some corporate property."

"You seem to like kids. Do you have any?"

"Never got the chance." She looked a little sad. "I married too soon, got dumped, then had to focus on feeding myself for so long, I never re-married. I am alone in life, but I have friends and that helps."

"Where are you from?" I fidgeted with a lounge chair.

"From Cuba. I came when I was a child in 1960." She frowned. "I was part of the Pedro Pan operation. Cuban parents sent their children to the States because they were afraid of what Castro would do to us." She sighed. "The vast majority of us were reunited with our parents after a couple of years or so. I was one of the rare children who wasn't. My father was already in jail for opposing Castro when I left. My mother apparently died of cancer that same year, or that was the letter I received from our neighbors in Havana. I was placed in a foster home and grew up in Denver."

"That's quite a story."

She smiled. "I don't tell it often. You have a family here whose parents immigrated around that time and your friends were born here. They know several Pedro Pans."

"That's interesting." I smiled, but inside I was wondering why Lita hadn't mentioned it. Then again, I hadn't had a chance to talk to her since the week before.

I said goodbye to Ms. Sanchez, then made my way up to their room and found Lita inside. Pedro had the kids on a horse ride.

"I talked to Ms. Sanchez today," I said.

"She tell you her story?" Lita looked a little guilty.

"Yes. Why didn't you tell me?"

"I haven't seen you and…" Lita winced. "I wanted to verify it first. It checked out."

"She seems clean otherwise." I frowned and thought of something else. "You know, I may have a way of verifying where she's working, too. Thanks." I stopped. "And, Lita, thanks for being so nice to her."

"It was a terrible time for us." Lita blinked and frowned. "My dad still hates Castro."

I hurried down to my parents' house and Desmond. He said that he still had friends at the hotel where Ms. Sanchez was supposedly working and agreed to make a few phone calls.

"How's Dusty doing?" I asked.

"Moping a lot." Desmond shifted. "I think he's going to try to bolt. I'm not sure if I should hold him."

"That's a good question. Let me talk to Sid, but if Dusty bolts before I do, page Nick and Frank and tail him, please."

"Will do."

I went back toward the restaurant. It was near the end of the lunch rush, and I was getting hungry as well. Sid, however, was not in the restaurant. Neither was Nick. I found them out back next to the dumpster bin.

"What's going on?"

"I screwed up," Nick yelped, obviously distraught.

"It wasn't your fault, son." Sid's tone strongly hinted that he'd already told that Nick more than once. He hefted himself up and into the bin. "Good thing the trash guys came this morning. Here it is."

Nick came over and took the trash bag. "I threw away somebody's false teeth. They were wrapped in a paper napkin. I didn't see them."

"It happens," Sid called from inside the bin.

"He was so mad." Nick trembled as he opened the trash bag. "I hate this job!"

"I know, sweetie. Do you want me to help?"

"I know what to look for," Sid said, climbing out of the bin, then dropping to the ground. "But why don't you stick around?"

They found the partial denture wrapped in a paper napkin near the bottom of the bag. Sid sent Nick to the front desk to let the guest know.

As soon as the boy was gone, Sid took my arm and headed me toward the staff lodge.

"I found something," he said quickly. "And I need to take a shower."

"You definitely need that," I said with a sniff.

Sid showed me what he'd found once we were in the apartment. It was a small, flat plastic case.

"A floppy disk," I said.

Sid nodded. "I don't know if it's the right one, let alone how it got in that can. I found it in a bag of old wires."

"You think Ty might have had it?"

"Possibly. The thing to do would be to find out if that's the disk we've been looking for."

"I'll go talk to Hattie." I took the disk. "Could Bracha have tossed it?"

"I'll talk to her after I get changed. I've got to go back to the restaurant, anyway. It's Janine's day off and we don't have a daytime assistant manager yet."

"You know who also could have had it." I pressed my lips together. "Donna. She was in that room and could have found it before she sounded the alarm on Lipplinger. Or maybe found it the day before and set the trap for him."

Sid thought. "We know she's got more on the ball than she appears."

"I'll ask her about it. She knows she's not supposed to take things that guests leave, except obvious trash."

I held my breath and gave him a quick kiss - he did not smell too good after being in the dumpster.

Hattie was in her room, fortunately, and all but pounced on the disk when I showed it to her.

"Where did you find it?" she asked.

"In the main trash bin," I said, deciding not to tell her how. "We're trying to find out how it got there. But if that's not the right disk, it won't make much difference."

Hattie turned on her brother's computer and we waited while it booted. A few minutes later, we had our answer.

"This is it," Hattie said.

"Yeah." I pointed at the screen. "There's the correct spelling."

Hattie sighed deeply in relief. "But how did it end up in a trash bin?"

"I don't know yet." I bit my lip. "It shouldn't have, but let's face it, Hattie. Not everyone knows what these things are. I've got some work to do. Um. Do you have a blank one I could borrow? Or one that doesn't have anything significant on it? I may need to show it to some folks."

Hattie nodded, gave me another of the plastic-covered disks. I also copied the plans onto a regular five and a quarter disk and left.

I found Donna finishing Cabin Eleven.

"No toys in the vacuum?" I said with a smile.

"Nope." Donna grinned. "I think I've got that one. Finally."

I pulled the smaller floppy from my shorts pocket. "Donna, would you have any idea where this came from?"

Donna's brows creased. "What is it? Some sort of weird coaster?"

"Not quite." I smiled. "One of the guests lost something like it and I'm trying to find out where the lost one might be."

Donna shrugged. "I have no clue."

Frankly, I thought the odds were relatively even on that point, but I let it go. I went to find Mira. She was finishing a spot check on Cabin One.

I looked around. "It's looking really nice."

Mira grinned. "Beatrice and Yesmenia."

"Yesmenia? I thought she considered the second floor her personal domain."

"I know." Mira smirked. "But I convinced her that she might want to try something new. And Beatrice helped."

I couldn't help grinning. "Looks like you've got this down." I shifted and pulled the disk out of my pocket. "Do you know where this came from?"

"I gave it to Ty," Mira said.

"You what?" I blinked. "Where did you find it?"

"In three-oh-five. I did a deep clean right after the stiff happened. You saw me."

"Yeah. But I didn't see this."

"It was behind the dresser. I think you'd left by then. Anyway, I had no idea what it was, so I took it to Ty, figuring he'd know. And the owner was dead, so…"

"I see." I bit my lip. "Okay. Thanks."

As I left the cabin, I looked back at Mira. I had to believe that if she was involved in the plans sale, it was only by accident. Admittedly, that wasn't evidence. But it was enough to get me looking elsewhere first.

I did have to question Ty Larson. He had the most contact with Dusty. He had a boxy build with dark gray hair and more wrinkles than a cotton shirt that had spent all week in the dryer. I found him in the facilities shed instead of somewhere else on the resort.

"Hey, Lisa. Something plugged?" He knew that I tended to grab the plumbing equipment and take care of the plugged toilets myself.

"Not this time." I pulled the plastic disk from my shorts. "Have you seen one of these recently?"

"That is the strangest coaster I have ever seen." Ty shook his head. "Mira brought one by a couple, three weeks ago. I tossed it this morning. I'm trying to clean up around here."

Which Ty did every so often. It rarely amounted to much, but he did try.

"It's not a coaster." I paused. "Did Dusty see it?"

Ty scratched his chin, which was covered with stubble, as usual. "Dusty? I don't think so. I just dropped it on my desk. Found it under a bunch of papers I should probably throw out."

I bit my tongue. Ty was, unfortunately, not very good at figuring out which papers were important and should be saved, and which he could toss. Which was why he seldom got any papers that should be saved.

The problem was, I couldn't really see him under KGB control. Ty was utterly necessary to the resort in that he could fix anything much like Dusty could. But there wasn't much beyond fixing things that seemed to interest him. It didn't mean somebody hadn't found his weak spot, but, again, I had to believe it made more sense to look elsewhere first.

I went to find Sid so that we could conference on what I'd found and anything he'd found. He was in the restaurant kitchen, but not in a good mood. I pulled him into the break room and shut the doors.

"Bracha recognized it as a floppy disk," Sid said distractedly. "But she had no idea why it was significant."

"Oh." I sighed. "Okay. Do you want me to order dinner in from somewhere?"

"I don't care," Sid snarled. "I'll be stuck here all night. I had to fire Lee."

"Oh, no!"

"Oh, yes. He came in today, flying higher than the proverbial kite." Sid paced the break room, utterly pissed. "We can't have that."

"No." I started crying. "We're going to be stuck here."

"What?"

I glared at him. "We'll be here for the rest of our natural lives. I'll even bet Dale set Lee up so that he keeps getting stoned. Dale wants us here, dammit, and he always gets what he wants."

"So what if we do?"

I all but screamed at him. "You're having fun. I'm not! I hate working here. I hate the constant complaints about stuff we have no control over. I hate being on a walkie-talkie all day so that I can be reeled in on a moment's notice to take care of some piddly problem. And I really hate that my father got pulled into stuff that he shouldn't have, but it won't make any difference because we're stuck here."

"I see." Sid softened. "You're feeling the stress, aren't you?"

"And you're not?"

He sighed. "Yeah, I am." He chuckled. "But you and I have our usual avenue for relieving my stress."

He meant messing around. We'd discovered that was his favorite way to release whatever stress he was feeling. It also worked for me most of the time.

"It's not working for me right now," I grumbled. I blinked back more tears. "The worst of it is, I do kind of want to be here. It was one of the things I'd planned on doing for a career when I was a kid. It's not all awful." I squeezed my eyes shut. "And with things being so messed up with my PhD program, maybe this is where God is sending me."

"I don't know about that." Sid is an atheist. He pulled me into his arms. "I do know that I love you. I do know that things here in the restaurant are not that messed up. It's just a matter of getting everybody trained. And I do know that whatever else is going on in terms of our side business, we will come out on top one way or another. We always have. It just won't be as easy or as neat as we'd like."

"It never is." I sighed and leaned against him. "Maybe I am over-reacting."

"We haven't had a case yet where one or the other of us, or both, hasn't had a solid melt-down. So, it's your turn this time." He lifted my chin, and I gazed into his gorgeous blue eyes. "It will be alright, my sweet, sweet Lisa. I believe that."

I smiled in spite of myself. "Thanks. I almost believe it too right now."

Oh, there was some very nice necking at that point, but, alas, it couldn't continue to its natural conclusion. Sid did have to get back to the kitchen.

The next morning, I got up early and put on a nice skirt suit. I ate in the apartment kitchen. Sid was there to pour coffee and sit with me, then drive me to the airport.

It was time for the meeting with the department head at my school.

"Do you want me to go with you?" he asked.

"No. They need you in the restaurant."

"You're more important." He smiled softly and touched my cheek.

"Thanks, lover." I blinked my eyes and took a deep breath. "I just want to get this over with. I'm so afraid they're booting me."

Sid pulled me up and held me. "And if that happens, then that may just be that sign from God you're looking for."

I couldn't help chuckling. Sid may be an atheist, but he does know how I operate that way.

"Honey," he said. "You don't know that it's about kicking you out. Weren't you told that the department head was talking to all the candidates?"

"Yeah."

"Hang onto that and we'll work things out no matter what happens. Okay?"

"Okay."

He said much the same thing as he put me on the plane to Los Angeles. I hung onto how much I loved him and how much he loved me. Once the plane landed, I rented a car because getting my own from the garage in the San Fernando Valley would take too long and headed up to the university where I was studying.

Dr. Chris Stevenson was a pleasant man in his mid-fifties, with a round figure and a gray beard. He didn't keep me waiting, but brought me right into his office within seconds of me getting there.

"Alright." He settled behind his perfectly neat desk and tapped a sheaf of papers on its bottom edge. "How's your summer been?"

"Interesting. I'm helping my father out with his business." I smiled nervously.

Stevenson looked at me and chuckled. "It's not bad news."

"Oh." I swallowed. "Thanks."

"The reason I'm talking to all of the PhD candidates is that we've had some personnel changes." Stevenson cleared his throat. "We, eh, convinced Dr. Barber to retire, and Dr. Clemmins was so pissed off, he retired as well. He may have thought he would be the next to go."

"Oh. Umm. I don't know what to say."

"Your complaint was the last straw for the Dean, and…" Stevenson cleared his throat again. "There may be other, um, complaints in process."

I looked innocent, but had to figure that complaints meant ongoing investigations or lawsuits that Stevenson couldn't talk about.

"It was about time." Stevenson grinned. "Barber was resting on his laurels. Hadn't produced any new scholarship in years. Clemmins' student evaluations were getting worse and worse. We even got Miriam back with us."

"That's wonderful!" I smiled happily.

"However, I have to re-arrange the advisory committees, which is why I want to talk to everybody before I do." He looked at me, then down at his notes. "Lisa, I have to tell you, we almost didn't accept you." He held up his hand. "I was the one who wanted you. The others were concerned about the gap between your master's degree and now."

"Well, it's like I told you in the interview. I had to teach to earn enough money to get my doctorate. But then I got laid off and when I couldn't get another job that year, I lost my confidence."

"And I remember how hard it was to find work in eighty-one, eighty-two. But you got such stellar recommendations from your superiors and your teachers, and the way you went gangbusters during your undergrad and master's, doubling up on credits, graduating early and getting your master's in one year. Everybody thought you were going to be on the tenure track before you were twenty-five." He looked at me. "What really happened?"

What had happened was the spy business, but I couldn't tell him that.

I swallowed and looked away. "I did lose my confidence. After I couldn't get a new job that year, I really wondered if I was cut out for academia. I was about to get evicted when I met my husband, and he offered me a job as his secretary. He even had me live-in. We weren't sleeping together. He slept around a lot, and I didn't sleep with anyone, period. We became friends, and I got to like the work, and then we fell in love." I shrugged. "Things just happened. But two years ago, we'd gotten married, and I was having trouble getting used to the idea that I was a wife and mother. Sid was worried about me, and asked me one day what I'd liked so much about teaching. It was all about helping students." I looked up at Stevenson. "Most people don't realize it, but teaching someone to write clearly can change their life. It's such an important skill, and I loved doing that. So, Sid talked me into going for my original dream."

Stevenson pressed his lips together. "I can see where you might have gotten off-track. But I also know something that you didn't at the time." He looked a little guilty. "I happen to know Stacey Keating."

"My mentor teacher." I smiled. Stacey had also been the associate dean of the department at the community college where I'd worked. "She's a terrific teacher."

"She says you are, too." Stevenson cleared his throat again. "But it wasn't just that you had the least seniority at that college. There were two of you in that position. They kept Roy Church."

"I didn't know," I said, my gut tightening. So, it hadn't just been being new, and to lose out to that jerk? I couldn't help feeling really angry, but tamped it down.

"Stacey is still pissed about that one. You were clearly the better teacher, and you had the most potential for finishing your doctorate. Roy's still there, but he's just skating along, hasn't even finished the course work for his." Stevenson took a deep breath. "I know you had a really tough first year here, although you did get your essay published. That was quite a coup."

"And put me in Barber's crosshairs." I grumbled.

Stevenson looked at me again. "But you're not that interested in Shakespeare."

"I love Shakespeare!"

"Yes, but you love teaching more, and even just now, when you talked about it, it was in terms of teaching writing skills, not iambic pentameter." Stevenson chuckled. "Your essay on keeping Shakespeare relevant was great, well-supported, with some excellent citations. But it was an opinion, not scholarship." Stevenson smiled again. "I like your work, Lisa. I think you are an asset to this department. But I don't think you have the right focus, and that's where your problem is." He again straightened his sheaf of papers that didn't need straightening.

I thought about it. "Then what do I focus on?"

"That." Stevenson cleared his throat. "How about English education? I've been talking about doing this for a while now, and I decided it's time. I'd like you to be part of a new pilot program focusing on teaching writing skills, not just the skills, themselves, but how do we teach them better so that kids go out there ready to succeed? Your doctorate will still be an English degree, but in English education and you can keep Shakespeare as a minor, so your credits from last year will still count. I've talked with Carol Parsons, over in the Education department, and she likes the cross discipline approach."

"Wow."

"Don't give me an answer now. I imagine you'll want to talk it over with your husband. But you'll also need to think about taking on a classroom assignment. In fact, I'm strongly encouraging you to." He handed me a sheet of paper. "Here's a list of openings. Tell the contacts that I sent you."

I looked the list over and smiled. "My son goes to this one."

"Your son?" Stevenson looked confused.

"He is only fifteen, and will be a sophomore in September at his high school. But he's also a bridge student and takes classes at this community college you've got here."

"Funny. You don't look old enough to have a fifteen-year-old."

I laughed a little. "Well, I am, but just barely. However, I adopted my husband's son. He's whip-smart and an absolute sweetheart. I'm so proud of him."

"I can see that." Stevenson did the throat clearing thing again. "You talk things over with your family then, and I hope to hear from you by the end of the week about how you want to proceed. I do have to get the graduate committees assigned." He got up. "And if you have any questions, please call me."

"I will. Thanks." I got up and shook his hand.

The inside of my head whirled as I got the rental car returned and then to the right ticketing desk for the flight I wanted. There weren't a lot of flights to South Lake Tahoe, but Lyle had given me a list the day before since I hadn't known exactly what time I'd be heading back. I called the resort restaurant and left a message for Sid about what time I'd arrive, then hurried to catch my plane.

I was surprised to see Daddy at the gate when I got off the plane.

"Where's Sid?" I asked.

"He asked me to come get you. He's stuck at the restaurant."

"Oh, no."

Daddy shrugged and walked me out to his jeep.

"So, how did it go?" he asked as he pulled out of the parking lot.

"It was very interesting." I looked at him and bit my lip. "Daddy, how badly do you want me to take over the resort for you?"

He laughed long and hard.

"I was serious!" I snapped.

"Lisle, baby, you weren't ever going to do that."

"That doesn't mean you don't want me to."

Daddy shook his head. "Of course. I'd love to hand my business over to my daughters. And maybe I'll yet find a way to do that so that you two can have your own lives. But neither of you were ever going to join me in the business, and that's fine."

"I tried to," I said, sulking. "I had this big idea that I was going to take over for you, so I tried to do everything on the resort."

"You did." Daddy chuckled. "You tried just about every job, and you hated every one of them. I'm glad you kept at the laundry and the store. And I really appreciated the way you stepped in on the housekeeping side that one summer. But it wasn't your passion, and I didn't think it should have been."

"What do you mean?"

"I'm in the hotel industry because my daddy was. When I was a boy about Nick's age, I hated my daddy for saying that I was going to follow in his footsteps. Now, as it happened, I found out that I liked the business, and when it came time to get out of South Florida, that's the business I bought. But I was never going to make my girls follow in my footsteps. And, thank God, you girls knew your own hearts and followed them." He smiled at me, then turned his eyes back to the road. "Your mother and I raised you two to be independent and think for yourselves. We didn't want you stuck like we were or like our parents were. So, don't be afraid to follow your heart. You won't disappoint me. In fact, I'm most proud of you when you do."

"Thanks, Daddy."

Back at the resort, I found Sid in the restaurant kitchen, but could only reassure him that things had gone well with my meeting.

"That's good to hear," he said, giving me a quick kiss. "But we had two waiters call in sick tonight and we've got a full house. We'll talk later."

He went back to plating salads at the speed of light.

I hung around for a few, chatting with Kathy and Jesse in the dining room, only to see Sid come out of the kitchen and take an order at a table nearby. Oh, he was good as he smiled and chatted with the guests. He even flirted a little with the older woman, and she ate it up. I could well imagine he'd gotten terrific tips when he'd waited tables when he was younger.

August 10-11, 1988

S id was so tired that night when he came in, we went straight to sleep. Well, he had worked both the day and the night shifts.

The next morning, in the apartment kitchen, I told Sid over breakfast about Stevenson's option for me and what had happened when I got laid off after my first year of teaching.

"I have to say, I'm surprised how angry that made me." I pressed my lips together.

"It sucks, but it's not surprising," Sid replied, pouring us each a cup of coffee. "And, while I feel the same umbrage over the sexism, I can't say I'm unhappy that you got laid off. I wouldn't have you otherwise."

I munched on some toast thoughtfully. "Maybe it was God leading me to you and the side business."

"Whatever." He looked at me. "Daddy mentioned that you'd talked to him about taking over the resort."

"He said that he'd always known I wouldn't and that I should follow my heart."

"Are you still feeling guilty about not wanting to take your father's place?" Sid got up to get another couple slices of toast from the toaster.

"No. Not really." I smiled. "It does make it easier for me to think about it, though. After all, if I did, it would be because I want to, not because I felt I had to." I looked at him. "What do you want to do?"

Sid laughed. "I don't want to stay here. If anything, last night confirmed that one for me. I'm having fun, and it's nice to keep my hand in. But, damn, it's hard work. I'd rather be writing, thank you. How about you?"

He handed me a slice of toast, buttered just the way I like it.

"Hm." I thought about it, then shook my head. "No. I don't want to take over. I really don't like the work."

He sat and got a bite of the other slice. "What do you want to do about your PhD program?"

"Actually, I kind of like the idea of making it about English education, and I like that I'll be teaching." I frowned. "It's just going to make working around the side business a lot more challenging."

"We're already doing that with my teaching schedule." Sid taught piano at Stella's school twice a week. "We'll find a way to make it work. It's not like you have a deadline to get all this done, either, if that helps."

I took a deep breath. "True. Now I just have to start applying for positions. At least Stevenson gave me some places to try." I got up and picked up our breakfast dishes. "Anything on the case yesterday?"

"Esther verified Donna's attendance at Sac State. According to Hattie, since we have the real plans in hand, it's probably time to start thinking about getting the dummy plans to Dusty's contact, whoever that is. Hattie thinks maybe have Clint question Dusty. He can do it directly under an alias."

"That sounds workable. I'll hang around outside today and see if I can question some folks unobtrusively."

As I slid into a lounge chair on the edge of the playground, I saw the Winslow family heading out for the day. A minute later, the DiNovo kids burst out of their cabin, followed by their father. The kids ran to the playground and Mr. DiNovo settled into the lounge chair next to mine.

"Hi," he said softly, setting a large briefcase next to him. "It won't disturb you if I try to get some work done while sitting here, will it?"

I smiled at him. "Why should it?"

"Not a lot of folks are working while they're here." He held out his right hand to me. "I'm Avery."

"I'm Lisa." I shook it. "But both you and your wife seem to work all the time."

Avery shook his head as he pulled a small set of papers from his briefcase.

"We're not technically on vacation," he said. "The house is being remodeled, so we came up here. I used to when I was a kid." He looked at me. "You remind me of the owner's daughter."

I chuckled. "That's probably because I am." I looked at him. "Did we...?"

"I saw you necking with some other guy one year, but we never did that. I was far too shy. I just worshiped from afar." He sighed as he looked over the first sheet of paper. "You're better off that we didn't."

"Why?" I asked.

"I've been one lousy husband and father." He looked at me. "I'm a geologist and working for a major oil company. The problem is, most of my work had to be done on site, and you can't take a wife and kids to places like Saudi Arabia. So, Francine has stayed home these past ten years and raised the kids. I finally got a job that would keep me here, but the funny thing is, after all that time apart, we're practically strangers to each other. I'm still working all the time, and since I agreed it was time for her to do what she wants, she's been spending her time working on law school." He looked over at his two children, a girl and a boy. "They barely know me. I don't know what to do about that." He choked. "I'm sorry. I shouldn't be dumping all this crap on you."

"It's alright. I'm sorry you're having such a rough time. Have you considered counseling?"

"Francine's not that excited about it, but we kind of want to try to stay together for the kids. They deserve an intact family. I just don't know how it's going to happen. Anyway, I've got reports to review."

He went to work. I lounged for a little while longer, then wandered around for a while. But there really wasn't anybody to talk to. I went to eat lunch at my parents' house. Sid was there, so we ate lunch together, then headed back to the apartment to make up for the night before. We cleaned up, then I went for another walk. I don't know what started the fight, but when I got back to the apartment, Sid and Nick were in the living room.

"I don't get to do anything I want to do!" Nick yelled at his father.

Sid held out his hands. "You're learning to drive. You're dating girls."

"I wanted to go to science camp. I didn't want to work a crap job. You made me do that." Nick's eyes blazed.

"I need you here." Sid glared right back at him. "You can do things that no one else can, and we've got a hot case."

"Well, you could have asked if I wanted to help." Nick paced. "You didn't even bother to do that. You just came in and told me I was going to work a crap job, whether I wanted to or not."

"I thought you'd want to be up here with us." Sid looked bewildered. "You hate it when you're away and we're working."

"But did you have to decide that I'd be a busboy? I didn't get a chance to figure out what I could do around here. You just gave the orders and I have to toe the line."

"I did not order you to take that job."

"Yeah, you did, Dad."

The two faced each other, breathing heavily. Then Nick turned and left the apartment, slamming the door on his way out. Sid swallowed and looked at me.

"I did not—"

"I'm afraid you did, Sid." I went over and touched his arm. "I know why. You just didn't give him much of an option or even ask him if he'd mind."

"We've had to make decisions like that for him before."

"But he's fifteen now. And we asked him about coming to Kansas. We didn't assume he would."

Sid cursed. "You'd think I would have seen it."

"You don't like just taking orders, either."

"I'd better go find him and apologize." He sighed, then looked at me. "You wanna come?"

"Sure. I may need to apologize, too."

We found Nick upstairs in his room.

"Can we talk?" Sid asked when Nick opened the door.

Nick nodded and let us in.

"Son," Sid said. "I owe you an apology. I should have taken your feelings into account a lot earlier, and I didn't. I just had a lot of things to manage, a lot of pieces to pull together, and I forgot that I have no right to treat you like just another piece."

Nick looked everywhere but at Sid. "It wasn't doing the job so much as that you didn't ask if I wanted to or what I thought about doing it."

"I know. I should have. I'm sorry. You have every reason and right to be mad at me."

"It's okay." Nick sighed and winced. "It hasn't been that bad. I just... I don't know."

"I don't, either, sometimes," Sid said with an odd smile.

Nick reached over and the two hugged.

"I'm still mad at you," the boy said as they released each other. "And I still want to go to science camp. And I really, really hate bussing tables."

"Unfortunately, you're too young to wait tables and I could really use you bussing." Sid sighed. "I'll see if one of the other guys has somebody who can take over for you. Can you hang in until I get someone?"

"That's fair." He looked up at me. "Hey, Mom."

"Hey, sweetie."

He came over and gave me a hug, too.

"And depending on how things here break here, we'll see about a week of science camp," Sid said. "I'm sorry, Nick, but I really do need you."

"It's not my fault I'm good."

We all laughed at that one, then made our way back to my parents' house to make dinner together with Daddy and Janey. Dusty was still pretty mopey, but Desmond and Daddy got into an extended discussion on barbecuing. Nick looked over at Dusty as we ate, and sighed.

"You okay?" I asked Nick later.

"I'm fine." He made a face. "It hasn't been that bad a summer. I'm getting really close to Grandpa, and that's great." He glanced back at Dusty. "And other stuff."

I played with the lock of hair on his forehead. "Okay. I love you, sweetheart."

"I love you, Mom."

I was working with Irene on incoming reservations the next morning when Clint, apparently, talked to Dusty. Desmond told me later that Clint had asked to speak to Dusty privately. I had no idea that part of the operation had even been set in motion until Sid paged me right after lunch.

"What's going on?" I asked Sid when I got to the apartment.

"I've gotta get Dusty out of here," Sid said. "He's trying to bolt. Something Clint said scared him. I told him I can get him hidden, but I have to take him to Sacramento to do it."

"Where are you hiding him?"

"I don't know." Sid shrugged. "I called Liz Warner, my old friend? She hides battered women. I told her that one of the college kids here got messed up and the CIA is involved. She said she'd take care of it. We're meeting in Sacto in a couple of hours."

"Okay. Thanks for letting me know." I gave him a warm kiss, and he rushed off.

I went to find Clint. We found each other in the hotel lobby. It turned out Clint had been looking for me, too.

"Hattie said I should," he told me. "The kid. Simpson. He told me that Yuri Voskoff has been staying here."

"Then he's been doing it under an assumed name." I thought. "We're looking for someone just over average height, dark hair and eyes, right?"

"No. Yuri's bald. Well, not completely. Half-bald, really." Clint shrugged. "He sometimes wears a toupee."

My heart stopped. "Does he know you? As a CIA agent?"

"Don't think so. I've never met the fellow. I've just seen photos. Now, what name is he traveling under while he's here?"

I thought about it. "Pretty sure Brian Lane." I pulled Clint to the restaurant. "He might be in there right now. I saw him go past the front desk about half an hour ago before Sid paged me."

I pointed Lane out to Clint.

"Yeah, that's Voskoff."

"Good." I took a deep breath. "Now we know, and now we can get the dummy plans to him somehow. I'm going to talk to Hattie. Can you update Dale on this? I don't want him here, but he should probably know that we've found our target."

"Sounds good." Clint headed out to the front of the resort and into the parking lot.

I went up to Hattie's room. She wasn't in for some reason. So, I went downstairs to help Mira get started on doing the timecards. She picked it up fast enough, but I stuck around until Nick paged me.

He had a location and the code for help.

To Breanna, 7/20/00

Topic of the Day: Seeing Mom and Dad in action

I could just shoot Darby right now. I get that he can't help wondering about Mom and Dad sometimes, and that he'd love to see what they can really do. And Mom and Dad are really good. But seeing them work that way is not at all fun, because when they do, it's generally because something has gone wrong and it's fucking scary.

Not always. In fact, you have seen Mom in action. You just didn't realize that was what you were seeing. It was your first semester at JHU, about a month after we started sharing our tiny little lab tech's office. When you met Mom for the first time. She'd gone into the office and was leaving me a note and you couldn't figure out how she had because you swore you'd locked the door. You had. I saw you do it the night before.

Mom picked the lock. She and Dad are real good at that. I know. It's not legal entry, but sometimes they have to.

Then there was the summer I was fifteen. Grandpa had been teaching me to drive and had somehow caught on to the side business. There's a reason he's so good at poker. Anyway, we go out that afternoon. I think it was a Thursday. Grandpa had me practicing parking in the front lot of the resort. Well, he sees this guy getting into a car and points him out. And I knew the guy from meetings with my folks. So Grandpa says we should follow him.

I knew how to tail someone in a car. I had just never been driving at the time. And maybe I shouldn't have gone for it, but it was kinda fun. So, I start telling Grandpa how you do a tail and all that, and Grandpa was impressed.

The guy, Clint Foster, drives off and we tail him. And he meets up with this guy that Mom and Dad really couldn't stand named Dale O'Connor.

"Do we stay on Mr. Foster?" I asked Grandpa.

"No," Grandpa said. "Let's follow the other fellow."

"Sure."

I don't know how we didn't get made, because it's really not that easy to tail someone if they're looking for it. And O'Connor definitely should have been looking for it. Anyway, he leads us to this small warehouse north of town, then gets out of his car and goes inside.

I looked at Grandpa and we got out of the jeep, and went to look, only to run into this guy with a big-ass gun pointed right at O'Connor's temple. He pushed us inside, got Dale handcuffed, then Grandpa, then me. He also took our shoes and belts and taped our mouths. And that's how Mom found us.

I took my mother's sedan from the garage, thanked God that it was running, and hit the accelerator. I found the warehouse easily enough. Daddy's jeep was parked nearby, but neither he nor Nick were to be seen. My heart in my throat, I parked in the trees on the side of the road away from the jeep, then slipped up to the door in the boxy gray brick building with no windows.

I heard scuffling inside, then silence. I slid in through the door. It was a huge single room, filled with boxes of computers fresh off a truck. Nick, Daddy, and Dale were seated in a row along the nearest pallet, mouths covered with duct tape and hands cuffed behind their backs. Not far away, a man with a bald head walked toward the back of the room. I scurried to hide behind another pallet. Voskoff, or Brian Lane, heard me and spun around.

He ran up to the front of the room and spotted me immediately. I put my hands up.

"Please don't hurt us!" I begged. "I saw my daddy's car and came in and saw them and, oh my god! Please don't hurt us!"

"Don't worry, Ms. Wycherly," Brian Lane (well, Voskoff) said, kindly. "I have no interest in killing civilians. But I do have to get out of here without interference from your local police."

He cuffed my hands behind my back and taped my mouth and got me sat down next to Nick, then took my shoes and put them with the others on top of a tall stack of computer boxes on another pallet. He disappeared to the back of the room for a few minutes. When he returned, he stopped in the doorway.

"Now," he said. "I don't want you to worry. Dale, here, will get you free in plenty of time. Dale, you have twenty minutes."

Voskoff shut the door, then locked it.

As soon as he was gone, I gestured Nick forward with a nod. He nodded, scooted himself forward and toward me. I laid down with my mouth next to his hands. He knew what to do. The tape came off quickly and painfully.

"Dale, what have you got?" I asked, getting myself sat up straight.

Dale shook his head, then nodded at Daddy and laid down and Daddy got the tape off his mouth, then laid down behind Dale. Nick made a face as he tried to run his hands along the waistband of his board shorts.

"Why'd he take our shoes?" Daddy asked as soon as he could.

"Because he's good," Dale said.

"Thank God, I'm better," I said.

It took some effort, but I got my polo shirt untucked from my shorts and inched my hands up along my back until I hit my bra.

Nick yelped as Daddy got the tape off his mouth.

"My beard!" he sniffed.

"Looks like it took your zits, too," I said, grunting as I tried to get the back of my bra unhooked.

"But why take our belts?" Daddy asked.

"We hide stuff in those and in our shoes." I reached for the first snap on my bra strap.

My bra straps unsnap. That first year I was with Sid, he'd suggested that I wear bras with detachable straps to help me escape an enemy. It turned out that detachable straps aren't all that easy to detach. So, years ago, I got into the habit of cutting the straps on regular bras, then sewing snaps on them.

"You can always hide something," Dale said.

"Dad says that a lot," Nick said, still trying to wriggle his bit of spring steel out of his board shorts.

"Who do you think taught him?" Dale glared and tried to shift. "Damn it. It was in the belt."

I shook my head and got the second snap undone. "Why don't you carry something in your waistband?"

"I don't need it that often," Dale growled. "I haven't been captured in years."

"Three years," I said, trying to pull my bra off my chest and down my back. "And, come to think of it, we saved your backside then, too."

"Mom?" Nick sounded worried. "I can't get mine. It slid around to the front."

"That's alright." I finally pulled the bra free and felt for the reason I'd taken it off. "I've got something."

Daddy looked pained. "He said twenty minutes. Any guesses as to what that's about?"

"Looks like he's got evidence to destroy." Dale said. "And an explosion will keep the cops occupied while he skips town."

I felt for the slits I'd put under the bra cups, then started pushing the casing down to get to the under wire inside.

Daddy looked at Dale. "You know the fellow."

"I've known him for years."

I glanced at Dale. "You're a known operative?"

I finally got a hold of the wire, but it stuck in the channel.

"It happens." Dale shrugged. "And I'm not that well known."

I yanked the wire again and almost lost it when it suddenly pulled free.

"How long has it been?" Daddy asked.

"A lot closer to twenty minutes than I'd like," I grumbled.

Still, I had the wire and got my cuffs opened and shook them off.

I got Nick free next, then Daddy. Okay, I hesitated when I saw Dale, but Nick yelped.

"There's a bomb back here! It's set to go off in one minute."

"Nick!" I screamed.

"It's okay, Mom."

Like hell it was. Still, I got Dale free of his cuffs and grabbed my running shoes, and got them on. Daddy had his running shoes on and got Nick's.

"I got it reset." Nick came running up.

"Oh, thank God." I looked at him.

"Did you give it more than ten minutes?" Dale demanded.

"I gave us five." Nick shrugged. "There are only two sticks."

"Could be nerve gas," Dale said. "Evacuate. Now."

I was already at the door, but the push bar was jammed and I couldn't get it open. I took a quick look at it, then popped open the sole of my shoe. Daddy's eyes opened wide in surprise. I grabbed a screwdriver and went to work.

"Do I need to reset again?" Nick asked.

"Can't you set it off that way?" I glared at him.

"That's only in the movies." Nick shrugged. "I mean, you can trigger a charge by trying to dismantle it. But not by resetting the clock. Most of the time."

"We shouldn't reset it, anyway," Dale said. "We don't want Yuri coming back here wondering why his bomb hasn't gone off."

The pin holding the push bar shut finally popped out.

I let Daddy and Nick out first. Dale followed us.

"We've got to get out of here now," I said.

We'd just barely made it to the jeep when the bang happened. It didn't sound like much, but soon smoke poured out of a hole in the back of the roof. Dale got in his car and took off. Daddy took me to where Mama's car was and we left immediately.

Sid's Voice -

The drive out to Sacramento was completely uneventful. It was nice seeing Liz again, but the whole encounter was about business and nothing else. I drove back to Tahoe wishing that Lisa had had a chance to meet Liz.

When I gave up sleeping around, I promised myself that I would never give Lisa reason to doubt my fidelity. I haven't. At least, I hope I haven't. It still amazes me that Lisa trusts me to the extent that she does. Back in '88, I was a lot more worried about appearing to violate that trust than I am now.

Liz was one of the very few women in my life who'd had an impact beyond the bedroom. She is an amazing broad, one of the things I'd always liked about her and still do. There was part of me that really wanted to share that with Lisa.

Nonetheless, we weren't in that place yet, at least between Liz and me. Which meant I wasn't exactly thinking about what I'd find in the apartment in the staff lodge when I walked in.

The good news is that I have been chronically on alert since I started intelligence work back in 1969. The man tearing apart the living room of the apartment startled me, but did not set me up for disaster. He was about my size, with dark hair ringing a significant bald spot on his head, and a deeply lined face.

"Who the hell are you?" I gasped, trying to look like a civilian.

"I am looking for something you have." He advanced on me, his huge automatic aimed at my heart, and I backed up into the doorway.

"What do I have?" I asked, gulping.

He spotted the computer, which was up against the wall under a window.

"This may be it." He grabbed the 5.5-inch floppy disk next to the drive on the table. "Where did you get this?"

I swallowed. "Um. One of the kids here had it." I gulped again, hoping like hell I was making it look good.

He chuckled and booted up the computer. It took several minutes, and I debated pleading with him. Not because I thought it would do any good, but it might make me look more like a civilian.

He inserted the disk into the drive. A couple minutes later, he looked at the screen and smiled.

"Good," he muttered, then shut the computer down and pulled the disk from the drive.

Then he cuffed me and taped my mouth, leaving me on the couch.

At the door, he turned and chuckled again. "I don't enjoy killing civilians. It's messy. Right now, I need to leave. Tell your wife that I like her. She gives good service."

He left the apartment, and I started breathing. I had a feeling he was trying to nettle me with the way he'd phrased things. He didn't know how well I knew Lisa. I got the spring steel from the back of my belt and got the cuffs off in short order.

August 12-19, 1988

When Nick, Daddy, and I got back to the resort, Sid met us in my parents' house. He didn't say anything about his little adventure beyond letting me know that Yuri Voskoff had the disk. I found a moment and went down to the main lodge to let Hattie know. I invited her to dinner at my parents' house, but she declined.

"Marge is back in town, and I'm going out with her." She sighed. "Apparently, she has a package for me. Not related to the plans, though." She shook her head. "It never ends."

Sid told me what had happened with Yuri in the apartment when we went to bed that night. How the operative had known that we had a disk with the plans, we never found out, but didn't really care, either.

The next morning, Hattie checked out, but waited for Sid and me to see her off.

"I got a message on my radio phone just now," she told us. "Overnight, a Soviet transponder sent a message that the Valient plans were on their way. And it was mis-spelled."

I sighed. "So he got away."

"Well, yes." Hattie looked at me. "That was the idea."

"Oh, I know." I looked at her. "He also murdered your brother. He had to have set up the trap in the TV set, probably to kill Dusty. He was right there in the hall when your brother set it up. It was just your brother's bad luck that the trap got him instead."

Hattie took a deep breath. "I know. It seems like we're sorely lacking in justice in this case. But there's not much we can do about it. Miles was just collateral damage, it seems." She paused and blinked.

"I'm so sorry, Hattie," Sid said, softly.

"Thank you," she said. "Both of you. For everything." She swallowed. "I've got to go get Miles' ashes, then get my plane ready."

"Your plane?" I asked.

"Yes. I have a Lear jet."

I sighed in relief. "That's how you got here so fast. Connecting flights always take forever. We were afraid you'd been here all along."

"Well, I was in Wyoming on a different matter." Hattie smiled. "We'll be in contact soon."

Sid and I hugged her and watched as she left. He slung his arm across my shoulders.

"I hate seeing the bad guy get away, too," he said. "But that's the business sometimes. At least he didn't spot us as operatives."

Sid went back to the restaurant for the morning rush and to oversee Janine interview a couple new bussers. Janine hired them both. Nick and Sid showed them their process, but the two guys already had some experience and Nick promptly quit.

Sid also found time to make a couple phone calls. Stella called the apartment late that afternoon.

"It's all arranged," Stella told me. "They didn't mind a last-minute registration at all. I'll see to getting him there and home, and he can stay with me and Sy until you get back."

Sy was Stella's lover, but he lived in New York during the school year and only spent summers in L.A. with Stella.

I let Sid tell Nick that he'd be going to science camp starting that Monday. Our ears rang with the whoop of joy that Nick let out.

"I love you, Dad!" Nick squeezed him, then pulled back. "When are you guys coming home?"

"I've probably got another week here," Sid said.

Nick's face grew worried. "You're still working?"

"Not a case, son." Sid squeezed him again. "If it was, I'd want to keep you here. You're good and I need that."

"Thanks, Dad." Nick stood tall.

I gasped. They looked at me.

"Sid, he's grown again," I said. "He's got to be almost six feet tall."

They laughed. And as it turned out, Nick was five-eleven, but only for the time being.

Saturday, the Fosters checked out and left, as did Kathy and Jesse and the Delgados. Lita and Pedro promised to return. They'd had a really good time there, and the kids loved the place.

Sunday, we took Nick to the airport earlier than we needed to. Mama and Grandma arrived, and we decided to let Grandma get a hug from Nick before he had to go. Grandma was happy to see him, but it was clear by the time Nick's plane left the gate that she was quite out of temper. Mama had mentioned several times that the packing up had not gone easily. We found out why when we got back to the house.

"Her doctor thinks she might have some neurological problem or the beginning of dementia," Mama told me. "I'll be taking her to San Francisco next week for tests." She sighed. "She's being difficult about it, though. I'm not sure if it's the dementia or her normal orneriness."

"Oh, no!" I held Mama. "Are you okay?"

"It's hard, honey. She is my mama. But she is seventy-eight years old and we're going to lose her sometime." Mama sighed. "That's also why she's so anxious to see you have babies."

Grandma chose that moment to waddle up. She's as short as my mother is, but much rounder.

"Well?" she demanded of me.

"Nothing, Grandma. I'm sorry."

"Mama," my mother cut in. "Will you please leave Lisle alone about that? She's not going to be blessed that way, and that's that."

Grandma waddled off, muttering.

Esther and Desmond came up with a new computer system for the resort, but decided not to install it until that fall. As it was, Desmond was going to take on the installation. Esther had her own security business to work on.

"I don't have any deadlines until winter," she told me. "But I need to think about it."

We did find out that Dusty got sent into the Witness Protection Plan, but didn't find out any more. Ty Larson was seriously annoyed that Dusty was gone. Ty had really liked the kid and had been hoping that Dusty would take over for him so that he could retire. Daddy set to work trying to find a replacement. He offered the spot to Judy Osbourne, who turned it down. She was actually quite content with her little business, although she offered to look around for another facilities person.

Donna and Marina both went back to school, however Donna changed her major from business to hospitality. Lee Whitney faded away, moving from Tahoe within a month. The DiNovos, the Winslows, and Ms. Sanchez eventually checked out, as well, and we never found out what happened to them. But that's the way of it at the resort. Guests go home and live their lives without us. Even if they come back, they seldom tell us what's been happening with them.

Liz Warner drove up for a day in the middle of that last week there. She was a delight and I'm pretty sure she liked me, too. [Oh, she did. - SEH]

Dale continued to be Dale, but it was generally agreed that getting taken down a peg helped keep him from going off on his own so much.

With Mama back, I didn't need to work so much, and, truth be told, things were pretty well running on their own. Daddy decided to hire Irene as the resort manager and offered her the apartment in the staff lodge as soon as Sid and I vacated.

Which we didn't do until a week after the warehouse explosion. The cops had dealt with that and didn't connect it to the resort, which was fine with us. Sid wanted to be sure everything was in place at the restaurant. Both Janine and Bracha insisted that it was, and I didn't really pay attention to which positions needed to be filled.

That Friday morning, I was packing the final suitcase when Daddy came into the apartment bedroom. Sid was taking the boxes and suitcases that had already been packed to his car, then getting Bowser and Motley ready to go. We were driving back to Los Angeles.

"Hi, Daddy," I said.

"You guys almost ready?"

"Just about." I folded up yet another Wycherly polo shirt.

"Sid says you two are going to Cancun on Sunday."

"Yeah. We're meeting Frank and Esther and Kathy and Jesse there." I stuck the shirt into the suitcase. "It's strictly a vacation. We set it up last spring, but had to put it off when things got set up here. Sid figures we've got the time, and he wants to do some serious sunbathing." I chuckled. "He can't here. You know he doesn't believe in tan lines."

Daddy laughed. Sid is a nudist at heart.

"Anyway, Kathy was able to get her sister to watch Keshon, and Esther figures she'd better take a vacation now before things heat up with her new business."

"Now, you've checked all the drawers and everything?"

"Yes, Daddy. I've just got this last bit of clothing here." I reached over and picked up my toy sword. "And this. Unless you want to keep it."

Daddy laughed softly. "Oh, no, honey. That's yours."

"Thanks." I grinned at him.

"Looks to me like you got one of your first career choices, after all."

"Which one?" I asked.

"Superhero."

I laughed. "I'm not a superhero, Daddy."

"Well, you're pretty damned amazing." He pulled me into his arms and squeezed. "I am so very proud of you, Lisle."

"Thanks, Daddy. I love you so much."

"I love you, sweetheart."

He went to help Sid with the rest of the luggage. I giggled as I packed the sword in the suitcase and shut it.

I'm not a superhero by any means. But I'm close enough.

THE ROOM WHERE IT HAPPENED

Book 14 in the Operation Quickline series (and the penultimate).

The job was a nuisance. The target was a disaster

Sid Hackbirn never knew his mother Sheila. When startling new evidence in Sheila's murder shows up, Sid isn't terribly interested until Stella, the aunt who raised him becomes hellbent on finding out who killed her sister over thirty years before.

As undercover agents in a top-secret organization, Sid and his wife Lisa Wycherly have the skills to investigate, but then get assigned to watch a congressman who was one of the main suspects in Sheila's murder.

With the congressman trying to make Sid into the son he should have had, and Stella recklessly diving into questioning suspects, Sid and Lisa are up to their armpits in a case that stands little chance of putting the demons of the past to rest.

Thank You for Reading

I do hope you enjoyed the book.

If you can do me one small favor, please. Can you go to one of the social media/retail profiles below and leave a short review? It doesn't need to be a lot, just honest.

a amazon.com/Paths-Taken-Operation-Quickline-Book-ebook/dp/B0DGMYM7GB

BB bookbub.com/books/paths-not-taken-by-anne-louise-bannon

f facebook.com/robingoodfellowent

g goodreads.com/book/show/218688480-paths-not-taken?from_search=true&from_srp=true&qid=eCL2BChH7v&rank=1

Other books by Anne Louise Bannon

I'm so glad you liked this book! Check out my other novels, available in print or ebook at your favorite retailer:

Old Los Angeles Series:
Death of the Zanjero
Death of the City Marshal
Death of the Chinese Field Hands
Death of an Heiress
Death of the Drunkard

Operation Quickline Series:
That Old Cloak and Dagger Routine
Stopleak
Deceptive Appearances
Fugue in a Minor Key
Sad Lisa
These Hallowed Halls
My Sweet Lisa
A Little Family Business
Just Because You're Paranoid
From This Day Forward
Silence in the Tortured Soul
Amateur Theatricals

Paths Not Taken

Freddie and Kathy Series:
Fascinating Rhythm
Bring Into Bondage
The Last Witnesses
Blood Red

Daria Barnes:
Rage Issues

Mrs. Sperling:
A Nose for a Niedeman

Brenda Finnegan:
Tyger, Tyger

Romantic Fiction:
White House Rhapsody

Fantasy and Science Fiction:
A Ring for a Second Chance
But World Enough and Time
Time Enough
And I would be honored if you left a review for this and any of my books on the below sites. It really helps.

BB   bookbub.com/profile/anne-louise-bannon

g   goodreads.com/author/show/513383.Anne_Louise
_Bannon

facebook.com/RobinGoodfellowEnt/

amazon.com/stores/author/B00JCRXST2?ingress
=0&visitId=bfadb491-d1ac-4575-84da-bb4f7d325a
d9&store_ref=ap_rdr&ref_=ap_rdr

pinterest.com/AnneLouiseBannon

instagram.com/annelouisebannon4/

Connect with Anne Louise Bannon

Thank you for sticking it out this long! Please join my newsletter. It's the best way to stay up-to-date on my upcoming projects, blog posts and even the occasional game and giveaway.

You can sign up for my newsletter on Substack, Subst ack.com/@annelouisebannon. or by visiting my website, annelouisebannon.com

And don't forget to connect with me on your favorite social media platforms:

BB bookbub.com/profile/anne-louise-bannon

g goodreads.com/author/show/513383.Anne_Louise _Bannon

f facebook.com/RobinGoodfellowEnt/

a amazon.com/stores/author/B00JCRXST2?ingress =0&visitId=bfadb491-d1ac-4575-84da-bb4f7d325a d9&store_ref=ap_rdr&ref_=ap_rdr

P pinterest.com/AnneLouiseBannon

O instagram.com/annelouisebannon4/

About Anne Louise Bannon

Anne Louise Bannon is an author and journalist who wrote her first novel at age 15. Her journalistic work has appeared in Ladies' Home Journal, the Los Angeles Times, Wines and Vines, and in newspapers across the country. She was a TV critic for over 10 years, founded the YourFamilyViewer blog, and created the OddBallGrape.com wine education blog with her husband, Michael Holland. She is the co-author of Howdunit: Book of Poisons, with Serita Stevens, as well as author of the Freddie and Kathy mystery series, set in the 1920s, the Old Los Angeles series, set in 1870, and the Operation Quickline series, plus several stand alones. She and her husband live in Southern California with an assortment of critters.

www.ingramcontent.com/pod-product-compliance
Lightning Source LLC
Chambersburg PA
CBHW072027220726
48293CB00016B/509